I0760444

Stephanie K. Clemens

All characters in this publication are purely fictitious and any resemblance to real persons, living or dead, is pure coincidence.

ISBN:
978-1-957508-02-3

To all the strong women in my life.
To those that push boundaries, find new paths, and create new opportunities

Prologue

Grantabridge, Brythion 1870

It wasn't hard to determine why so many of the members of the Shadowed Sword seemed to be stuck in the past. The grey stone walls of the chamber were decorated with more swords than one could possibly imagine, from dueling rapiers to broadswords and everything in-between. It was like standing in the middle of an armory from the medieval ages in so many ways. It's no wonder that the society's motto was lost to its current members.

"I just cannot believe you don't see that the Shadowed Sword has strayed from its purpose. I mean, just look at the motto." I pointed to the wall with the words Seek Knowledge carved into it, ignoring all the swords surrounding the words we were supposed to live by. "It doesn't say Seek Those with Societal Status, or Only Lords Allowed, or Enter All Those with Power. It says Seek Knowledge. The implication is knowledge is everywhere and we should try to find it wherever we can."

"Edmund, you may be a future Duke, but you have a sad misunderstanding of the world. Why would we want to let anyone but the highest echelons of society into the Shadowed Sword? It is secret for a reason."

"Because that's how this society was meant to be." I turned away from my companion; I might as well be speaking to the chamber walls for all the good it would do. I couldn't stop myself, though. Turning back so I could read his expressions, I continued on, knowing this conversation was a repeat of past discussions and would be had again in the future. "Adding intelligent individuals from every social class isn't going to make it less secret. In fact, go read the original member lists. There were professors, tutors, writers, and businessmen. It was so much more than just another men's club of elite society. I doubt you've noticed, but high society is not always the most intelligent or forward thinking. The discussions they must have had before, the philosophical pursuit—the impressions they left on society because actual topics that affected the country were discussed here. Now we have the likes of Lord Bradbury, who can't even string two words together unless it's about horseflesh or gambling." I needed to calm down. Arguments were never as effective when one was hot under the collar. And I, Edmund Fremont, the next Duke of Nordaoine, was nothing if not effective.

My companion looked at me, and I knew he was contemplating my brown skin and black hair. My status as a future duke was the only thing preventing him from actually uttering the contempt he felt for me. He had never done anything about it. But I could see it in his eyes, in the way he clenched his fists as I spoke, as if he was contemplating hitting me at all times. He hated that I had enough clout in society to effect change.

"Edmund, isn't it enough that your crusade to have women allowed at University worked? Do you have to go about trying to change everything? Especially the things in this world that don't need changing?"

"You think my crusade worked? The University is allowing four women to attend. Four. They aren't even allowed to sit for exams or get the degrees they will have earned by the time they have completed their studies. So these four women can come to University, use its resources, hopefully find a professor who will work with them in their chosen field, do all the work required by the University, and leave with absolutely no recognition of the work that they did. I'm sure these women risk being outcast by society, or worse, disowned by their family, to come here." The accomplishment of getting women into Grantabridge University was bittersweet. Just knowing what some would give up to come here, and how little they would potentially get from the experience, left me disheartened.

"The University buckled and allowed four women where women have no right to be in the first place."

"No right? You don't think women have a right to learn, grow, and invent? Just think of the interesting dinner conversations you could have with any of these four women." Just the thought of marrying an intellectual equal made me smile. And it was more than just her being intelligent. I knew women didn't need a formal education to be intelligent. Mother was a great example of that, always reading—whether it was fashion magazines, philosophy, or novels, it all led to Mother having a great mind and understanding of the world. But these women coming to University, I believed they wanted more. They wanted to change the world. They wanted to leave an imprint, just like me. And society needed more people like that. Especially individuals that flout convention like these four women, the first to attend university.

"Why would I ever want to have an intellectual conversation with my wife? Intellectual conversations happen at my club with other men, not at home, and definitely not with women."

On that note I threw up my hands, not in surrender, more like despair. "Change will happen, my friend. And if you aren't ready for it, you will be the one that becomes obsolete."

* * *

After months of arguing with fellow members of Shadowed Sword, I was thankful to be going home for the summer. Not that it felt like summer: Brythion was almost always overcast and cold, except for very late summer, and right now was no exception. I was looking forward to playing chess with Mother and harassing Kaiden. Being around my family was exactly what I needed. All my endeavors to push the Shadowed Sword towards progress were with resistance. The current leader of the society continued to let in the Lord Bradburys of the world and ignored anyone with potential but missing the title he considered a requisition for membership.

I decided I would run against the stubborn fool at the election during the next term. The society needed to change. Well, it needed to change if it was going to stay relevant. Apparently, staying relevant wasn't on many of the members' minds, but I was having some success campaigning quietly behind closed doors. Some members even agreed with the three new members I proposed. Hopefully, the new term would bring change.

The carriage came to an abrupt stop. I tried to stop myself from sliding off the red velvet seats with little success.

"Why are we stopping, John?" I said while knocking on the roof of the carriage.

"There's a tree fallen across the road, my lord. We might have to find another route. I don't think I can clear it," John Coachman said.

"What if we hooked the horses to it? Would they be able to move it out of the way?" I said, offering what I hoped was the most practical and efficient solution to the current predicament.

"That could work, sir. I'll get started on it."

I jumped out of the carriage, leaving my frock coat and hat behind. I could not leave all the work to John, but it would not do to arrive home overly disheveled. Mother would never approve.

We had stopped in a lovely little clearing with a bit of sunlight that was finally peeking through the grey clouds and filtering through the trees. It was clear to me that someone had moved the log there specifically to stop travelers, as it was in the middle of the road with space on either side of it, just not quite enough room to go around. A naturally fallen tree would have been much closer to the forest line.

"Halt!" a stranger yelled. He was quite well dressed, and

his horse was prime, quality horseflesh.

It did not shock me to see him there. Clearly, we had fallen, much like the tree, into a trap.

"As you can see, we have already halted, since the tree is blocking the road," I said.

"Then hands up. Don't move."

"You can have whatever coins I have on me, just please let us be on our way." I slowly walked forward, hoping to de-escalate the situation.

"Stop moving or I'll shoot." The man waved his pistol in my direction.

I stopped moving, noticing others going through my carriage and luggage. I stood there, believing my best chance to get home was to let them take what they wanted. That was, until I really looked at the highwayman. His extremely nice waistcoat had a familiar pattern, that same fabric lined his greatcoat, and his leather boots were way too nice for someone making a living divesting others of their belongings on a rarely used road.

I made eye contact with the highwayman and saw his eyes flash with contempt. Contempt I recognized. Contempt I saw almost daily. That's when I knew I was not getting out of this situation.

"Sorry Edmund, it simply has to be done." The highwayman was not sorry. He fired his pistol. Pain tore through my chest. I tried to look down to see what had just happened. Instead, I crumpled into nothingness.

Chapter One

Rosheen Terra, Brythion 1870

"Have you taken leave of all your senses!" exclaimed my mother, Olivia Stanhope, stopping me in the great hall of our manor, my hand already reaching for the doorknob to the front parlor where my mother and aunt were taking tea. "Under no circumstances will Philippa attend University. She already flouts convention with all her tinkering. There is no way her reputation could withstand attending university. People will think of her as a bluestocking and never consider her an eligible match."

Instead of entering the parlor as planned, I stopped and bent down to peek through the keyhole, my leather-clad derrière sticking out into the great hall with a complete lack of decorum. My indecorous position would not be a surprise to anyone that knew me. I had just come back from riding my steamer bike and hadn't changed into what Mother, and the rest of society, would deem ladylike clothing yet.

"Oh, posh," Honoria sputtered. "Is that all you want for Pippa? Marriage to some dull Brythionite. She would be gutted at such a life."

I couldn't actually see my mother or Aunt Honoria through

the keyhole, just the elegantly decorated room I had grown up in, with its light blue papered walls, mahogany and brocade side chairs, and a blue silk Latikan rug. I gave up trying to see into the room for now and just pressed my ear to the door so I could hear better.

"It would be a good life for her. Her life would be settled, have a purpose and stability. Not everyone can live the way you do, Honoria," Olivia said, the inescapable derision she felt for her older sister, Honoria, seeping in at the end.

"Not everyone can live happily? That's a bloody shame."

"Honoria, language."

I cracked the door open, quietly peeking in. Aunt Honoria was on her feet, pacing around my mother. It surprised me that my mother hadn't already lectured her about wearing a hole in the carpet. She was always telling me to stop pacing because she feared I would destroy her silk carpet.

Honoria was one of those women that just had a presence. Despite being short and petite like me, when she entered a room, she filled it. Which is what she was doing in her forest green silk dress, with her matching green hat sitting jauntily atop her flaming red hair. I not only shared her petite stature but also her bright red hair.

My mother, on the other hand, had a tendency to be a wallflower. And a wilted one at that, or at least that's how she looked now, semirecumbent on the cream-colored settee, her lackluster brown curls drooping, her pink frills looking smushed from the weight of the day.

"You want to destroy that poor girl. What you call purpose would leave her feeling adrift and purposeless. I don't know why you refuse to accept that not only is she not like you, she's talented. Have you even looked at the things she's built? What you call *tinkering*. Her steam motorbike is a work of pure genius. I would have loved to ride on it across Eletharis, the wind in my hair and sun on my face."

My breath caught at her words; I wiped away tears as they formed. Honoria understands. She seemed to be the only one. But those sensations she described were the reasons I built the steamer bike. And my *tinkering*, it's so much more than what my mother can deem to acknowledge. I want to change the world with one of my inventions.

"Honoria, it would behoove you to remember that Philippa is not your daughter. And, therefore, none of your concern. You have already dragged the family name through the mud with your antics. I will not allow it to continue with my daughter. Philippa will learn her place. She will not attend University. And you will stop encouraging her."

I couldn't take it anymore. My mother's words were like little cuts to my soul. All I wanted was to be the best at steam engineering I could be. If mother had her way, there would be no steam engineering in my life.

"But Mama," I exclaimed as I burst through the door, the lemony scent of the room filling my nose, mixed with the familiar floral scent I knew my mother put on every day. "I could do so much if I had an education. You plan on Percy going to university at some point. Why is it so wrong for me to do so?"

"Ladies do not have any need for university, Philippa, and that means you." My mother turned and got a good look at me. "What on earth are you wearing? Upstairs, now, change into something a young lady can be seen in." Her teacup chattered against the saucer, sloshing tea onto it, signaling my mother was more than a little distressed.

"I won't let you ruin that girl," I heard Honoria mutter while my mother shooed me out of the parlor.

* * *

My feet were heavy as I made my way up the stairs to my room. The soothing wall colors did nothing to soothe my mood. Especially since my boots thudded with every step on the hardwood floors. It sounded like I was walking the plank to my own doom.

At least one person understood what I wanted and, more importantly, why I wanted it. Too bad one person wasn't enough to actually get me to University.

I entered my bedroom, closing the doors behind me. I tried

to let the aqua colors of my room calm me down. The colors reminded me of the ocean, which always calmed my mind. I flopped down on my canopy bed, the white-and-aqua covers almost consuming me. I lay there twisting my braid of flaming red hair, deep in thought over what had just transpired. There's no way Aunt Honoria would convince Mother to let me go to university. Despite finding happiness with Father, my mother still blamed Honoria for, well, for being scandalous. I mean, Aunt Honoria was caught kissing a duke in an alcove at a ball and then flat out refused to marry him. Can you imagine having the strength of conviction to turn down a duke? Since then Aunt Honoria had been everywhere—Sindthia, the Arbaro Akva, Eletharis, Aikupita—oh, and the things she'd done! Climbing mountains, riding camels, it all sounded so amazing. I mean, she just returned from Hellias after exploring some of the excavation sites there. And all of it was so out of my reach. I didn't necessarily want to be just like Aunt Honoria, but I wanted her strength to tell my family I was going to University, and if they didn't like it, they could sod off. Which was unlikely because I was practical enough to realize I needed money to live off of, and without my family, I had none.

There was nothing for it. I might as well change and have a cup of tea. I sat up on the edge of my bed, looking at all the pieces of frill in my wardrobe, each one somehow more frilly and more pastel than the next. I didn't want to be seen in any of these. The ruffles would overwhelm my petite frame, and my hair was so bright, the pastels would fade away to oblivion. Clothing was just another area where my mother and I did not see eye to eye. I always thought I looked like an over-decorated cake with a top layer that clashed with the bottom layers when I put on the clothing my mother insisted I wear. I loved my practical leather leggings and blouses, and even my jodhpurs. The styles of the day were so restrictive, overly frilly, and truly ridiculous. Why did I need to pad my bum? I would throw away every one of those dresses my mother bought me if I thought I could get away with it.

"Knock, knock," Aunt Honoria said as she tapped on the door.

"Come in," I answered, gesturing to my maid, Sarah, to

open the door for her. Honoria always seemed so full of energy, like someone that had one too many cups of coffee each and every morning. I patted the bed next to me, inviting her to sit there. Instead, Aunt Honoria paced the length of my room. It was no surprise. I'm not sure I had ever seen her sit for a conversation.

"Pippa, your mother, well . . . That's neither here nor there at this point," Honoria began, her green eyes sparkling mischievously. "Since your family has their head so far up their own arse they can't see that the world is changing, I'm going to give you the ability to make your own decisions. Tomorrow morning, I'm going to see my solicitor. I'll have him set up a stipend for you to live off of and pay for your tuition, so if you choose, you can attend University. They only accepted four women this year on a trial basis. And I cannot see you missing out because your mother is afraid of change."

"Aunt Honoria, you can't. That's too generous." I couldn't take her money. I didn't want to be the reason she couldn't live her life the way she wanted.

"Hogwash, you're my favorite niece. And I will not see you waste away in some manor house in the country because that was your only option. You should be able to set the path you want for yourself. And I know you can't do that without money. Don't worry, I'm not giving you so much that I won't continue in my grand way. I just might have a little less champagne to drink every week. I would have given anything to go to university when I was your age. This will let me live vicariously through you. My dream was to be an archaeologist, but I could convince no one to let me join an expedition. At least you will have the opportunity to choose to follow your dreams of steam engineering."

"Auntie, thank you so much!" I squealed, hugging her in excitement. After a moment, she pulled back and looked at me.

"Just know the consequences of each decision you make, because there will be consequences. I fear your parents will disown you if you go to university; and if you don't, well, I don't know if you'll be happy living with Lord WhoeverTheyChoose." Aunt Honoria stopped in front of my open wardrobe. "Are these your clothes?" She picked through my closet with distaste, everything in pinks and yellows with an obscene amount of ruffles. "This is what your mother considers presentable? She never did understand what it was like to have red hair. Come to my room; we're the same size. Let's see if we can find something in my wardrobe that will flatter you. And bring Sarah with you."

I followed along quietly, my head spinning, thinking of what the future could hold now that I had options. It seriously felt like I could accomplish anything.

Chapter Two

"Percival Stanhope! I challenge you to a duel," I said, pushing myself into his room with the dramatic flair of a stage performer.

Percy did not appreciate my entrance; instead he rolled over with a groan. "Pippa, go back to sleep, it's too early for your exuberance."

"It's ten a.m. and we aren't keeping city hours here. Get your lazy arse up before I do something drastic." I dramatically tiptoed closer to Percy's bed, foil at the ready.

"All right, I'll get up. Give me a minute to get ready." Percy sighed.

I bounced up and down a bit, awkwardly clapping my hands while still keeping hold of my foil. "Thank you, Percy! Just hurry, I don't want Mother to catch us on our way out. I'm not in the mood for another one of her lectures."

I gave a quick salute with my foil, then turned on my heels and ran down the stairs. My steps slowed as I reached the bottom floor. Looking to avoid my mother, I quietly made my way to the kitchen. The door loomed in front of me, freedom just on the other side. Glancing over my shoulder one more time, I quickly opened the door and scurried through. Relief coursed through me as I eaned back on the door. Whew, I made it.

Wait, what was that I smelled? The scent of sticky buns and berry jam surrounded me, making my knees go weak as my stomach protested in the most vocal and unladylike way. I needed to pack some for Percy and me. It smelled too good to leave without grabbing at least one each. I pushed myself off the door, the snatching of sticky buns the only thing running through my mind.

“Ah, Miss Pippa, I see you’ve found the sticky buns,” Cook said, laughter filling her voice.

“Yes, Cook, would it be too much to ask to bring some with me for a picnic this morning? Percy and I are going to practice and this would be the best snack in the world.” I can’t remember a time when Cook had said no to me. There was always the possibility of a first time. Hopefully, today wasn’t that day. I was already salivating over the thought of cramming one of her delicious concoctions into my mouth.

Cook bent over and pulled a basket from the shelves. “Lucky for you, Miss Pippa, I’ve already set aside some buns for you and Mr. Percy. Somehow, I knew you would be up to your normal antics today. Now skedaddle, before your mother sees you with them sticky buns.”

“You are wonderful!” I said. Then grabbed Cook by the shoulders and planted a kiss on her cheek. “Thank you!” I grabbed the basket and sprinted through the door, relishing in the freedom of just being outside with the summer breeze caressing the bit of skin I was showing and tugging at the wild hairs that framed my face. I continued to run through the meadows surrounding my family’s estate. When I was out of sight of the manor house, I plopped down on the grassy knoll Percy and I always practiced on and grabbed a sticky bun. Popping the warm, gooey ball of freshly baked dough into my mouth, I couldn’t help but close my eyes and savor the blissful moment.

“You better have saved some for me, Pippa. Especially after I trudged out here because you insisted.” Percy may have sounded grumpy, but I knew he loved these moments just as much as I did.

I patted the grass next to me, then offered him a bite. He sat, folding his lanky body as he did so. Then he grabbed the sweet treat. Like me, his eyes closed. I liked to think that he felt what I did when I took that first bite: a wonderful escape with the sun, grass, and wildflowers for our only company.

Percy was a handsome cross between our sister Penelope and me. His dark blond hair had reds in it and a tendency to curl, and his blue eyes always sparkled, lighting up his face. Right now, at eighteen, he could still be described as gangly but would grow into his limbs probably before I had the chance to see him again.

Just the thought of not seeing my brother had my eyes welling up with tears. I glanced away from him and surreptitiously wiped my eyes. I would not let thoughts of my eventual departure ruin the time I had left here. Which was the main reason I had decided not to tell him I was leaving. I didn't want both of us counting down the days we could spend together. It was bad enough that I was doing so.

I jumped up from the ground. "I believe, good sir, I had challenged you to a duel."

"And a duel you shall have, Pippa. But can't I enjoy this sticky bun for just a bit longer?" Percy's eyes were alight with laughter as he watched me grab and unsheathe my foil. He shoved the last bite into his mouth. Jumping to his feet, his foil at the ready, he shouted, "En Garde," through the mouthful of delicious baked dough, and our battle was on.

The two of us lunged, riposted, retreated, and sidestepped atop our grassy knoll until exhaustion overcame us. Like always, Percy had the upper hand in our matches since he insisted I follow the gentleman's rules of the sport. I only beat him when I started throwing extra punches and strategically tripping him. And that always put him in a sour mood. I wanted today's practice to be remembered fondly for a long time, so I kept my shenanigans to a minimum. That was, until there was only one bite of sticky bun left. It wouldn't have been very sisterly of me to just let Percy have it. I grabbed it and bounced to my feet.

"Pippa, I'm going to get you for that!"

"I'd like to see you try!" Hiking my skirts up above my knees, I sprinted away from him.

Running until the grass under my feet became sand and the smell of the ocean filled my nose, I breathed with the waves in and out, over and over again. When Percy collapsed next to me, I handed him half of the last bite without a word. I was going to miss these moments.

* * *

I could feel my palms sweating inside my gloves. My legs were wobbly, and my brain, well, it was telling me flight was better than sticking around for the fight that I was about to cause. I was nervous. But at least I looked smart. Aunt Honoria had given me her stunning teal silk dress. The color not only suited my hair but matched my green eyes to perfection. Not to mention it was ladylike, with fitted, three-quarter sleeves, a slight V-neckline with just a hint of lace, and covered buttons down the front of the bodice. The skirt had a slight bustle and just enough pleated ruffles that embellished the long drape and bottom of the skirt to look stylish, but not so much that the ruffles overpowered my slight frame. Right now, I hoped the proper clothing would please my mother and make what I was about to do easier.

"Good evening, Mama, Papa," I said as I entered the parlor, running my hands over the front of my dress, trying to quell my nerves.

"Philippa, why do you insist on wearing that dress when you have so many lovely ones upstairs? That one is way too bold a color to be considered proper." Apparently, my idea of wearing proper clothing to ease into this conversation did not go according to plan.

"Oh, Livy, the dress suits her nicely," my father said. He always tried to lessen my mother's sting, to no avail most times, and definitely not tonight.

"It's okay, Papa, I know the dress suits me better than those frilly frocks upstairs. However, the dress is going to be the least of Mama's worries when she hears what I have come to announce." I took a deep breath, trying and failing to steady my nerves.

"Always so dramatic, Philippa, out with it. What have you

come down to say?" my mother said, almost dismissing my words before I had a chance to speak them.

"Well," I paused, "I have decided that I will attend Grantabridge University. I cannot turn down the opportunity to forge an exciting path for women, opening up different opportunities. This year there will be four of us, but imagine what could happen next year, and the next? And the head steam engineering professor has decided to let me attend his classes. So, I will get the opportunity to learn how to properly assemble a steam engine and so much more. I sent in my acceptance a few weeks ago, and the dormitory opens tomorrow." The words came out one atop of another as if they were racing to leave my mouth.

"I do not care if you sent in your acceptance or not, you will not be attending university." My mother fumed, her normally pale face red with anger.

"I'm afraid, Mama, that you cannot stop me. I am more than old enough to make this decision for myself. In fact, if I was a man, I would have already been at university for years." I stood my ground, not giving an inch, even though it was the hardest thing I had ever done. The censure in my mother's voice was strong and made me want to run to my room and forget I had ever started this conversation.

"However, Philippa, you are not a man. Women are not suited for university, and I will not allow you to drag this family's name down by allowing you to go off on your own. And to a male-dominated institution. No, I simply will not allow it."

"Mama, we do not know that women are not suited to university, because the universities have never let us attend. And I will not be alone. There are three other women that will attend with me. All daughters of gentlemen. The ladies will have their own dormitory with a headmistress. It's all very proper."

"This is unheard of. Do you have nothing to say?" My mother turned to my father, pleading.

"What do you want me to do, Livy? Pippa is correct. She's old enough to make this decision and, short of imprisoning her in this house, we can't stop her." My father, ever the pragmatist.

"Well, Philippa, if you insist on this course of action, don't come crawling back here when it does not go well. You will not be welcome. And I hope you've figured out how you will pay for everything, because you won't get one pence from us." There it was, what I knew would happen from the beginning but had hoped to avoid. My mother always lamented how stubborn I was. She just failed to realize that my stubbornness was from her.

"I assumed it would come to this, Mama, and I'm prepared for it. I don't like it and wish we could find some common ground. Someday, I hope we can." I had played out this conversation in my head so many times over the last few weeks, and while I should probably be angry, I was just hurt. I didn't want to fight with her any more than necessary.

"Livy, you can't mean to disown Pippa. It's just a little schooling," Papa said.

"Schooling! It's more than that, and you know it. I will not let Philippa ruin Penelope's chances of making a good match. Lord Bainbridge is about to propose, and if he were to find out about this, all would be lost." My mother was set to have a fit of the vapors at any moment. I wanted to avoid the dramatic fainting spell if I could.

"It's okay, Papa. I'll be fine. Aunt Honoria has given me a stipend to live off of. I'll miss both of you dearly. But I don't want to ruin Penelope's chances of wedded bliss." I couldn't hide the sarcasm from the last bit, but at least I tried.

"Honoria did what? My sister is always trying to ruin my life." With that, my mother's hand went to her forehead, and she crumpled on the velvet settee.

My father moved swiftly to her side, fanning her. I left the room, dashing the tears from my eyes as they formed. It's not like I wanted to be disowned by my family, but I could not let my mother's antiquated views rule my life. Hopefully, she would see this one day. But for now, this was the only way.

"What have you done now, Pippa?" My perfectly coiffed sister sighed, exasperated with me as always. Penelope's perfect blonde curls framed her heart-shaped face, round blue eyes, and rosebud lips. Her pastel blue dress was somehow perfectly pressed and covered with frills. She was older than me but frivolous and self-centered by nature. As much as I wanted us to have a close relationship, we never developed one. The two of us were just so very different.

I rolled my eyes, "I just told Mama and Papa that I'm leaving for University."

"Are you trying to destroy all my chances?" She stomped her foot, emphasizing her question. "It's bad enough you are always tinkering, but now, before I get a proposal, you're off to university. I'll never get married now thanks to you." Penelope wailed with a foot stomp for extra emphasis.

"Penny," I said, knowing she hated the nickname, "I don't see how my actions will affect Lord Bainbridge. You'll be engaged any day now." I pushed past her, running to my bedroom before she could lay more blame at my feet.

I continued down the hall, stopping outside my room and sighing happily at the peace that lay right beyond the closed doors.

"You're really doing it, Pippa. You're off to Grantabridge tomorrow. Why didn't you tell me sooner?" Percy said as I entered my bedroom. My small traveling cases were already packed, sitting next to the bed.

"Percy, you know this is my room." I looked at him, hands on my hips. I wasn't really upset with his intrusion. In fact, I was happy to see him before I left. I was going to miss him the most.

"You mean it *was* your room. Mother will probably turn it into something else as soon as you're gone. She's so upset with you."

I looked around and sighed. "You're probably right, Percy. Please try to save what you can of mine. Just in case they eventually allow me back, once Penelope is married."

"Now that we've settled on saving your things, I'm going to ask again. Why didn't you tell me you decided to go to University, Pippa? You know I'm all for it. First off, no one deserves it more than you. Second, you can teach me all about it when I'm up there next year. Think of the grand time we'll have. Plus, we could have squirreled away your things a long time ago so you wouldn't worry about them being thrown out if you had shared your plans to leave with me."

"Oh Percy, it was hard enough deciding to go and knowing I was going to have to say goodbye to you. It was just too much. Who's going to get you into mischief without me around?" I was always getting my little brother into trouble, from taking his fencing lessons for him at one point, to convincing him to help me on a few explosive experiments on another, and a general affinity for doing things just outside the boundaries set by society.

"Mother will come around eventually. And who knows, maybe you'll land a duke at University and then she'll have to eat her words. Wouldn't that be grand?"

"No duke is ever going to want me. They'll all think I'm too eccentric, just like Mama. But I hope she comes around at some point. I would hate to be cut off from all of you forever. Try to visit when you can, Percy, or at least write a letter or two while I am down there. I don't know what I'd do if I didn't have you and Aunt Honoria in my life."

"Probably would have turned out to be just like Penelope."

I stared at him for a moment, then hit him with a pillow. "Don't ever say such things."

Chapter Three

I kicked the stand on my steamer bike, steadying it while pushing my goggles up over my leather helmet, and looked around. The Grantabridge Dormitory for Young Ladies: it had a nice ring to it, but in reality, as things rarely do, did not live up to the posh name. The red of the brick building seemed to have run away, and the door was grey and peeling. Definitely not an ostentatious start.

Maybe my sister was right. I shook my head; those thoughts are not allowed to enter my brain. To even think that Penelope, whose only goal in life was to find a husband rich enough to allow her to continue her insipid life, could be right went against everything I believed in.

I squared my shoulders, chin jutting forward in stubborn resolve, and swung my leather-clad leg over the bike, careful not to knock my meager belongings off the back. It was my lifelong goal to study steam engineering at university, and I wasn't going to let a slightly dilapidated building dissuade me from my goal.

At that moment another woman arrived. She was tall and willowy. Dressed to the nines with two footmen bogged down with suitcases, her mauve dress was the height of style, with its fitted bodice, bustle, and ruffles. Ruffles that suited her to perfection.

Her brown hair was perfectly coiffed with a jaunty hat atop that served no purpose other than highlighting the caramel tones in her hair. I overheard her say she expected better than this, but alas, we had to make do. Looking at the newcomer was like watching Penelope float into the dormitory. I thought Grantabridge was only admitting the intellectually elite, not socialites.

Looking back, the dormitory (if you really wanted to call it that) was more like the home of someone that had lost their fortune decades ago and the home had been sitting empty ever since. Clearly, we women were truly welcome here at Grantabridge, I thought sarcastically. No wonder I was always so sassy; my thoughts were even more sarcastic than what I said aloud.

I grabbed my two suitcases off the back of the bike and followed the socialite to the front door. Trying, and failing, not to roll my eyes, I watched her attempt to delicately open the door. Her petite nose scrunched as she finally gave it a good yank, and she scowled as the hinges protested loudly at being forced to work after so long. She sighed as she looked down at her no longer pristine-white glove. It looked like she thought about trying to wipe off the dirt, but then thought better of it, she lifted her skirts up by her fingertips and crossed over the threshold.

I slowly followed her in. If the outside looked decrepit the inside was just as lackluster. Dingy and dusty were two of the nicest descriptors that came to mind. An older, stern-looking woman stood in front of us. I don't know how she did it, but she managed to match the building. Her grey dress was somehow both fashionable and looked like it had seen better days. Her hair, also grey, was pulled back tight, accentuating her frown and furrowed brow. I would have thought she would be expecting the first female class allowed at University to be arriving. But she seemed a strange combination of put-out and surprised.

"Georgiana Spencer," announced the socialite, her calling card magically appearing. Wait, calling card? Were we supposed to have those? "I've been told this is where the entering class of lady students will be living." Her pristine smile was so out of place here.

The older woman turned towards me, scowling. "Philippa

Stanhope," I responded to her unasked question. I dropped my suitcase and held out my hand, which the older woman looked at with a sniff of disdain. Fine then. I picked up my suitcase. "And you are?"

"Millicent Pierce, the proprietress of the dormitory."

"How wonderful!" Georgiana clapped in delight. I rolled my eyes. I could not see how anything about Millicent Pierce, proprietress, was wonderful. "If you are the proprietress, you can show us to our rooms. I've been so looking forward to settling in."

Millicent huffed, but it was like she was infected by Georgiana. I'm sure if I had shown up on my own, I would still be standing in the entryway trying to get acknowledged. Granted, I barely looked like a girl—well, that's not exactly true. I looked like a girl, but I definitely didn't look like a proper lady. In my leather leggings, oversized shirt, and mini-pack belted around my waist, I might have been a boy at first glance. Until you looked, then you noticed that my bum did not look like that of a young man. And then you had my hair: right now it was braided in two long pigtails that hung over my shoulders. My leather helmet hid most of my hair, or at least hid the color that people always found shocking.

I followed them to the stairs, wondering if our rooms would be on the upper floors, the rooms reserved normally for servants. That made me wonder what Miss Spencer would do with all her things if we ended up in the servant quarters.

Our mismatched troupe headed up the stairs, each step a new protest, a new sound. They creaked and groaned, communicating more than the three women walking up them. It was a symphony of complaints only a house could make, and my immediate thought was that there would be no sneaking out of this dull grey behemoth. Yes, everything just looked grey. Like someone had come in, said that there was just too much color, and muted everything. The fact that it was grey and threadbare in places just added to the impression we were not truly welcome at University. This seemed like a test they hoped would scare us away. I hoped the four of us were more determined than whoever assigned us this building to make our home.

When we reached the top of the stairs, Millicent nodded her head to the right, her eyes meeting mine for the first time, then pointed to the room at the end of the hall. "The one at the end is yours, Miss Stanhope," she bit out.

I nodded, glanced at Miss Spencer and her minientourage, who were just now making it up the stairs, then turned towards my room. At least I was able to afford a room at the University, silently thanking Aunt Honoria. My very dignified parents—well, my mother anyway—might not approve of what they called my bookish habits, but I thought she would have expected better than what the University had offered us as our dorm. She may have disowned me, but she would never tolerate me being treated as less than her status required. Penelope had just looked on as our parents disowned me. I'm sure she agreed with Mother that I was a disgrace to the family and would see the dilapidated dorm as something I deserved. At least my brother, Percy, was, well, my brother. He understood why I needed to be here . . . maybe not in this building, but at Grantabridge. The years of him sneaking me his lesson books had paid off. I made it into University and my dear younger brother would always be on my side.

I opened the door. Surprisingly there was no creak or squeak. I stepped in and looked around. The room was surprisingly large—like, unexpectedly large. There was a bed that actually looked inviting off to the right. I was terribly sad I had to leave my decadent, fluffy bed behind, but I figured I was going to have to sacrifice a lot for this experience. On the other side of the room was a table and chair. Set up like a desk, but the table provided a larger workspace than most desks I'd seen. However, the corner did not provide nearly enough light to make a good study space. There was an empty bookshelf and a small chest of drawers by the table. Closer to the bed was a wardrobe and a nightstand.

My belongings looked quite meager up against the background of the large room, but dashing off to University against my family's will led to grabbing things in haste and not looking back. Thank goodness for Aunt Honoria; if she hadn't shown up out of the blue and set me up with a monthly stipend, I don't know where I would be right now. Actually, I do, and it wouldn't be unpacking my bags at Grantabridge University. It would be sitting at home waiting on Lord WhatsHisName to call my mother, hoping for a quick marriage that would keep me out of trouble.

Luckily for me, Aunt Honoria had turned her nose up at that sort of life, showing up for a visit every few months after some grand adventure and telling Percy and me stories of traipsing through the Omazenas rainforest, riding on a camel in Junhar, climbing mountains in Eletharis, and so much more. I looked around after putting away the last of my things and flopped on the bed, ready to start truly living my life, like Aunt Honoria lived hers.

* * *

What in heaven's name was that noise? Some sort of cross between a bird dying and a bell clanging was all my foggy mind could make out before the banging started on my door.

"Tea!" someone yelled from outside my room.

Groggily I rubbed my eyes as I contemplated holing myself up in my room, maybe even finishing the nap I hadn't realized I started but now desperately wanted to finish in peace. The grumbling of my stomach informed me it had other ideas and I'd better make my way downstairs. Tea meant food, and at this point I had no idea when there would be food served at the dorm, or if it would even be edible.

I made my way downstairs, the same creaks and groans betraying my every step as they did on the way up. I peeked into each room I passed. Nothing stood out as being particularly well appointed; it was all rather shabby. I'm sure long ago, it had been quite nice. I heard commotion behind a set of double doors. It sounded like I found the place where tea was being served. I pulled open the door with a loud creak and stopped.

Everyone turned to stare at me. I looked down. Bloody hell, I had forgotten to change my clothes. I was still in my steamer bike attire, definitely not dressed for tea. There was nothing I could do now; I shrugged and continued into the room. There was a seat next to Miss Georgiana Spencer, but I was sure she wouldn't want to sit next to me. She still looked so put together, something I struggled to achieve even on the best of days. There were two other ladies my age who must have arrived while I slept, my fellow university mates I assumed. One was wearing the most stunning color of emerald green that complemented the rich tawny tones of her skin and her black hair, the shiniest I had ever seen. The other looked like she was doing her best to blend into the background, and if the house wasn't so grey, her light tan dress would have done the trick. There was absolutely nothing remarkable about her in appearance, until she looked at you with her icy blue eyes. Eyes that stood out because everything else about her seemed to be from the same neutral color palette.

Georgiana waved me over and gestured to the seat next to her. "Philippa, do come sit by me. We didn't have a chance to chat earlier, and I do so want to get to know everyone." Energy radiated off of Georgiana, and my post-nap brain wanted to be able to siphon some of it off from her and use it for myself.

"Miss Spencer . . ."

"No, no, no, you must call me Georgi. We are going to be living together for at least the next year. We can't go around calling each other Miss this and Miss that. Let's dispense with the formalities immediately. We are modern women after all."

I smiled despite myself. It seemed I had judged Miss Spencer quite harshly and inaccurately. "Then you should call me Pippa, only my mother and my incredibly stuffy sister call me Philippa."

"Pippa, that's splendid." Georgi clapped her hands in delight.

"I feel the overwhelming need to apologize to you, Georgi. I wasn't very nice when we first met. I hate to say it, but your appearance reminded me so much of Penelope, my sister, I assumed you were going to be quite a bit like her. I have never been so happy to be wrong." I probably shouldn't have said anything, Georgi was so nice, and I had not been nice at our first meeting.

"Oh tosh! It's all part of the game we must play as ladies."

She glanced at me. “What are you here to study? How did your family take it when you decided to come to University? Do you know anyone here yet?” Georgi rattled off question after question, then turned to the other ladies. “Pippa, this is Madeleine Cavendish.” The dark-haired beauty nodded; she seemed to be fighting back a smile. “And with her is Wilhelmina Schulz.” Our monochromatic companion looked wide-eyed, as if she was surprised anyone realized she was there.

“I’m hoping to study steam engineering. I built the steamer bike I arrived on, but I know there’s so much more I can learn. And . . . well, my family isn’t the least bit supportive. My mother disowned me and my sister accused me of ruining her life. But hopefully, my brother, Percy, will be attending University in a year or two.”

“Maybe I should be more offended you thought I was going to be like your sister. How unfortunate about your mother. My parents were chuffed when I got the acceptance letter. All the money on tutors finally paid off. Although I’m not sure they knew what to do with me next. I’d already read every book in our library at least once. And they were done bringing in language tutors, especially after the last one.”

The last one, I thought. I wonder what happened there.

“I’m sorry, I ramble when I’m nervous and I’m always nervous meeting new people. It’s either sit in awkward silence or I can’t stop talking. There is no in-between.”

“But you were so efficient earlier,” I said before I could stop myself.

“Oh, it was all an act. When I’m in a new situation, I like to pretend I’m my mother and try to handle it the way she would.”

I was shocked, Georgi was nothing like I expected. I guess I really shouldn’t be all that surprised. But after our first almost-meeting, I had thought of her so much like my sister. And I couldn’t be more pleased with how wrong I was. “What are you studying, Georgi?”

“Politics and the law. I’ve been reading all these theories on society, social contracts, laws, and I think we can be so much better. I really don't understand how the four of us are the first women to attend the University. And they haven't decided to confer a degree when we finish. We are just supposed to be thankful to have the opportunity to attend class, study, pass tests, and not get our degree."

"One step at a time, Georgi. We had to get our foot in the door before we could dismantle the institution from the inside," the third woman at the table said gracefully. I'm not sure how you speak gracefully, but she did somehow. She looked over at me, her golden eyes bright. "I'm Madeleine Cavendish, but please call me Mads, all my friends do. Madeleine is just so formal and Brythionite. Georgi and I had just discovered that we share an interest in languages before you came down. Although for different reasons. She learned them to read books in their original language. I just love the patterns they form. Each language is like its own code. Secret, until you finally figure them out."

Mads was stunning, with thick, black hair and bright golden eyes that set off her tawny-colored skin. And her dress was so bold. My mother would just die if I ever wore something so bold. But it suited everything about Mads. This was a woman that was meant to stand out, and it looked like she was comfortable doing so.

"Interesting, I've never thought of it that way. Are you studying language then?" I asked.

"Heaven's no. I'm a mathematician. I love code breaking and other puzzle solving. My sisters are always mocking me about my deciphering."

I turned to the last woman at the table. She was studying her nails with great interest. Her blonde hair was pulled away from her face, showing off a light tan. And she wore a very simple, beige dress. I looked up, Georgie and Mads both shrugged. Georgi mouthed, "Wilhelmina."

"What about you, Wilhelmina? What are you studying?"

"It's W-W-W-Willa, I'm g-g-going to study herbology. I want to open my own apothecary." Her nails continued to be her main focus as she spoke.

"That's fantastic, Willa. It'll be like having our very own

doctor on-site," I said.

"Oh, and m-m-my brother, Toby, is here. He really didn't want me to come." She glanced up as she finished her sentence, her eyes darting from each one of us and back.

"Well, I'm so glad you didn't listen to him," Georgi said, taking Willa's hand in hers. "If you hadn't come, then we would have never met you, and that would have been quite a loss to us all. I just know it."

And just like that, the four of us became fast friends.

Chapter Four

I tossed and turned in the foreign bed I now called my own all night: drifting off to sleep in spurts, waking up not knowing where I was, remembering where I was, and then starting the cycle all over again. As much as this is where I knew I should be, where I wanted to be, I was still nervous.

There were so many people that did not think women were capable of attending University and succeeding. They believed the stress of learning was too much for the feminine constitution, and the tax on a woman's system would prohibit her from her only purpose in life: bearing children. The theory seemed ridiculous, yet it's exactly what the high court case in Eletharis stated when a woman had petitioned to attend law school and was denied simply because she was not a man.

I knew some of the faculty fought to allow just the four of us in, and even then, there were some professors that would not teach us because they believed working with us would be a waste of their time and a distraction from the male students. Then, there were even those outside of the University who were opposed to the advanced education of women. I was also concerned with the other students. Namely, the male students. There had been such an uproar among the current student class when women attending

University was discussed. It's one of the reasons we wouldn't be conferred a degree, just work our arses off like we would get one but have the symbol of our achievement withheld from us.

I contemplated what I was going to wear for my first class. The class was alchemy, and I knew it would eventually have a lab portion. Part of me wanted to just dress practical, but practical was scandalous because it involved me wearing my leather leggings and showing that I did, indeed, have legs. I should dress properly in one of my bustled gowns Aunt Honoria gave me. But I was afraid the dress would get in the way. Either too much bustle or too many ruffles and I could go up in flames, or something equally dramatic. I was probably overthinking this completely. I mean, it was the first day. Maybe we wouldn't even cover much. Or it would just be a lecture. I seriously doubted they would give us access to fire on the very first day.

With that in my head, I grabbed a cobalt-blue skirt with matching vest, one of my tailored white shirts, and a decorative scarf I normally fashioned like a cravat. I laced up my boots, threw on my rather small bustle, and I shrugged on my short, refusing to wear the longer corsets (much to my mother's dismay), quickly cinched it, and grabbed my shirt. Next, the blue skirt and vest went on, along with the cute scarf. I turned back and forth in front of the mirror; I looked rather studious, without a hint of the wildness that came so naturally to me.

Next, I had to deal with my hair. I took my long braids and twisted them on the back of my head, shoved some pins in—it was the only thing I knew how to do with my hair without the help of a lady's maid—and walked out my door.

And immediately ran into Georgi.

"Pippa, I'm so sorry. I'm so nervous, I wasn't even watching where I was going." Georgi stopped speaking long enough to look up and take a breath. "Don't you look rather smart? I adore your outfit choice for the first day of class. I swear Hannah was at her wit's end."

"You look splendid, Georgi! But who's Hannah?"

"Oh, did I not mention her last night? She's my lady's maid. I can't do anything without her. She always helps me decide when I'm at a bit of a loss on what's best." Georgi glanced down at her ensemble. "I've been going back and forth all morning, unable to decide how to proceed. How do we maintain we are 'normal' women, but also that we are meant to be at university? Wanting to be unique, but encouraging all who see us to believe women should be able to attend university."

Georgi looked stunning in a dusty blue ensemble with too many pleated ruffles on the skirt to count. Her apron drape fell over the bustle perfectly, and her bodice was high-necked with piping that accentuated her waist. The entire ensemble was perfection on her.

"Oh, Georgi, and I thought I was overthinking it. I was just trying to decide if I should dress practical but scandalous, or if I should risk setting myself on fire by wearing clothing with a bustle and ruffles." I shook my head. "I've never thought this much about what to wear out, not even for my coming-out ball. My mother and sister are both obsessed with clothing but I've never understood it."

Georgi's head jerked towards me, her effervescent smile wavering. "Did you say you didn't understand the obsession with clothing? Pippa, it's one of the few tools a woman has in her arsenal. Clothing tells everyone your status, your values, even your profession. You can tell the world that you are coy, prim, scandalous, and so much more. It's one of the few things we have in this world where we have more options than men. Just think, you were worried about what to wear today, and I can see your practical concerns, but you chose something that was feminine in form, with masculine accessories. I assumed to let anyone you interact with know that you belonged."

"I've never thought about women's clothing like that at all. It has always seemed so frivolous to be so caught up in it. I'll have to give it some thought."

"What class are you off to now?" Georgi said.

"Alchemy with Professor Marcus Aneurin. I'm hoping by

studying transmutation I can discover a new method of heating water. Right now I use heating stones, but I'm hoping for something that lasts longer and is easier to transport. Just the process of transmutation causes heat, so there has to be a way. Plus, he teaches steam engineering, which is my absolute passion. And I want to fix my steamer bike. So far, I've only been able to ride it wearing pants, which will not sell to women. I want to create a cage for skirts to go over, but I can't figure out a safe spot for the steam pipe. The only way this is going to take off is if it's safe and somehow proper." I lost myself in my musings. "I'm sorry, Georgi, I didn't mean to continue on so. What class are you off to today?"

"My dear Pippa, it is exciting to hear you go on. We women need to support each other, especially in this new endeavor. Just think of what your inventions could do to change the women's place in society. Especially if you can make something proper by society's strict rules. I'm off to Greek political philosophy. My studies at the moment won't have a tremendous impact on the future like yours will, but I'm hoping by studying the ancients, I can find some logic that will promote advancement."

With that, we said our farewells for the day, going to our different corners of town where each of our classes was being held.

* * *

I made my way to class, walking through downtown Grantabridge. The women's dorm was about as far away from the University as you could get and still be considered in town. It would be so much easier to get there on my steamer bike, but until I figured out the venting problem, I was going to have to walk. I don't think the almost-all-male university was ready to see me in leather leggings. Of course, I say that now, on my first day of class. I wonder how long it will take before I'm riding to class, barely thinking of what is or is not proper.

Grantabridge was a rather lovely town with old stone buildings and cobblestone streets. Every now and then, you would cross a street to find brick sidewalks under your feet or brick buildings rising above your head, some newer than others, although calling them new was a misnomer. I thought the newer buildings were still around a hundred years old.

I reached the market at the center of town, where locals were selling fresh vegetables, jars of jam, and even some lovely wooden sculptures. Passing the market, I stopped for a moment on the famous Granta Bridge that allowed one to safely walk over the Granta River. I already knew the bridges in this town would become my favorite spots. There were over five bridges crossing over the river as one walked through town. The Granta Bridge was just the largest, with its arched stone structure. As I stood on the bridge, I could see the reflection of the next bridge on the calm river water, as well as the townhomes on either side of the river. Each side of the bridge had a lovely park, and early as it was, there were nannies out with their charges already. I smiled as the young ones frolicked by the water's edge, their guardians yelling at them to stay out of the river.

Percy would have been in the river in less than a second as a child, I thought.

After passing by the modiste, milliner, and cobbler (the shopping trifecta), and then the ice parlor and a steam mechanic shop, I finally arrived at the university building that was supposed to hold my class. The building must have been around since the 1600s, maybe even earlier. Even though the building was old, it was in much better shape than the women's dormitory.

I looked at the heavy wooden door that could lead me to so many things, took a deep breath, and pushed it open. On the other side of the door stood an empty room. Well, not an empty room. There was one man in it standing at a workstation that looked like a project had exploded papers on it, but it was too much trouble to clean up the debris, so he just kept working. He was on the tall side, spectacles sliding down his sharp nose. His clothes were stylish, but not quite what I would expect from a student here. University learning still preferred the rich, and especially the extremely rich, as students, and not much else. The room itself had paneled walls with wall sconces evenly spaced around the room, multiple bookcases, two wingback chairs, rows of tables and chairs, and a fireplace.

I cleared my throat cautiously. The man looked up from whatever he was doing, quite startled.

"Hello," I said with a bit of hesitation. "I'm here for the alchemy course."

"You must be Philippa Stanhope," the man said, wiping his hands on his waistcoat. "I apologize for the disarray. I hardly ever see any of my students at the beginning of the term. It's only around exams that they come to my workshop or my office." He focused on allowing me to study him further. This man seemed to vibrate with frenetic energy. He was tall and lanky, with a slight hunch to his shoulders, probably from spending all day hunching over his desk. His wavy brown hair was in complete disarray, with a set of spectacles—well, some unique cross between regular glasses, opera glasses, and goggles—perched atop of his head in addition to the set on his nose. His waistcoat was made of fine fabric, but he had missed a button here and there. He was not at all what I expected, to say the very least.

"What? But I thought we had class today; isn't it the first day of classes?" I questioned.

"They didn't tell you ladies how things worked? Obviously they didn't tell you because you're here now. That is disappointing," he said, trailing off to a mutter. He looked up at me. "Well, Miss Stanhope, most of the students complete their studies here independently. While there are professors for certain subjects, we are here mostly to continue our own work and guide students when they need guidance. Which is normally around exams."

I stood there, perplexed. This did not fit in with my view of university at all. I was hoping to be able to work with other like-minds, learn from those that had been on this path for longer than me. If all this would be was independent study, what was the point of, well, everything?

"Professor—"

"Marcus Aneurin," he interrupted with a slight bow.

"Professor Aneurin, I didn't come to Grantabridge for independent study. I'm not allowed to take exams, which means I won't get an actual degree, but I still risked everything to come. My mother has disowned me for ruining the family name, and I thought it was okay because, well, because I was going to be learning from the best. But learning on my own? I've been doing that at home forever. I could have continued doing that and still be living comfortably, not any closer to solving the problem of long-term heat dispersion, or how to make my steamer bike run longer and also account for a lady's attire," I rambled, my heart sinking in my chest.

I felt tears start to well in my eyes. I willed myself not to cry now, to wait until I was back in the decrepit dorm. But I wasn't sure if my will was enough to stop them. I couldn't help but think I had given up everything, for absolutely nothing.

Chapter Five

I turned away quickly, attempting to wipe the tears from my eyes before they actually started to fall. Apparently willing them not to fall wasn't working as well as I hoped. Not that I thought it was really going to work.

"Miss Stanhope, did you say 'long-term heat dispersion?' "

I turned back to him, assuming he would actually be looking at me. I assumed wrong. He was rather frantically sifting through papers on his desk. The complicated glasses contraption slipped down onto his forehead, while his actual spectacles slipped off his nose.

"Yes, I've been trying to determine how to travel long distances on my steamer bike," I began. "Right now, I have what I call heating stones, and they work, but the water cools off so quickly. You have to constantly add stones, which is a distraction from the road, and while a handful of stones isn't heavy, if you wanted to make a long trip, you would weigh down the bike before long. I've tried everything I can think of to create something better, but nothing seems to work. I was so hoping in coming here I would get to work with others that are interested. Finally have someone to discuss ideas with. But if there's no formalized instruction, I don't see how that's going to work." My voice trailed off as he looked up at me. Everything about him was slightly askew, however, his brown eyes gleamed with intelligence.

"I can see where heat dispersion would be a problem, especially trying to keep the vehicle lightweight for ease of movement."

I watched as Professor Aneurin shuffled papers around his desk, writing a note here and there, muttering under his breath.

"Professor, I'm not sure what to do? Do you want me to stay or not?" The longer I stood there, the more awkward I felt. I had no idea what I should be doing at this point. I felt like my dreams had been crushed only for this small beam of light to push through, maybe getting brighter with each moment that passed.

"Do you have the steamer bike with you? I've never seen a powered bike before."

"No professor, I have to wear leggings when I ride the bike. I was worried about appearances if I showed up to class looking, well, scandalous in the minds of many."

"Yes, I see, I see." More mumbling, more shifting of papers, however, there were no answers to my questions.

I stood there, mouth agape. It was like I had disappeared as soon as I stopped speaking. Professor Aneurin paced around the room, grabbed a book here, moved a paper there, jotted down a note, then grabbed another book. None of it seemed structured. Then there was the constant muttering. I couldn't make out what he was saying. Just that something was being said.

"Well, Professor, since there's no class, I guess I should be going." I turned to leave. Where I was going to go, I wasn't quite sure. Maybe see if Grantabridge had a flavored ice parlor? I thought I saw one on my walk over here, and an ice parlor seemed like the place to go to figure out what to do when everything started to fall apart and if, god forbid, my mother was actually correct in not wanting me to attend university.

"Wait, what? I thought you said something about giving up everything to be here and wanting to solve these problems." He looked at me expectantly.

"Well, yes, but I'm not sure how my standing here is going

to solve anything." I really didn't know what to do, but clearly he expected something.

"Of course, standing there isn't going to solve anything, so find a way to be useful. At the very least, grab a book and start reading. I suggest one of the books on transmutation. Just the process that creates heat, there could be something there." He gestured to the books closest to the fireplace.

"I was just saying that to one of the other women in my dorm this morning. It's why I was so excited to take alchemy. I think it will apply to steam technology. I'm just not exactly sure how." I felt excitement start to bubble. Maybe this university thing would work out. In fact, maybe, just maybe, it was going to turn out better than expected.

I walked over to his shelves and looked at the titles, looking for something I hadn't read yet. The excitement of working with someone on these projects poured through me, putting an extra bounce to my step. I don't know why the professor was changing his plans, but I wouldn't have wanted it any other way. I grabbed what looked like an introduction to alchemy text since my knowledge was rather limited on that subject and went to the corner to read.

As I settled into the chair, I looked around the room. In some ways it was just like what I thought a classroom would be. There were tables and chairs lined up for students to listen to a lecture. Then there was everything else. Professor Aneurin's desk was a mess of papers and scribbles in piles that covered every single inch of his desk. The chalkboard behind the desk had about a dozen equations on it and three drawings of new technology. One looked like it might be a steam-powered wagon of some sort. I would think it was similar to the horseless carriage or steam carriage but adjusting the body design to allow for transporting goods rather than people. It was all so fascinating to me, almost like looking inside a person's brain and seeing how it worked. I thought about asking the professor about the designs, but I stopped myself; the way this was going, I was sure I would have plenty of time to ask about them in the future.

Finally, I settled into the chair fully and started reading. I almost tucked my feet under me as I read, then remembered I was not in my home or room but in someone else's workspace. I wasn't ready to expose myself as the truly improper lady I was, at least not quite yet. The subject itself was absolutely fascinating, even if it was a combination of review and new things. I could see where there might be a path to fixing the current drawbacks with steam engineering.

* * *

Moments later, or potentially hours, two gentlemen burst through the door. Both tall, fit, and wealthy. Or at least their clothing was extremely well tailored. However, the similarities ended there. One gentleman had brown skin, black hair, eyes that looked like amber, and a full mouth that seemed to be on the verge of a smile, and I was pretty sure the smile would lead to dimples. The other was almost the opposite in looks: sandy hair, blue eyes, and tight lips that were already smirking. Probably always smirking. He made me uncomfortable.

"Professor Aneurin, we need your time," the man with the smirk said.

"Ah, Lord Middleton, how nice to see you. Rather unexpected this early in the term," Professor Aneurin said.

I looked around, observing the demeanor of both Lord Middleton and Professor Aneurin, and I was at a loss. Do I continue my research in the corner? Should I pack up and head back to the dormitory? At the moment Lord Middleton had yet to notice me, but I was sure it wouldn't be long before he did, and I wasn't sure I was comfortable with him knowing I was there.

"Simon, it appears that the professor is busy at the moment. We should schedule a time to come back," the other gentleman said as his eyes met mine. I felt my heartbeat quicken as we held eye contact just a second longer than I was used to.

I then looked away quickly, not sure if I was thankful or annoyed that he had brought attention to me. I was feeling just a little thankful I had caught his attention. He was quite attractive. However, I watched Lord Middleton as he realized the professor was not alone. Surprise, and then contempt, registered on his face, his mouth going from smirk to sneer. At that moment, I decided I was annoyed, definitely annoyed.

"I'm sure the professor has time for us, Fremont. He does not appear to be too busy to speak to me," Lord Middleton said, dismissing my very presence in the room. "And Fremont, you should not forget you are the next Duke of Nordaoine. You should not be put off when you need something."

"Really, Middleton, it is not that important." Lord Fremont shuffled his feet, his hands clenched and unclenched. It was clear he was uncomfortable being here right now. Seeing his discomfort was almost enough for me to forget that I was annoyed with him.

"You dragged me all the way down here, Fremont. Are you really going to let some upstart girl stop you from getting the information we came for? After all, it was your brother who was murdered," Lord Middleton said.

I looked up in shock. Murdered? I'd read about the death of Edmund Fremont in the papers over the summer. The papers had attributed his death to a highway robbery gone terribly wrong. What could Professor Aneurin know about the heir to a dukedom's death? And why would the new heir think the professor knew anything?

And then this "upstart girl" business. With the dorm and the utter lack of information of what University was going to be like, it was clear no one wanted me or the other women here. What else could people do to make it clear that I didn't fit in and shouldn't be at University? The petty child in me wanted to pack up and walk out, saying, "Sticks and stones, Lord Middleton, sticks and stones." But my knowledge about people like him implied even that would be an unsatisfactory experience.

"Professor Aneurin," I said, "I would love to take a few books back to my dorm, if you don't mind. I think I might have an idea that could help create a controlled heat transference, allowing for longer travel."

"Already? Yes, yes, take any books you need. We should meet later this week to see if the readings bear any fruit. Say, Thursday afternoon?" Aneurin said.

I leisurely looked over the titles as Lord Middleton stared at me, mouth agape. Lord Fremont inched his way closer to the door, looking like he was trying to escape unseen, which was impossible since he had to be over six feet tall. Someone that tall and that striking did not just leave a room without being noticed. Eventually, I grabbed the three books I planned on taking all along and sauntered past Lord Middleton, then nodded at Lord Fremont before turning to Professor Aneurin with a wave.

"I will see you Thursday, Professor." With that little show, I left the room, stopping the door from shutting completely, annoyed at being judged on the basis of nothing other than my gender.

"I do not understand why you argued to have women allowed into the University, Professor. They are nothing but frivolity. I mean, how long does it take to pick out a few books to read? Assuming she actually reads them and that wasn't some act in the 'How to Catch a Titled Husband' play," Lord Middleton said.

"Lord Middleton, I've seen Miss Stanhope's designs. They are . . ."

"She probably copied them from a book she saw somewhere."

I rolled my eyes listening to this drivel. Of all the excessively chauvinistic things I've heard in my life, this was the worst! I really should stop eavesdropping. I never heard anything good.

"I can assure you, Lord Middleton, they are not copied. I'm looking forward to working with her the rest of the year, hopefully."

"Aneurin, I know you and Edmund fought for this travesty. Really, women attending university, but I'm prepared to move on if . . ."

The door I was listening through opened. I jumped back, startled, narrowly avoiding being run over by Lord Fremont.

"Excuse me, Miss Stanhope, I didn't expect anyone to be outside the door," he whispered.

"Oh, it's nothing. Lord Fremont, I assume. Although, I'm

not sure of your title, heir to the Duke of Nordaoine seems a little ostentatious at this point." I was rambling. I rambled when I was flustered, and I was flustered. He just caught me eavesdropping but seemed nice enough to ignore my actions.

Up close, I could see his eyes were multiple shades of brown, darker on the outside and lighter next to the pupil. I noted his fingers were long, strong, and calloused as he pulled on his black gloves. Calloused—not what one would expect of an aristocrat.

"It's Fremont, Kaiden Fremont." Apparently he didn't notice how discombobulated I was, or was considerate enough to ignore it. "Future duke, but not by choice."

"Thank you, Lord Fremont. It's a pleasure meeting you," I responded like I was at a ball and had just been introduced by a society matron during my first season. I needed to get out of there before I actually said something stupid. "I'm sorry about your brother." I turned to leave but was stopped by his crisp voice.

"Thank you, Miss Stanhope. I appreciate your kind words. My brother would have been so encouraged to see you here at University." He paused for a beat, then hesitantly asked, "Can I help you carry your books back to the dorm?"

I turned back to see his gaze flick to Aneurin's workshop and watch him tug his sleeves down, as if the clothes were not made for him. Although, his clothes were definitely made for him. The fit of his black coat and magenta waistcoat left no question to his station or that the fabric was covering quite broad shoulders.

"There's no need. I can manage just fine. Plus, I wouldn't want some upstart of a girl to inconvenience you," I said, shocking myself. Where did that come from? Lord Fremont hadn't said any of the awful things his friend had spewed.

"Miss Stanhope, I don't believe any of the nonsense that Lord Middleton was spouting."

I tried to say I know and I'm sorry. Everything Lord Fremont said had been kind. Nothing like Lord Middleton. Instead, nonsense leapt from my mouth. "And yet you seem to be close acquaintances, friends even, one might say." With that, I turned and walked away, leaving Kaiden Fremont agape, standing outside the alchemy classroom.

I thought I heard Lord Fremont say, “I never claimed we were friends,” as I continued on my way.

Chapter Six

By the time I walked back to the dorm, I was absolutely famished, still somewhat embarrassed, and dying to tell my new friends about what had happened. Thankfully, as I entered our perpetually grey building, Miss Pierce was setting out luncheon. My stomach grumbled just thinking about it.

The rest of the ladies were already sitting around the table. Miss Pierce had set out buttered bread, slices of cold beef, and a plum pudding. The meal on the table was definitely not as sumptuous as the ones I would have at home, but it looked to be enough to satisfy my hunger, at the very least.

The ladies didn't stop chatting when I entered the room. I was surprised to see all of them here together already. I hoped their day had gone as well, if not better, than mine. I realized we might all have had an interesting and potentially disappointing morning. The fact they were already back at the dorm did not bode well for a good start on this educational journey.

I flopped—yes, flopped—down into my chair. Nothing graceful about it. Then tossed the books I had onto the end of the table where no one was sitting. Georgi, Mads, and Willa looked on with some amusement. I guess I was being a tad dramatic. But it felt like I had lived a week in one morning, so maybe the drama was well deserved. Plus, who doesn't like a little drama in one's life?

"Good afternoon, ladies. How was everyone's first day? Was it what you expected? Because mine was nothing like I expected and I'm not sure how I feel about it yet," I said, taking a small plate and filling it with a couple pieces of bread and slices of beef, then returning to my seat. I couldn't wait to hear how everyone else had handled the change in expectations. I assumed we all confronted today.

"Well, if you're asking, Did I get to sit in a room with other like-minds interested in Greek political philosophy and expound on the pros and cons of democracy with them? The answer is a resounding no," Georgi said. "I showed up to the professor's room to find out University is just more independent study. Which is absurd. You would think formal instruction would exist. Some people here want to become barristers and solicitors. Including me, but apparently I have too weak of a constitution to handle the stress. I'm distraught that those upholding the law are barely forced to learn it."

"Finding out that attending university could be the same as staying home and studying is discouraging, to say the least. That being said, the resources are much better here. I did get to meet the math professor," Mads said.

"That is true. I have access to so many treatises. Books I would never have even thought about if I stayed home. Oh look, what did you bring back with you, Pippa?" Georgi grabbed the books I brought back with me, perusing each title in short order. "Pfft, there's only science books here, these aren't even fun."

"Speak for yourself, Georgi. I happen to love science books," I said, smiling. "Mads, what was your math professor like?"

"He was interesting. I spent the most of my time there proving to him I knew the basics of mathematics. It was difficult not to speak my mind. I managed to hold in all my unnecessary comments," Mads said.

"At l-l-least the p-p-p-professor was in the room for your

'class.' No one was there when I showed up."

"Oh Willa, that is so disappointing! It truly feels like they didn't plan for us to be here," Georgi said.

"Seems more likely they are doing whatever they can to drive us out. I don't think we are actually welcome here." I then recounted what I had overheard after leaving Professor Aneurin.

"You met the new Lord Fremont? Did you know his brother was a driving force behind letting women attend the University? If it wasn't for him, we wouldn't be here. The fact highwaymen overtook him is such a loss. Not just to the marriage mart, but to the world. He was constantly on the forefront of progress. I really wish I had met him at some point." Georgi delicately wiped her eyes with her handkerchief. "I can't even imagine being his younger brother right now. The freedom of being the younger son, and out of nowhere, you are next in line for the dukedom. I have heard that they were very close. None of that rivalry you find in so many other families."

"Lord Fremont seemed quite out of his element. Lord Middleton walked in, throwing the weight of his title around." I shoved my chair as I stood. Just the thought of Lord Middleton had me pacing like a caged animal. "Lord Fremont refused to act that way. In fact, he seemed kind, and I treated him like he was Lord Middleton, or at least as arrogant as Lord Middleton. I do not know what came over me. I was so mean, it felt wrong, but I couldn't stop myself." I flopped back into my chair with a groan.

"I always f-f-f-feel awkward around new people, especially men. I think they are judging me," Willa said.

"Titled men do seem to like to judge others and their harshest judgment falls on women. When really they need to take a closer look at themselves," Mads said.

"It was something more, though. I think I was thrown off by everything that transpired this morning. First, there was no class, and I felt like I was lost, but then I spent the morning studying with the professor, even if we didn't speak much. Then Lord Middleton came in with Lord Fremont. And it was just so awful being there. Of course, I couldn't stop myself from eavesdropping after I left. And then I was caught by Lord Fremont. Not that he even alluded to it, but it was so embarrassing. It was nice to hear that Professor Aneurin was one individual championing for us to be here, though." My braids had fallen from the pins that had at least held them up through the morning, and I was nervously twisting the end of one braid around my finger. The day had been too much, and it was only halfway over.

"Did anyone else set up a time to meet with their professor regularly?" I asked.

"I think I will convince my math professor to work with me at least semiregularly. He sent me home with a stack of basic problems. I've looked them over, and saying they are basic is putting it nicely. He assigned the math I was doing for fun when I was ten years old." Mads rolled her eyes. "I'm really hoping to find someone here to work on cryptography with me. I want to both create and decode. And with cryptography having such ancient roots, some even from my country, I want to know so much more."

"Chances are you could actually teach the course on cryptography with your knowledge, not that anyone here would let you, or any of us," Georgi said. "I mean, you are already proficient at different ciphers. Pippa's already built her steamer bike. And Willa, you know more about natural remedies than anyone else I know."

I looked at Georgi, a bit surprised. First, she was able to get Willa to talk? And they talked about remedies? Second, how did she know so much about us so quickly?

"Pippa, you were the lucky one today. We were sitting here forever before you arrived. And Willa made this marvelous tea that cured my awful headache. I was so disappointed that I was stuck reading political theories and not discussing them. I worked myself up into quite a state," Georgi said, answering the questions in my head.

"We are going to have to do something about what is considered formal education here. I'm glad Professor Aneurin will work with me one-on-one. But each of us should be able to do more with this opportunity. Not just what we were doing at home but with a better library." The entire situation we found ourselves in frustrated me. Each of us had so much to offer. But no one seemed to want what we had to offer.

"D-d-d-does anyone smell that? Is something b-b-b-burning?" Willa looked around, frantic.

I looked around and saw smoke sneaking in around the door to the garden. Which made absolutely no sense at all. Covering my mouth and nose, I rushed to the door. Hesitating, I decided opening it was the right course of action, although risky. There at my feet, flames licked the bricks coated in the dead leaves of autumn. "WATER!" If the flames moved to the dried-out garden, it was over, everything would be burned to an absolute crisp. And I couldn't just stomp on it because of my skirts. I definitely preferred not catching myself on fire in the process of extinguishing it.

"Here, it's lemonade but it should work." Georgi thrust the pitcher towards me, and I poured it over the flames, dousing as much as I could, then stomping on the embers that refused to extinguish.

Chapter Seven

For the first day, it had been quite a doozy. All I wanted to do was lay down and recover from everything that happened. Instead, my mind was whirling like the cranks and gears of a steam engine. And what I wanted to do no longer matched with what my mind and body were telling me I had to do. So, instead of flopping onto my bed in the most unladylike of demeanors, I rearranged my room. Whoever designed the room to begin with had not taken the time to actually think about where things would be the most useful.

The desk had to move under the window so I would have some natural light to work. Right now, it was as far from the window as it could possibly get. I tried to drag the desk over, but bloody hell, the thing was heavy. I stopped and scowled at my current nemesis, the giant block of wood currently thwarting my will. This would not do. Hands on my hips, I looked around the room; I had to find a better way. As it was, I was nowhere near strong enough to move the blasted thing on my own.

The floor was smooth wood. If I could lift the desk enough to put something slippery under the legs, I might have a solution. Fabric seemed the best option, but I couldn't afford to use any of my clothes. I grabbed so few, and with all these men around, my leather leggings were not the thing. And leather did not have the right texture to slip across the floor. Plus, I would ruin them if I used them to move the desk, and I hadn't given up on their comfort completely, at least not yet.

Blankets. I needed extra blankets, or at least one. Assuming I could get it under the legs of the desk, a thick blanket should glide it across the floor. Opening up every drawer in the room, I finally found a nice, thick wool blanket. I crawled under the desk, carefully aligning each corner of the blanket with a leg, scooting out from under the desk by the time the last corner was in place. Then, leg by leg, I went over and lifted it, using my booted foot to push the blanket under the desk. Sweat dripped from my brow as I attempted to blow errant strands of hair out of my face. Mother would be at a loss for words if she saw me now, moving furniture like a commoner. Well, it wouldn't be the moving of furniture, it would be the perspiration. Ladies did not perspire, they glistened. And I was well past the point of glistening. I was also huffing and puffing, which was even more of a decorum faux pas.

Blanket situated securely under the desk, I wiped my hands on my skirt and pushed. Bloody brilliant! While the desk didn't necessarily glide effortlessly across the floor, it did move fairly smoothly and wasn't nearly as noisy as I expected. I got the desk, my workstation, situated under the window, happy the window wasn't right by the bed. I did not want to have to move the bed as well. Next, I grabbed the chair and slid it under the desk, placed the handful of books from Aneurin's library on my shelves, and then spread all my notes over my workspace.

What I wouldn't give for a chalkboard for this space as well. I also needed to find some water storage and matches or some other fire starter. At least the room had a small fireplace, so it should be a normal request. My list also included some storage bins. I had all the materials for my experiments I needed to keep in my room. I cleared out the chest of drawers by the bookshelf and moved the extra blankets onto my bed. The supply closet was ready. I would just have to place a bit of my stipend from Aunt Honoria aside every month to actually restock my supplies. I should talk to Mads and see if she would help me set up a budget.

Satisfied with my work, I plopped onto my chair. And well, I don't think I had ever felt something so comfortable. This must be why men always stayed in their study. If I had a chair I could sink into like this at home, I might never have left. Just as I was about to drift off to sleep in that big, comfy chair, fully dressed, boots and corset still on, surprisingly, there was a knock on my door. I got up with a groan, my body angry because I was leaving the chair and hadn't rid myself of my infernal corset yet. It may only be a half corset, but after a while, the restrictive nature of it was too much.

"Pippa, you have to tell me more about your run in with Lord Fremont! I have heard he is absolutely dreamy." Georgi burst through the door as soon as I opened it.

"Ugh, I made such a fool of myself, and was rather, well, mean." I rolled my eyes just thinking about my behavior. "There's no way Lord Fremont would want to be around me ever again." I sighed. I rather thought it would be nice to be around him again, if I could behave like a normal person.

"I just can't believe we are here testing out this program because of his brother. Edmund fought tooth and nail to get us in. And he was up against so much opposition. Even Lady Corinne St. Gramflurri said it was not the purview of ladies to attend University. She believes the very act of learning would inhibit a lady from her purpose in life. And can you guess what that purpose is? Producing an heir and a spare. I did not know I was nothing more than a broodmare. Just good for breeding and nothing else. Old hag."

"Georgi, you can't say stuff like that. What if someone hears?" I agreed with Georgi, but some things were left better unsaid.

"Who's going to hear me express my opinion anywhere, much less in your bedchamber, Pippa? Oh, I like how you moved the desk. Is that what all the racket was earlier? You know Miss Pierce won't like it at all."

"She might not, but I need it set up so I can at least do some work here. Especially since it's not like we are meeting and having class. I don't know why I expected something so structured. But I pictured it more like a formal salon, not well, this."

"Quit trying to distract me, Pippa." Georgi walked around the room, picking up an item here and there, looking at it and then setting it down. I was familiar with that pent-up energy. Those moments where even my body craved something more. "Tell me about the new Lord Fremont."

"Oh, Georgi, there's not much to tell. He attempted to be the perfect gentleman. He offered to walk me back here and carry my books. It completely flustered me. I had just heard Lord Middleton say I was an upstart girl that copied a man's work to get in. And then Lord Fremont almost knocked me down when he opened the door. Catching me eavesdropping, of all things. It was awful. Then I acted like he said all those awful things about women being at the University, the things Lord Middleton said. After that I stormed off in some sort of misplaced righteous indignation. I don't think I can see him again. It was mortifying."

Georgi stopped. "What did Lord Middleton say?"

"Nothing surprising. He pontificated on the fact that women should not be here. Then accused me of copying all of my designs. That's when Lord Fremont came out of the room. Probably a good thing, because storming in and all but admitting to eavesdropping wouldn't have been very ladylike. Bloody hell, I hate trying to be poised and collected all the time."

Georgi started pacing again.

"Are you all right, Georgi? You seem rather out of sorts."

"I'm just reeling from the day. I don't know why, but I expected it to be different here. And then the fire. There's no way it was an accident. Thinking about that and what Lord Middleton said today, I'm just frustrated, and I know tomorrow is another day, but I don't feel ready to put on the smile everyone expects. It's exhausting always being cheerful."

"I have an idea. Shall we have a little adventure?" I ask. "Well, adventure may be too strong of a word, but I think I can teach you something completely new. I sat in on my brother's fencing lessons and after the lessons, with his practice partner. We did this for years. Sometimes I would even stand in for him when he didn't feel like taking his lesson. It would be so much fun to have regular lessons here," I said, already planning a lesson in my head.

"Oh my! That sounds wonderful. Not quite as much fun as sneaking into the library to steal books. But maybe a close second. We can set up in my room, it's much larger than your room." Georgi clapped her hands in delight. I figured she would love something that gave the illusion of control.

"I'll go grab my foils." Yes, in all the things I brought with me to school, my fencing foils had seemed necessary. "Do you want to see if Mads and Willa are interested? I would hate to leave them out. We could set up two areas. One for training with the foils and one for conditioning, since I only have two foils."

We made plans to reconvene in her room. I would gather what gear I had and she would gather our friends. I turned to her with a smile. "Oh, and Georgi, change into something that allows more freedom of movement."

In my room, I quickly changed. First, I put on what I liked to call my sports corset. I designed it after a short corset I found in some old trunks in the attic at home. I left the boning out, just wearing it tightly around my chest. It offered even more movement than the short stays I wore earlier. It allowed me to bend and move at the waist but limited any uncomfortable bouncing. Was it completely comfortable? No, but without it I felt like I was pushing the bounds of society further than even I wished to go. Then I hopped into my leggings and a white shirt, cinching it around my waist with a long, thin piece of teal fabric I had sewn for just this purpose, then grabbed my foils. Georgi was right. I really did think about clothing more often than not. I just didn't think about elegant ensembles. My mind was always looking at ways to make clothing more practical.

I made my way to Georgi's room, keeping my eyes open for Miss Pierce. I really did not think she would approve of fencing lessons happening in her dormitory. But truly, we were grown women. What was the harm in learning new things? I opened the door and found Georgi, Mads, and Willa waiting expectantly, all still wearing long dresses. Although none of them were as frilly as what Georgi had been wearing.

"If we keep this up, we are going to have to make you something less cumbersome than those skirts with all the petticoats. I don't want us tripping over skirts and petticoats that wrap around our legs as we move."

"I want a pair of leggings like yours, Pippa. Those are fantastic," Georgi said.

"I normally only wear them when I'm on my steamer bike. Leather is harder to tear, so it makes for a bit of a safer material both for riding and fencing. I've made all my clothes, so we should be able to work something out that each of you will be comfortable wearing."

"Pippa, did you say you made what you are wearing right now?" Mads said. "That's unbelievable!"

"If w-w-w-we d-d-d-decided to m-m-make something, I could help. I've always been good with a needle. I hope this isn't too impr-pr-pr-proper of question, but what are you wearing underneath that allows you to freely bend at the w-w-w-waist?" Willa said, blushing ever so slightly. Wow, Willa was so pretty when she blushed.

"Oh, I call it my sports corset. I designed it off some short corsets I found in my parents' attic. It's perfect because I still feel ladylike but have a pretty broad range of motion."

"That would be so helpful while gardening."

"Willa, that would be a wonderful use of the corset. Let's get your measurements and I can show you how to make one." I was excited to share more of the things I made. "Shall we get started?"

With that, I created two stations, and we rotated through them until we were all laughing from exhilaration and exhaustion. Well, I didn't rotate since I was the only one who knew how to use a foil. While I worked with Georgi on fencing techniques, like her stance and the proper way to hold the foil, a riposte, and a parry, Mads and Willa worked on balance exercises: standing on one foot as long as possible, lifting one leg behind and holding, and lifting one leg in front and holding, and then push-ups done on the wall for some core strength. All these things we never did as ladies, but I enjoyed because I felt more alert and alive when I was active like this. After we went through a round of exercises, I started fencing techniques with another of my new friends.

Each time we rotated, it became apparent how difficult the balance exercises were. The ladies were struggling. Balance exercises done in corsets and petticoats were difficult because not only would we be fighting against our own weakness, the corset didn’t allow natural posture. So it created a disconnect between where the body wanted to go and where it could go. Needless to say, everyone ended up falling while trying to balance, and after who knows how long, one by one, each of us stayed on the floor. Lying there, I contemplated this amazing group of women and how lucky I was to have found them.

Chapter Eight

Thursday came, and this time I rode my steamer bike to class since Professor Aneurin said he was interested in seeing it. I felt seeing it might help him understand what I wanted to accomplish, and maybe we'll even figure out why I was falling short. Of course, that meant traveling across Grantabridge in my least ladylike clothing, but at least I would be comfortable. Plus, when did I really care about being ladylike? I'd rather run around like this than in an overly fussy ensemble, anyway. If people judged me for it, well, I was used to it.

I filled the tank with water, straddled the steamer bike, pulled my leather cap and goggles on, dropped the heating stones in, kicked the kickstand up, and twisted the accelerator. I loved the heating stones; the transfer of heat to the water happened in an instant, allowing me to be on my way rather quickly. The stones retained the heat until they were immersed in water, so I could heat them in my room and then carry them around in my waist pouch until I was ready to use them. I sped through the narrow streets, taking in everything around me while carefully watching for pedestrians. Even with everything to watch out for, riding the bike always helped clear my head. Maybe it was the breeze caressing me as I sped up, pushing all thoughts away, or the fact that riding left little room to think of anything other than what I was doing—whatever it was, by the time I reached Professor Aneurin's classroom, I felt refreshed, vibrating with energy.

"Professor Aneurin," I said, knocking on the door.

"Miss Stanhope, why don't you just come in?" He stopped, his eyes darting around, taking in the steamer bike. "Oh my, this is your invention. Spectacular! Much more impressive than the drawn-out plans, which were stunning." He held the door open as I moved my invention inside.

Aneurin walked around the steamer bike, muttering to himself as he stopped and looked at some parts more closely. Every now and then he shook his head. I used the frame and wheels of a bicycle as the base of my creation. Removing the pedals, I put my tank in the center body of the bicycle. Attached to the handlebars was the pressure readout, as well as the conveyance for my heating stones. Once the water in the tank was hot, the steam activated the piston, causing the back wheel to turn. The accelerator allowed me to control the pressure of the steam that reached the piston, thereby controlling the speed at which the wheel turned. I'm sure there were adjustments that could be made; the placement of the tank was not the most convenient, to say the least, but I was rather proud of my invention.

"Quite impressive, Miss Stanhope. You designed this on your own?"

"Yes, Professor, I used the principles established by James Watt when he first made his steam engine. I was trying to limit the energy loss, which is considerable, and hopefully create something the average person could use. I want to make adjustments, because I would love more women to use this; however, its design is not conducive to ladies' attire."

"It's a testament to the functionality of your design that you can even consider these changes. I think we have to start with the tank. Scorching hot water that close to the body could be quite dangerous." He picked out one of the biggest problems with my steamer bike right away.

"Professor, I was wondering if there was any way to

insulate the tank? If the tank could be insulated, it would help with two problems. First, the loss of heat would be reduced and it would help prevent burns. I just don't know what to insulate it with?" I asked. Talking about my designs and ideas with another person was new to me. I felt out of my element and unsure of myself.

"What a fantastic place to improve steam engineering. It will not only help your project, but it could have a tremendous impact on the rest of the field. Anything that helps produce steam for longer is essential. Let's focus on finding different insulating materials we can test." He took to my idea right away, heading straight to the bookshelves.

I sighed with relief as we scoured his bookshelves for anything that could help us. I did not know what to expect after our first meeting. Today Professor Aneurin was incredibly focused, and he listened to my thoughts on the subject, which was refreshing. My brother was the only other person who actually listened to me when I talked about steam technology. I should include Aunt Honoria on the list of people that listened, but neither my aunt nor my brother truly understood what I was saying. My aunt was just thrilled with my inventions, and my brother normally spent the time looking for a way to use my inventions but not caring how they worked. The rest of my family considered my inventing a nuisance. So to be here, to be heard, it felt like . . . Oh, I don't know what it felt like, but it was one of the best feelings in the world.

"Professor, what if we sandwiched wool and corrugated board between two metals? Maybe even do multiple layers. More layers should increase the effectiveness of the insulation."

"Hmm . . . that could work. We just need to ensure the insulation could not catch fire. Which would mean a vacuum seal. If there's none, or very little oxygen in the insulation compartment, it should be unable to catch on fire."

I felt like I could work on this all day. Unfortunately, someone had other ideas. Lord Simon Middleton threw the door open and walked through. It appeared he enjoyed making an entrance.

"Professor Aneurin, a moment of your time." Lord Middleton didn't even glance around to take in his surroundings. Barging in and interrupting as if it was his due, he clearly believed that any human must do what he wants, when he wants, simply because of who he was.

"Lord Middleton, I'm busy at the moment. Perhaps we can schedule something later today."

It was then that Lord Middleton looked around, his eyes falling on me. Lounging in a comfy chair, reading about vacuum seals, my leather-clad leg hanging over the armrest while the other leg tucked under me on the chair, I'm sure I looked like a child. At least I still had my boots on.

"Oh, she's here," Simon said, rolling his eyes then instantly dismissing me. I could tell he didn't want me here.

"Professor, why don't I take some of these books back with me? We can meet again on Monday. Maybe run some experiments," I said.

"Oh, thank you, Miss Stanhope. That would be most helpful. I'll see what I can do about supplies."

I gathered my things along with the extra books, walked over to my steamer bike, and rolled it outside, where, quite literally, I ran into Lord Kaiden Fremont. It was like running into a wall. Beneath all the finery of today, Lord Fremont was, well, he seemed to be . . . That is . . . I couldn't even acknowledge what I felt in my own mind.

"Forgive me, I didn't mean to." My eyes stayed cast down, my face heating up, definitely turning an unbecoming shade of red. I couldn't speak to him after I was so rude last time. And now I was looking down at my legs. Bloody hell, my legs were on display in public, in front of a future duke. Why I cared now, and not moments ago, I didn't know, but it seemed to matter at the moment.

"Pardon me, Miss Stanhope." Lord Fremont nodded his head in a polite but perfunctory bow.

I needed to say somcthing to him. Preferably something nice, since I was so awful the last time we met. Instead, I shifted my weight back and forth, wanting nothing more than to jump on my steamer bike and disappear.

"Is that your invention? Professor Aneurin mentioned some of your designs on Monday."

Startled, I looked up. "Yes, I designed and built this." Bloody hell, he was handsome. His brown eyes were soft with kindness, and his lips twitched like he was trying not to break into a smile. Then there were his broad shoulders, tapering to a narrow waist, and he was so tall. I felt like I could have been a woodland sprite next to his warrior-like height.

"Can I look at it? I didn't think I was going to have a chance to study anything like this. I was headed back to the military until . . ." He drifted off.

"Of course you can look at it. Just, um, well. Of course you can look at it."

He walked around the steamer bike. It was a strange experience having two people actually inspect one of my inventions. Then to have it happen on the same day was overwhelming.

After a thorough look, Lord Fremont let out a low whistle. "This is fascinating. I like where you put the water tank. I would think it helps to maintain balance."

"It does, but I'm concerned someone will burn their legs while riding because of its location. It's one of the many reasons I want to figure out a way to insulate the tank. I can imagine the water boiling hot inside the tank, and the outside of the tank feeling lukewarm to the touch."

"That would be quite an accomplishment, Miss Stanhope. Do you have any idea what materials you are going to use?"

"Not yet. Well, I have some ideas, but right now they are too dangerous. I don't want to risk fires starting."

"I could see not wanting to start fires between the legs of anyone using your invention. That definitely would not be top notch. And, Miss Stanhope, this invention is really quite top notch." His deep amber eyes made contact with mine and he smiled, slowly, as if he had all day to stand here and smile at me. And I felt heat rise to my cheeks. God, my face probably matched my hair right now. But really, what was a girl to do when someone complimented her creation so nicely?

“You are too kind, Lord Fremont. This was just me tinkering back home.” Why did I do that? This was a lot of hard work, thoroughly annoying my mother to no end for months and months. Well, she should be proud that all that etiquette training had actually worked. It seemed I wasn’t capable of taking credit for my accomplishments. How very ladylike of me.

“Miss Stanhope, if this is just tinkering, I can’t wait to see what you come up with now that you are at University. You could very well change the world as we know it.”

“I would settle for changing here first. The world can come later,” I said. I had only been at Grantabridge for a few days, but it was quite clear that making it through school was going to be an uphill battle, with constantly proving that I and the other women admitted were as capable as the men, if not more so.

“The world won’t even see you coming. I’ve kept you long enough, Miss Stanhope. Although,” he paused, “I would be honored to walk you back, if you would allow it.” He glanced down at his shoes as if some of the confidence he had just moments ago had left, leaving him out on a limb.

“Are you sure? I was so awful to you the last time we met. I can’t even fathom why I said the things I said.”

“Well, I’m fairly certain it had to do with Lord Middleton being an absolute arse. I see now why my brother just barely tolerated him.”

“It’s kind of you to make excuses for me. Perhaps, I can redeem myself by allowing you to escort me home.” I grabbed my bike by the handlebars, rolling it beside me.

As we started towards my dorm, Lord Fremont clasped his hands behind his back. He still wore black gloves, indicating he was in mourning for his brother. I held up the steamer bike as we walked. I was certain we made quite the awkward-looking pair.

“Why bother yourself with Lord Middleton if you don’t like him?” I asked.

“At this point, I need his connections here to help establish myself. I spent the last two years in the military, and just happened to be on leave when my brother was shot. Unfortunately, my past has led to a set of acquaintances that aren't quite up to snuff, as they say." Lord Fremont pinched his nose briefly. The loss in his voice was both sad and bitter to my ears.

"Lord Middleton does have the appropriate pedigree to help you out, even if everything else about him is lacking," I said.

"Everything changed in an instant, it seemed. The life I knew, ripped away by some unknown individual." Lord Fremont clasped his hands behind his back once again. He continued on, his words clipped, "I wasn't supposed to attend university or be next in line to become duke—second son, and all. But now that I'm here, I need the same connections my brother had. No one ever intended for me to be a duke, not my mother, certainly not my father, and not me. I just don't have the gravitas Edmund had. I've never wanted to." Anger and loss swirled together in his words, mixing until I couldn't decipher one emotion from the other.

"It must be difficult to lose your brother and the life you knew all at the same time. I can't even imagine what you must be feeling." I reached out to comfort him, but changed my mind, my arm falling back to the handlebar of my steamer bike.

I watched as Lord Fremont shook his head, the movement ever so slight. Like he was trying to shake off all the emotions he didn't want to feel. "And then, I want . . . This may seem ridiculous, but I want to figure out who killed my brother."

"Wasn't it a highwayman? That's what the papers said."

"That's what they said. But I don't think so. Edmund created so much havoc here. And he wasn't done. I think whoever killed him did it to stop his progressive ideas from taking hold." Lord Fremont looked at me, expecting me to say something.

"I hope that's not the case. I wouldn't want my presence here being the cause of your brother's death. Especially because you can't stop progress. While I would love to think that without me, this steamer bike wouldn't exist, eventually it would've. Because that's what happens. So, even without your brother around, someone is going to challenge the status quo. That's just how the world works," I said, looking at him. Then I was afraid I said too much, so I looked away.

"I didn't mean to imply it was his fight to get ladies admitted to university that got him killed, although I'm sure it was part of it. Edmund wasn't happy with what he had accomplished. He knew some of the ladies that would be admitted were going to have to give up so much. And while the access to materials you get from being here is nice, he was worried some ladies wouldn't find a professor to work with them. Then, if they did, what were they really getting with no degree conferred on them? To come here and not be able to actually graduate still means you can't be a barrister or solicitor or doctor, or so many other things that shouldn't be only the purview of men just because they are men. Edmund was also trying to get the Shadowed . . . Um, he was trying to create a more inclusive space for philosophical and political discourse. And he would have taken his seat in the House of Lords before long, with ideas of supporting women's suffrage, and so much more." Lord Fremont may have been discussing the reasons why he thought his brother was murdered, but it didn't change the pride he had for his brother and his actions.

"He sounds impressive. It's clear that you truly admired him and the two of you were close," I said. I wanted to comfort him but didn't know how, so instead, I changed the subject. "Did you just allude to one of the secret societies here at Grantabridge? I've always wanted to know more about them. Why do they exist? How does one get invited to be a member? Is there any reason to actually become a member?" I fired question after question.

"From what I can tell, they are completely underwhelming and run by fools." Lord Fremont dismissed the entire group of individuals with a wave of his hand.

"Oh." I sighed, disappointed. I wanted to meet with like-minded people and have amazing discussions in secret. It all sounded so mysterious.

"From what I have seen, my brother was correct. These societies have lost their purpose and become archaic in the worst sort of way, stilting progress by pandering to the wealthy and the titled." His experiences with these secret societies clearly disgusted Lord Fremont.

"This is the ladies' dormitory."

"This building? It looks almost abandoned."

"It isn't as bad as it looks. I too was discouraged when I first arrived. But the bedrooms are quite large and comfortable. There is space in each room to set up a workspace. Some of us even have more room. So it's perfect for the lost ladies of Grantabridge University," I said, smiling. The building looked sad in so many ways. But by spring it would be blooming with flowers, if Willa had anything to say about it. She had already started to tackle the back gardens with a vengeance.

Lord Fremont took my hand and gave a slight bow; I might have curtsied in response. Yes, curtsied holding up my steamer bike while wearing leather leggings.

"Thank you, Miss Stanhope. I very much enjoyed our walk. It was refreshing to hear new ways of thinking about life. I hope we can do this again soon." His words sounded so formal after a conversation that had felt almost intimate.

"I should thank you, Lord Fremont, for going out of your way to walk with me. I hope I haven't taken up too much of your time."

"Not at all, but I should return to Lord Middleton." With that, he turned and walked away. I just stood there, watching him until he was out of sight.

Chapter Nine

"It looks like Lord Fremont has forgiven you for everything you said last time," Georgi said as soon as I entered.

"He was certainly friendly during our walk," I said, blushing. I really needed to stop blushing. It's not something I did delicately. More like my entire face turned beet red, making my freckles stand out more than they already did. It was not dainty or cute.

"A walk he had no need to take," Georgi said with a sly smile. I could see machinations happening behind her eyes. It seemed she was a matchmaker at heart. A matchmaker who wanted to change the world, but a matchmaker nonetheless.

"I think he wanted to be away from Lord Middleton. They don't seem to see things the same way. Lord Fremont is more like his brother in his views of the world."

"Is that so?" Georgi looked at me with a raised eyebrow.

"What? Please, just say whatever it is you have to say."

"I have nothing to say. You were the one that walked home with a handsome future duke. I've just been here studying Plato in Ancient Greek all morning. You've been gone for hours, and when you show up, it's with a gentleman. A very handsome gentleman at that. And it looks like you have a letter from another gentleman by the name of Percival." Georgi laughed. "Whatever are you going to do, Pippa?"

"Percival is my brother," I said, rolling my eyes.

I pushed by Georgi, snatching the letter from her hand as I passed. I ignored her peel of laughter while trying not to storm up the stairs. The stairs creaked and groaned in protest, making my efforts seem futile.

Is this what having a sister you're close to was actually like? Maybe I didn't mind having Penelope as my sister. I wasn't even fooling myself with those thoughts; I loved the teasing, even though it made me uncomfortable. I really didn't want Georgi to realize how much her teasing was getting to me. At least, not until I took some time to figure out exactly why her teasing bothered me so.

"Thank you f-f-f-for always listening," I heard Willa say when I reached the top of the stairs. I took a few steps towards her door, then stopped. Did I really want to interrupt her and whoever she was with?

"It's been so hard here. The botany professor has no interest in teaching me. My brother is still constantly telling me I made a mistake. I normally feel invisible, unless I'm taking care of you, my lovelies," Willa said, her stutter completely gone.

"Oh, Willa," I said. "I didn't mean to eavesdrop, but you sounded so confident and so sad. I had to come in here."

"P-P-P-Pippa, it's okay. I was talking to my plants. I stutter less around them," Willa said, blushing. "I think it's because the plants never judge me."

"Willa, that's one of the sweetest things I've heard. I feel the same way about my inventions. I hope you feel like I, and the rest of us here, see you."

"I actually d-d-d-do. It has been amazing to meet the rest of you. It's the first time I've felt accepted by someone other than my plants. You are all so patient when I speak." Willa's eyes never left her hands as she spoke. I wanted to lift her chin up, but didn't, knowing it would make her jump out of her skin.

"I'm so happy we met and are going through this thing

together. If you ever need anything, to talk, anything, let me know. We will figure it out." I hugged Willa before leaving her alone with her plants and making my way to my room.

* * *

I closed the door to my room and stayed there, leaning up against the door for a moment. Georgi's teasing aside, there was nothing happening between Lord Fremont and me. I didn't have time for any distractions, and handsome men definitely counted as a distraction.

Pulling myself together, I gathered two copper cylinders, some corrugated board, wool, and my heating stones. What was I missing? A timepiece—I had to have a pocket watch somewhere. I pulled open drawers, rifling through them until I found what I was looking for. Percy's pocket watch, the gold-and-silver timepiece, shined in my hand. Through the glass you could see the gears turn, especially from the back. I wanted to take off the cover so I could see all the gears that made this small object keep time. I knew Percy liked the running wolf etched on the cover; it was his favorite part, so I couldn't get rid of it. I gave it to him on his sixteenth birthday. Hopefully, he hadn't realized I had taken it back, like any good sister wouldn't.

I started my little test by pouring the pitcher of water I always liked to have in my room into the smaller of the copper cans. Then, I put it in the larger copper can. Carefully, I placed the wool between the two cans, then bent the corrugated board into a circular shape, placing it between the two cans as well. This was a pretty informal experiment. Normally I'd set up a control canister of hot water as well, but I was out of copper cans. I could take whatever I learned back to Professor Aneurin on Monday. It would feel so good to impress him by taking the initiative on this idea. I could only imagine my excitement if it worked.

I looked at the time on the watch and recorded it. Then dropped a few heating stones into the water. It wasn't long before steam rose off the top of the water. Everything looked good. Maybe my idea would work. I could see the water boil, and the steam was coming off faster and thicker. Just like I wanted. The key was whether or not the water would stay hot and steamy with the insulation.

But then, the steam mixed with smoke, and the acrid smell filled my nostrils. Blast, I should have known this would happen! I had even thought about what I could use for the vacuum seal Aneurin and I had discussed. I was supposed to be looking up how to create a vacuum, not setting fire to my room.

I looked around.

What was I going to use to put out the fire?

My water was inside what was on fire.

"Bloody Hell!"

"What's wrong, Pippa?" Mads burst through the door.

"Water, I need water, or something to smother it."

"Willa, get Pippa water and dirt. Do you have dirt in your room?"

I looked up to see Willa running off. Then Georgi came in, turning away, coughing.

Willa was back, tossing water on my experiment and then throwing dirt on it. I pushed the dirt in between the two copper cans, singeing my fingertips as I did so.

Then the fire was out. Thank god it hadn't spread farther than my disaster of an experiment. Shockingly, the worktable didn't show any signs of the fire, other than the mess of dirt and water, but no burn marks.

"Where's Miss Pierce? I don't want her to know about this. It'll probably get me kicked out." I was frantic. "I can't get kicked out. My mother won't let me go back home after I made the choice to come here."

"She's out for her afternoon stroll, or whatever she does every afternoon. Open the windows to air out the room. We won't let anyone kick you out," Mads said. At least we knew which of us here would keep her cool in an emergency. It definitely wasn't me.

I didn't know if I wanted to laugh or cry at this point. It had been ages since I had started a fire. The last time was at least in my workshop. Not the house. I swear the only reason I had a workshop was my mother's fear of me burning down our home. With that thought, I felt the tears break through and I couldn't make them stop. I also couldn't catch my breath as the situation, or what could have been, crashed down on me. Mads took my hand and pulled me to the bed, where she pushed me down to sitting and mimed slow breaths with me until I could mimic her and gain control of myself.

"Oh, Pippa, don't give it a second thought, we're here for you," Mads reassured me, softly patting me on the back. I felt like she had done this many times before.

"Thank you. I don't know what came over me. Well, that's not true. I started a fire and could have burned down where we live. I don't know why I didn't think this through better before starting my tests. Like always, I jumped into it too quickly, not thinking things through. I must have made the water too hot."

"We all make mistakes. I would prefer to keep the indoor fires to a minimum in the future. We should try to find you a place to work." Mads was so reasonable it made me laugh. Nothing about this seemed reasonable.

"How are you always so calm, Mads?" I asked.

"Growing up with three younger sisters who were always getting into trouble helps with the calm. That, and I was working on scheduling everything for the first semester, figuring out schedules, codes, math problems. Anything like that has been my time for myself since my mother passed. It always calms me down."

"How intriguing. Sometimes, I wish I was calmer." I wiped the tears from my face, then pulled my hand back, wincing. Well, that's not good. I had burned myself.

"P-P-P-Pippa, let me l-l-l-look at your hands." I let Willa take my hands in hers. She tsked, then left the room. I stared after her, then glanced at my friends. They shrugged. Willa was the silent one. If words weren't needed, she didn't use them.

"This should help those b-b-b-burns, Pippa. It's a salve of Calendula and Propolis. J-J-J-Just rub it on the burns, and they should heal in no time. But don't eat it." Willa looked at me, expecting a response.

"Of course, Willa. Thank you, I promise to use it on my fingers only and not to eat it."

* * *

I paced the length of my room, trying to quiet all the thoughts roaring through my head. Every few passes, I would lie down in my bed, tossing and turning until I twisted the bedding around my legs. Sleep was impossible. I didn't want to be alone with my thoughts. Hoping Georgi was still awake, I slipped out of my room and knocked on her door ever so quietly.

"Are you okay, Pippa?" Georgi asked.

"Not really." I sighed, entering her room. Our makeshift mats were still set up, a reminder that my little escapade had caused us to cancel fencing lessons, something we were planning on doing every evening. I paced along the length of her room, causing the floor to groan in protest every time I stepped on one particular spot. "I just feel so bad, and I don't know what to do. Experiments are part of what I need to do to develop more steam technology, but there's always a risk. Everything I do involves high temperatures. And I can't risk everyone here."

"It seems like you need an actual workshop," Georgi offered, moving the books strewn all over her bed to the bookshelf in her room.

"How am I going to afford a workshop? My aunt was generous, but with supplies, books, and food, there's not much left over." I was in one of those moods where I didn't really want solutions. Wallowing in self-pity, that's what I wanted. I would figure it out soon, but I wasn't in the mood for reasonable solutions this very moment.

"We just have to find someone that will share space with you. And maybe you can ask Mads to help you with a budget?"

"With my propensity for starting fires, just how are we going to go about finding a space." I stopped my pacing and threw myself on Georgi's bed.

There was a soft knock on the door. Both Willa and Mads came in and made themselves comfortable. Apparently, Georgi's room had already become our meeting place, even though we had only been here a short time.

"Are you moping over a little fire, Pippa?" Mads said,

winking at me.

"Well, I could have burned down the entire place."

"But you didn't, and you know, nobody would have missed it—well, maybe Miss Pierce. This place is dreary." Georgi's irreverence was contagious. I felt the corners of my mouth twitch, creeping up into a smile despite my obvious intentions of throwing myself a very elaborate pity party tonight.

"You are correct, Georgi, this place is dreary. I wonder what Miss Pierce would do if we spruced it up a bit. Added just a bit of color downstairs. And then started hosting salons. Do you think her face could become any more pinched?" Mads's eyes sparkled with mirth.

"A salon isn't a bad idea. Maybe we should do something to really establish ourselves here in Grantabridge. I mean, we will be here for a few years before we finish with whatever coursework they think about giving us. And the more ladies here that are interested, the more involvement there will be, the more there will be a catalyst for change." So much for self-pity. I was taking this idea and going with it. I loved the idea of creating a space for intellectuals like us.

"Miss P-P-P-Pierce would never let us. Plus, sp-sp-speaking in front of others is so hard." Willa's stutter worsened just at the thought of what Mads and I suggested.

"But Willa, we could do so much. It's the perfect way to break the structure from within. Plus, think of all those connections we could make." Georgi sighed, slipping off into her dream world, one where she was in control.

"Georgi, I can see you building your very own empire in your mind over there."

"So what if I am, Pippa, so what if I am?" Georgi rubbed her hands together maniacally.

I thought she was joking, at least in part. Maybe. With Georgi, it was hard to tell.

"What if we did more than salons? Maybe we start with that. But Kaiden . . . I mean, Lord Fremont was talking about this secret society on campus. What if we created one of our own?" I loved the idea of a growing group of women who would support each other in, well, in whatever each woman wanted to pursue.

Just coming to Grantabridge had already changed so much of my life. Even though it hadn't been long, the four in this room were a huge part of it. It was incredibly freeing to be around other ladies like me. Especially compared to home, where everything my mother allowed me to do was begrudgingly and with the intention of keeping it secret so I didn't ruin the family name.

"Kaiden, is it?" Georgi said, teasing me once again.

"I don't know why I said that."

"I do. He is handsome and apparently nice, with a tragic backstory. What more could you want?" Mads held her hands to her chest and batted her eyelashes.

Apparently, someone had been speaking out of turn. I glared at Georgi.

"He is qu-qu-quite swoon worthy," Willa said.

"Willa, even you?"

Willa shrugged her shoulders. I meant, he was quite handsome and intelligent. But this wasn't some romantic periodical, and I wasn't sure a tragic backstory was something that I should look for in a man.

"Enough of this talk of boys. It's like being around my sister," I said.

"Don't be harsh, Pippa. We may all have our intellectual pursuits, but a handsome gentleman is always going to be of interest. Unless he's a fool. Have you seen Lord Bradbury around campus? I met him during my season. While he is quite dashing with his tall good looks, the man only speaks of horseflesh and gambling. And that was while we waltzed. I can't imagine he's learning much here," Georgi said.

"Another seat here that could have gone to someone that deserved it rather than a gentleman whose only reference was a title," I said, frustration tinging my tone.

Georgi jumped up off the bed, shifting the mood of the room and demanding our attention. "I think we should seriously think about starting an organized secret society. But first things first, we need to find Pippa a free, or inexpensive, place to work nearby. Let's avoid any more mishaps. Then, I think we should try to host some salons, which means finding the proper space for it that won't peak unwanted interest that could shut us down. From the salons, we can start to think if we should add anyone to our merry band. Until then, it will just be the four of us."

"We should call ourselves the Women Adventurers' Consortium of Knowledge." My sense of humor was ridiculous.

"Pippa, you realize the acronym for that is WACK," Mads said.

Then all the lights went out, leaving us completely in the dark.

"Georgi, do you have any candles in here?" I asked. The darkness was all-encompassing, without any light trickling in through the window.

"I think so," I heard Georgi say. Then there was quite a bit of fumbling around, some running into things, followed by a few curses.

It would be hard to find anything in the dark. We had been here for almost a full week, but that didn't mean anything was truly familiar yet.

After what seemed like forever sitting in the dark, but was probably only a few minutes at most, Georgi lit a candle for us, casting a dim, flickering light throughout the room.

I made my way downstairs with my friends by my side. Mads and Georgi had the candles, holding them high above our heads. They were our main (well only) source of light at this point. The house was creepy at night. It was kinda creepy here during the day, but the long, grey shadows went above and beyond to establish a creepy ick-factor I would not forget anytime soon.

As a group, we made it to the basement. The small turbine that provided electricity for the dorm had stopped. It was quite similar to what my parents' house used. The room felt cooler than I would have expected. It should have been warm from the hot water that created steam that caused the turbines to move. I walked over to the water tank and it was cool to the touch. Removing the lid and looking over the edge, I saw there were chunks of ice floating in it. At least there was an explanation for the lights going out, just not one for the presence of ice in the water of our turbine tank.

"There was ice in the water tank," I said.

I tossed some of my heating stones still in my pouch from my ride earlier today into the water tank. Hopefully, it would be enough to get us through the night with at least some light. Then I gestured that we should head back upstairs.

"Ice in the water tank would be a strong indication that the power outage was intentional. Who would want to create an electrical problem here? Especially so late into the evening?" Mads asked.

This was the first time we had been up this late. And it was all because I couldn't sleep. Maybe the staff turned it off every night. It could happen every night and none of us would have noticed.

"I w-w-w-wonder if it's connected to the leaf fire outside the dining room?" Willa said.

I had assumed the leaf fire was an accident, even though both Georgi and Willa thought it was intentional, but could not make the same assumption about the lights.

"What does anyone gain from turning off the lights once we are all in bed?"

We all looked at each other with no answers. Just a lot of confusion.

Settling back into Georgi's room, worry filled the air.

"I don't understand what they were trying to accomplish. Even if it had been earlier in the evening, what would turning the power off actually do? It's such a simple fix," I said.

Mads looked over at me in disbelief. "Pippa, it might be simple for you, but I don't even know if I would have gone to the basement to see what was wrong first. I probably would have assumed the problem was more widespread, or something I couldn't fix on my own."

"I agree with Mads. I may have eventually thought to check the basement and the home's steam-power setup. But it wouldn't have been my first thought. I hope I would have made it there eventually because it is very logical. But it would have taken me a bit," Georgi said.

"So what would have happened if we woke up and there was no power?" I asked.

"Not much. I mean, one night wouldn't have been enough for any food to go bad in the icebox. It would have just been an inconvenience," Mads said.

"It's too strange. But there's no way it was an accident. There were chunks of ice in the water tank. I don't even know how a person could have transported that much ice. I mean, if you think about it, the water was boiling to have constant steam and filled with the condensation trap, and at some point, someone replaced any lost water. Any ice thrown in would have melted almost instantaneously."

"Maybe the lights are turned off every night, and we just didn't realize it? We are normally asleep by this time," Mads said.

"But wh-wh-wh-what about the leaf fire? Even if the lights were nothing, the f-f-fire must have been intentional," Willa said, wringing her hands.

"We are probably looking at this completely the wrong way. We've created an elaborate plot by having overactive imaginations and the stress of earlier today," Georgi said. "We should all try to get some sleep. There's nothing to be done, at least not tonight. And our minds will be fresh in the morning."

"Yes, but ice chunks?" I pondered.

"Rest, Pippa, we will think on it later." Georgi was done.

I plodded back to my room, two thoughts fighting each other in my mind. First, how could I catch steam and create condensation to use and heat again? Two, was there a chance that the ladies attending Grantabridge University were being sabotaged, and if we were being sabotaged, what was the purpose of it?

Chapter Ten

It was hard not to obsess over the strange things happening at our dorm. At least, I was struggling. Over the last few days, it seemed like minor things kept happening. Some of my books were missing. All the work Willa did in the garden was dug up. Georgi's translations were found partially burned in the parlor fireplace. So far, Mads was the only one who hadn't had something happen to her, but I figured it would happen soon enough. I was sure of it. The problem was everything that occurred could be explained. I could have left my books somewhere, a gopher could have got in the garden, and the papers, well, Georgi might have thrown them in the fire in frustration. I was so frustrated because I was sure someone was up to something. The only other one of us convinced something nefarious was going on in the dorm was Willa, and it all came back to the leaf fire for her. Georgi might have some concern that we were being sabotaged, but she and Mads were happy to dismiss it by explaining it away.

I didn't know what to do about it. I hadn't come up with any solutions to anything else either. Well, that wasn't exactly true. I had a fantastic idea to add a condensation trap to the steamer bike; recycling the water could solve part of my distance problems as well as make the steamer bike more skirt friendly. I could not wait to discuss it with Professor Aneurin. It seemed so simple, I can't believe it never occurred to me before, but after seeing our basement steam room, the idea just clicked. But as for the saboteur, I was at a loss. At least today was a class day. I could use the distraction and the comfort of working with Professor Aneurin. I really loved spending time in his workshop. While he muttered and mumbled his ideas, sifting through papers and taking notes, I curled up and read some book he thought would help me in my studies. The book almost always inspired new ideas. And after a few meetings, his workshop felt like an extension of home.

I arrived at the classroom after riding through town. It seemed like some of the locals were getting used to seeing me ride through town in goggles, pants, and boots. Some shop owners came out of their shops and waved to me as I rode by, and the baker always had a small bag of baked goods waiting for me when I rode by on Mondays and Thursdays. I never intended to actually stop, but the look on his face . . . I couldn't just ride on by. It felt so good, even if it didn't mean that much.

I jumped off my bike and released the steam, then burst through the door.

"Professor Aneurin, I just had the most fantastic idea to help with long-term travel."

Professor Aneurin was not alone. With him was an older, meticulously dressed gentleman. His frock coat was amazingly tailored, his grey cravat both subtle and complicated at the same time. Everything looked in place on his tall frame, everything except his dramatic mustache. He turned his grey eyes to me with disdain.

Apparently it was going to be another one of those days, and I didn't even have my ladylike clothing on to help prevent judgment today. I was standing there in my jodhpurs, boots, leather corset, belt, and a teal blouse. I hadn't even taken my leather hat off, just put my goggles on top of it. And then, there was the fact my hair was in pigtails. So, when this man looked at me like I was a child interrupting the adults, it kinda hit home.

"Ah, Pippa, can you give us a few moments? Professor

Gates and I are just about done with our meeting." Professor Aneurin seemed more scattered than normal. Which was saying a lot: Professor Aneurin was the most scattered person I knew.

"Yes, Professor, I'll wait outside until you're ready." I grabbed my bag since I had dropped it on the floor when I entered, turned, and walked towards the door.

I felt the heat of Professor Gates's gaze as I walked out of the room. I wanted to look back to confirm what I felt was really happening. His gaze made me so uncomfortable I kept my eyes straight ahead until the door blocked his view of me.

"Are you telling me, Marcus, she's the reason you've been so distracted recently?" I heard an unfamiliar voice question. It must be Professor Gates, another man questioning my capability.

It may be impolite to eavesdrop, but it was also rude to talk about people behind their backs. I left the door open just a little bit, standing close enough that I could hear, but not so close that Professor Gates would run into me when he left. I really needed to hear how this man thought working with me was a waste of time.

"William, I have not been distracted. I have been working on progressing steam technology with Miss Stanhope a few times a week. And alchemy experiments when I'm not working with her."

"Steam technology won't last, Marcus. You should be focused on finding formulas that will change the world." I almost snorted at his statement, but kept silent to avoid being caught. Steam technology was clearly the future; a person had to be blind, or intentionally ignorant, not to see that.

"William, I'm afraid you are falling behind the times. What Miss Stanhope and I are working on has the potential to really change the world. The way her mind works, it's astonishing. Right now, the only byproduct of her invention is steam." I felt tears prick my eyes at the professor's kind words.

"But Marcus, I need you to focus on alchemy, not this steam engineering, or that girl."

"What's your concern, William? We've been working on the transmutation formula forever and we aren't getting any closer. Taking some time away could be refreshing. I'll come back to it soon. What am I saying? I still work on it multiple times a week. This is the first time you've stopped by this semester. And let's not forget, I am the only professor here working with steam engineering. I have to spend some time on it."

"Just make some progress. I can't wait around forever. And you . . ."

I jumped away from the door as I heard the striking of heels on the wood floor. I missed whatever else Professor Gates had been going to say, but I inferred he was not happy with Professor Aneurin. I wondered what transmutation formula Professor Aneurin was supposed to be working on at greater speed. Professor Gates swung the door open, not caring if there was anyone standing nearby or not. Soon after, Professor Aneurin popped his head out.

"Oh good, Miss Stanhope, you're still here. What has you so excited this morning?"

"Are you sure you have time today? Professor Gates seemed rather displeased. I don't want to get you into any trouble. I know how often we meet is not normal here." I walked through the door while expressing my concern. I really admired Professor Aneurin. No one else in my life had ever treated me like I actually knew what I was doing. I didn't want to lose that.

"Don't concern yourself with Professor Gates. He's impatient and out of touch. He doesn't see the importance in what we're working on. He's hoping for a quick solution to his problems. And I'm not sure if that solution exists." Aneurin ran his hand through his hair, tousling it even more than it was naturally.

"What were you so excited about earlier, Miss Stanhope?"

Excited about—what had I been thinking about earlier? This is why people had notebooks. If only I could remember where I put my notebooks. I had at least a dozen of them, all with great ideas, but I could never find the one I was looking for.

"Miss Stanhope?"

"I'm sorry, I was going to tell you about my idea to trap the steam and have it condense and feed back into the water tank. There would still be some energy loss, but just think about it. If we can reuse the water, then we can travel farther. In addition, it shouldn't take as much energy to heat up the water we get from the steam because it will already be warm just from the process."

"That's a fantastic idea, Miss Stanhope. We'll need to use gravity to ensure the water flows back into the water tank. Which shouldn't be too difficult."

Professor Aneurin and I fell into our routine, this time working at his desk drawing up different plans for the steam catcher. It was comforting to sit, passing papers back and forth, changing things here and there, working on finding the completed, working design. Every now and then, one of us would get up and start walking around. More often than not, that was Professor Aneurin. He always had this frantic energy about him. It seemed if he sat still for too long, he would come apart at the seams. The frantic energy was part of our process though; I was no longer distracted by it. He would pace, and I would sit there lightly biting the end of my pencil until I could see my idea clearly in my head, then I would try to draw it. Unfortunately, drawing was not one of my strengths. But for some reason, Professor Aneurin could look at what I tried to draw and fix it until it matched what was in my head.

"Lord Middleton, how nice to see you . . . again," Professor Aneurin said.

He was back *again*. Did he always have to interrupt while I was here? I looked over and met Lord Middleton's ice-blue eyes. I didn't realize it was possible to see so many feelings in a person's eyes. I shivered. The contempt I saw in his eyes felt like it could freeze my very being.

"Professor, I'll be on my way. Maybe I'll find somewhere to build the device." I grabbed all of our papers and shoved them into my bag.

"I see you're still wasting time with that girl, Professor."

Bloody hell, twice in one day I had to hear that I was wasting the professor's time. Lord Simon Middleton was an arrogant arse. Sadly, he was also going to be a duke. Which meant he had power. Why was it that the worst of society were the ones that were able to maintain control? If he had his way, I would be gone by the time the next semester started.

He made me so uncomfortable that every time he showed up, I left, even though Professor Aneurin made it clear I belonged here, both in the workshop and at the University. He also told me with both his words and actions that he wanted to work with me. However, as soon as Lord Middleton walked into the room, it was like hearing every voice that had ever told me I was wrong for pursuing steam engineering speak to me all at once. I could not stay another moment longer than necessary if he was in the room.

"Ah, Miss Stanhope, it's a pleasure to see you again," Lord Fremont said.

"Is it? Really? Are you always with him?" I tossed my arms in the air and continued walking.

"What . . . Oh . . . What nonsense did he spout this time?"

"The same nonsense, I'm just so tired of hearing it. Two different men implying, actually stating, that I'm a waste of the professor's time, even though they have taken no time to do any research on me or my work." I stopped midstride, causing Kaiden to run into me. I felt his hands on my arms, which tingled where he touched, steadying me. I turned towards him, and we were nose to nose, well, nose to chest, as I glared up at him, ignoring his enticing scent.

"Does he follow me? Why does he show up every time I'm here? I don't understand. Is he trying to torture me?"

Throwing my hands up into the air, I turned back and walked over to my steamer bike. Which was sitting in a large puddle of water. The tank, which had been fine earlier, now had a large hole in it.

"Bloody hell, what is with people today? Is it Rain on Pippa's Parade Day and I just didn't know it? I must have forgotten to look at the calendar." I'm sure I looked like I had absolutely lost my mind, stomping around and gesticulating wildly. Enough was enough. With that thought, I sat down on the ground and burst into tears.

"Miss Stanhope . . ." I looked up, and somehow Lord Fremont had folded his lanky frame into a kneeling position in front of me, holding out his handkerchief. Lord Fremont's kindness was out of place with the harsh words of the other men continually implying I was not worthy.

"I'm sorry." I sniffed, and the citrusy scent of Lord Fremont's cologne filled my nose. He smelled of citrus and salt, reminding me of the ocean. "I don't know what's come over me. Hearing 'that girl' one more time, and then seeing my bike sabotaged. It's just too much." I wiped my eyes and handed back the wet cloth, embarrassed by my outburst.

"Here, let me help you up." Lord Fremont unfolded himself and held out his hand. I offered mine; taking it, he pulled me up effortlessly, but I had also pushed off the ground. The extra force had me crashing into his chest, leaving me staring at his deep-red ruby cravat pin. I grabbed onto his frock coat to steady myself. Then I looked up. His amber eyes met mine and time stopped. My eyes fell to his lips; I licked my lips. Then suddenly his hands were at my waist, moving me back a few steps.

"Miss Stanhope, do you have a place to take your steamer bike to fix it?" I wasn't sure I understood what he said, even though I was watching his lips move.

"What, my steamer bike? My bike . . . No, I don't. At home I did all the repairs myself in my workshop. But I don't have a workshop here, and after almost setting fire to our dormitory, I can't work on it there. Plus, I couldn't get the bike up to the second floor."

"I have a friend that has a shop in town. He's the local steam mechanic. I could introduce you to him. Maybe he'll let you work in his shop." Lord Fremont's eyes and smile were bright. He was excited at the thought of being able to help and unable to hide it.

"Did you not hear that I set fire to the dormitory? Are you just too nice and ignoring it? You didn't even blink." I looked at him, astonished at his lack of appropriate reactions. A person should not smile when talking to a person who sets fires.

"Edmund set fire to our house a few times before we banned him from doing experiments in the house. I assume fires are the danger of living with anyone that works with combustible materials and high heats," he explained with matter-of-fact precision.

"Does anything phase you?" I stared at him with a mixture of anger, helplessness, and sadness. A turbulent set of emotions.

"Yes," he said. His clipped tone should have clued me in to drop the subject. I didn't. I was stubborn, emotional, and didn't understand why he was so calm.

"Like what? Just today I've yelled, sobbed, and told you I set stuff on fire. And you are so even-keeled, it's frustrating. And then you offer a very reasonable solution to my predicament. I don't understand it." I was pretty sure I needed to be locked away in a tower somewhere. I was completely irrational.

"Would you rather I not be calm? I'm actually rather concerned that someone put a hole in your bike, even though you haven't even acknowledged that this had to have been intentional. That being said, you seem to have the anger aspect under control, so I thought it would be nice if I had a calmer approach, hopefully to be able to offer useful suggestions. If you would like me to stomp around waving my arms, wildly yelling, I can. I just don't think it would be of any use." Kaiden glared at me. Finally, his stoic demeanor slipped; I was not used to so much calm.

"So where is this mechanic? We should go before it's too late. Maybe I can even fix my bike today." I looked at Lord Fremont from the corner of my eye. He threw up his hands, clearly frustrated by the emotional trip I had just taken him on.

"Of course, Miss Stanhope. Come with me."

Chapter Eleven

Lord Fremont and I walked in silence for a while. I wouldn't say the silence was comfortable, but it wasn't quite uncomfortable either. I wanted to break it, but I didn't know what to say. So, I just kept glancing over at him. He easily maneuvered my bike through the crowds as we walked through Grantabridge. I had informed him I was perfectly capable of taking my invention to the mechanic, but he insisted. And while I felt awkward and didn't know what to do with my hands, I actually found his actions rather thoughtful. I glanced over again. His cravat looked a bit wilted, like he had been tugging on it all morning. Dark stubble emphasized his strong jawline and his full lips. I wonder what . . .

"Do not finish that thought, Pippa," I muttered under my breath.

"Did you say something?" he asked.

"What . . . No . . . Of course not," I said, blushing profusely. My face was probably the color of my hair. I always turned bright red when I felt like I had been caught doing something I shouldn't.

"It feels like you want to say something, Miss Stanhope."

"Pippa, it's Pippa." I almost clapped my hand over my

mouth. Why was I always saying unplanned things around him? At least this was friendly. But also bold, oh so bold.

"Well, Pippa, you must call me Kaiden." I liked the way he said my name.

"Of course, Kaiden. Tell me, how do you know this mechanic? I haven't seen you actually expressing an interest in steam engineering."

"We met in a faraway land and an ancient time." I glanced up at Kaiden sharply. "I kid, I kid. Edmund was having a steam carriage built before he was murdered. And he hired Finnigan to build it. He just finished, but something was off. It doesn't handle right. But I can't put my finger on what exactly is wrong."

"Sounds like he does way more than just fix steam engines. Sounds like he builds."

"He does. He's extremely good at what he does. His designs are clunky, lacking some of the finesse I've seen in your work, but he's improving."

"You've seen my work?"

"Yes, while Lord Middleton harasses the professor, I look at your drawings. They are quite good. I don't know much about steam engineering, but the designs I've seen make sense even to my untrained eye."

"I thought Lord Middleton was talking to the professor to help you solve your brother's murder?"

"He seems to think that as well. However, I know Aneurin doesn't have information about Edmund's death. The evidence I've found leads a different direction. Not that Middleton will listen."

"Where does the evidence point?" I asked.

"Everything I can find points to Edmund's politics. And a man that worked by his side makes little sense as also being his killer. In addition, everyone in town saw Aneurin and Lady Adelaide out for a stroll right around the time Edmund was shot."

"Oh, I see." I did see, but I also didn't know what to say. So I changed the subject. "Are you studying anything while you're here?" I could smack myself. Why did everything I say come off so rude?

Kaiden sighed, his laugh brittle. "I am, actually. Right now, I'm focusing on law and politics, with some crop management thrown in for good measure. I have to learn everything I can about being a duke and property management. So I spend my days studying things that had no interest to me."

"Had? Are they of interest now?"

"Only out of necessity. It's so much responsibility for one person. I don't know how Edmund did it. I never wanted to know. We were both living the life we wanted to be living. And now, I'm living his life. Not mine," Kaiden said, his words tinged with bitterness and grief. It made me think he wasn't just mourning the loss of his brother but also the loss of the life he had planned on living. "At some point, I'll have to take my seat in the House of Lords. I want to be informed so I can be reasonable and logical in my decisions. And still carry out the legacy Edmund wanted for himself. At least I believe in the things he believed in. It makes it easier. But I know I'm going to be fighting every step that's made towards change. On top of that, I have so many tenants counting on me to keep the estate thriving. Edmund was learning all these things since he was a child. I had so much more freedom. Now I have to learn it all in a very short amount of time."

"That's quite a burden. The combination of loss and change can't be easy. And now you think Edmund's murderer is here in Grantabridge? That it wasn't a random highwayman?"

"I do. Edmund was, to put it nicely, difficult. But in all the best ways. He was passionate and hard-headed. He pushed people in ways that made them uncomfortable. Like fighting to have women admitted to the University. When he took his seat in the House of Lords, he would have been advocating a change in almost everything because he saw a brighter future. Unfortunately, not everyone saw the same things he did. I think that's what got him killed."

"Your brother seems like he was quite astonishing. I wish I could have met him."

"He would have enjoyed your company, Pippa. Do you have any brothers or sisters?"

"Yes, one of each. I'm surprised you haven't met my sister, Penelope. She's normally in Fintan with my mother during the season. And then there's my younger brother, Percy, that is, Percival. He should attend here next year."

"And are they anything like you? Does Penelope ride around Fintan on her steamer bike, red hair flying in the wind?"

"Oh, my god, no! Penelope wouldn't be caught dead near anything I've invented. She's determined my attending university will ruin her chances for a match. And she has very normal blonde hair. As does Percy. I was lucky enough to inherit my Aunt Honoria's flaming locks."

"Honoria, as in Honoria Porter?"

"Yes . . . Why?" I felt my guard go up.

"She's quite infamous and rather inspirational. No one would really think much of what she did if she were a man. But she did it all and with such finesse. I've always just admired her courage. Honestly, most men wouldn't even do what she did."

I let out the breath I'd been holding, preparing to defend her. "She's my favorite person in the entire world. Percy is a close second. He used to sneak all his books to me. The only reason I'm here at Grantabridge is because of Aunt Honoria. When I told my parents I wanted to attend, my mother gave me an ultimatum. Stay home and be part of the family, or leave and she would never speak to me again. If it wasn't for my aunt, I would be completely on my own here."

"I would love to meet her one day. Has she really been to Junhar?"

"She's basically been everywhere. I think her most recent travels were to the Omazenas."

"Amazing. I had planned to use my status as the second son to explore once I had done my duty in the military. But now, who knows if I'll ever leave this country."

Kaiden's words had tears welling up in my eyes. Just the sadness in his voice was enough to affect me. He lost his brother and his future in a single moment.

Kaiden opened the door to the mechanic shop, and I walked through. The space smelled of steam and metal and it was humid, which was to be expected in a steam mechanic shop. Everything was organized, with different projects lined up against one wall. I saw what I assumed was the steam carriage Edmund had ordered. It was hard not to walk over to it right away, but I needed to meet the mechanic first.

"Ah, here we are, Pippa, the mechanic shop I was telling you about. Let me introduce you to . . ."

"Colin Finnigan, I did not know you were in Grantabridge." I practically catapulted into his arms. "How long has it been?"

"I take it you two know each other," Kaiden said.

I looked at Kaiden. He seemed so stuffy suddenly. He always seemed quite proper, but not so stiff. It was a strange change I couldn't explain.

"Oh yes! Colin is the son of our head stable groom. He wanted nothing to do with horses. We used to sneak off and try to build things all the time. We learned so much together." I looked over at Colin. He was short, compared to Kaiden. His auburn hair fell unruly over his forehead, making his freckles and green eyes stand out.

"Miss Pippa Stanhope, funny seeing you here. Last time I saw you, you had just about blown up the workshop we were in."

"I see some things never change," Kaiden said.

"Don't pay attention to him. I just told him I accidentally set fire to my room here on campus. I'm not sure if he's recovered from the shock of that information yet. Or, taken the time to process my genius." I looked over at Kaiden, flashing him a sassy smile.

"More like an evil genius," Kaiden said, laughing.

I hadn't expected that. The teasing. It seemed out of character for him, it broke away from the formal demeanor he always presented, it made me feel all fluttery inside. I wasn't sure if I liked that or not. Wait, that's not true. I did like it, I wanted more of it.

"Colin, how did you end up in Grantabridge?" I asked, looking around his shop, pretending I hadn't already taken it all in, and processed the different projects along the wall. “Is this what you’re working on? What are you using as insulation? Actually, are you using any insulation? How are you keeping the water tank full? How far can you travel on one water tank?”

“Same old Pippa, a million questions, never waiting for an answer. I’ve been in Grantabridge since I left your family’s home. And yes, that’s my current project. I’m calling it the steam carriage. I didn’t see any sense in putting in the insulation and increasing potential fire hazards. What else was there, oh yes, distance. I don’t actually know, but I can get to Fintan for sure.”

“That’s spectacular. Have you thought about adding a steam catcher like they have in homes to the steam carriage? I want to add it to my bike, and have spent the day trying to design it correctly to capture, condense, and reheat. Which reminds me, Ka . . . Lord Fremont brought me here to see if I could get my bike fixed. I was at Professor Aneurin’s and someone drilled a hole in my water tank while I was inside.”

Examining the damage, Colin asked, “Who did you upset? That’s some serious damage. But I can have it fixed by tomorrow, maybe the next day.”

“If I knew who did this, I would have dragged them over here by the ear and forced them to pay for it to be fixed. Maybe I would have challenged them to a duel. Instead, I’m stuck trying to determine how I am going to pay for it.”

“What? You’re a Stanhope, how can you not have the money to pay for it?” Colin was shocked.

“I’m afraid the name doesn’t mean anything as it applies to me specifically. But that’s neither here nor there. I’ll figure something out. I’ll just have a few less supplies to set on fire over the next few weeks.”

“Don’t be ridiculous. If you help me finish Lord Fremont’s steam carriage, I’ll fix your bike, and if you want, you can use some space here as a workshop. We can’t have you burning down your dormitory.”

My jaw dropped. I must have looked utterly ridiculous as I stood there, mouth gaping. I glanced over at Kaiden, and he shook his head almost imperceptibly, indicating he hadn’t set this up.

"You know I'm likely to burn this place down if you let me back here?"

"Unlikely, I've taken precautions."

"It's too much, Colin. I don't think I can."

"Don't assume I'm being altruistic. I need help; there's some things I'm struggling with. And if I remember correctly, you're an innovative problem solver. It would really help me out."

Could I really be this lucky? A workshop, and someone else to design with. It really was too much to process.

"Well, if you insist, how can I refuse? After all, who am I to say no to anyone that needs my help." I winked at Colin. "Are you just going to weld a patch where the hole is?"

"That's my plan."

"Can you do it on the inside of the tank? The water pressure will reinforce the patch."

"Yes, Pippa, I can do that. Are you sure you don't want to just patch it yourself?"

"Oh Colin, could I? Not that I don't trust you. But I'm the only one that's ever worked on the steamer bike. It's my pride and joy."

"I was joking. But if you really want to, by all means have at it. Come by tomorrow and fix that mess you call your bike, but not until tomorrow." I wanted to throw my arms around Colin in a huge hug, but there are some rules of society that I knew I was better following.

"I'll be back tomorrow. Take good care of my baby."

Kaiden held the door open for me and then followed me out.

As we walked, fog rolled in over the river, hugging the bridges and caressing the banks with its gentle touch. It was a picturesque scene, one typical of a late afternoon here in Grantabridge, where the sun tended to hide away more than show its face.

"You were quiet at the workshop, Kaiden."

"I didn't want to interrupt the reunion, once I knew it was a reunion. What are the chances you'd actually know the mechanic I was talking about?" Kaiden said, sounding just a little annoyed. Or maybe that was just my imagination. Was there any reason for me to want him to be annoyed at my relationship with Colin?

"That was very kind of you. I haven't seen Colin in years. Percy, Colin, and I used to get into so much trouble together." I smiled, thinking back to all those memories.

"You, in trouble. I can't imagine that." His lips twitched into a half-formed smile.

"Why, Lord Fremont, are you teasing me?"

Kaiden stopped, grabbing my hands. "I thought we agreed you would call me Kaiden. And why would I be teasing you? It couldn't be because you are brave, intelligent, and beautiful."

I looked down at my feet after that. It wasn't the most debonair of compliments, but I was at a loss for words. Kaiden was easy to be around, and handsome. But, calling me beautiful and intelligent was a form of flirting I wasn't used to, and I had no idea how to respond. I was not the lady gentlemen flirted with.

"I'm sorry, Pippa, I didn't mean to overstep." The bashfulness that came over him was present once again. "It's just shocking to know what you gave up to be here. And then listening to you talk about steam engineering, it's like watching a child talk about their favorite toys."

Glancing over at him, I raised an eyebrow. Not the most flattering of comparisons, but he might have a point.

Words continued to rapidly fall from Kaiden's mouth. "It's the excitement and pure joy. It seems that as we get older, we lose those things. But when you start talking about what you love, you light up with excitement. I'm pretty sure you forgot about me and everything around you while you were talking to Colin. Because the subject of modifying technology makes you light up like fireworks."

It was definitely the nicest thing anyone had ever said about me. "I guess I'm going to have to learn how to take a compliment. Even ones that compare me to a child."

Kaiden smiled. "I guess you will."

"And Kaiden, I didn't forget that you were there."

Our eyes met briefly and held. Then he grabbed my hand

and tucked it into his arm. In reality, we must have looked ridiculous. I was still in my steamer bike attire, and he was dressed like you would expect a lord. That is to say, he looked nice in his frock coat, silk waistcoat, and grey-striped pants. We walked like this, in silence, for a while. There were very few people that were comfortable with silence. It was nice to be around someone that got it.

"Pippa, why doesn't your family want you to be here?" Kaiden asked, interrupting my silent reverie.

"My mother believes that if it is known that I am attending University, I will ruin my sister's chance of ever making a good match, and mine as well. My mother would blame me if Penelope failed to marry. All because she doesn't believe anyone would want to marry into the family with a well-known bluestocking."

"But that's utter nonsense."

"Are you sure? My mother isn't the only one who thinks that way. I figure I gave up on marriage, especially marriage to a peer, the moment I stepped foot in Grantabridge as a student. I've turned my nose up at all of society's requirements for a young lady. I don't have a chaperone or lady's maid. There's no one here to protect me from, well, men. I'm ruined just for those reasons alone."

"I don't think you're ruined. I can't imagine growing up with that sort of pressure. Being around those beliefs seems soul crushing."

"It can be. I was lucky, I had my younger brother. He would sneak books to me, and I would help him practice his fencing and boxing."

"Boxing?"

"Yes. You should be careful. I have a mean right hook."

"Somehow that does not surprise me."

"Do you have any other siblings?" I asked.

"It was always just Edmund and me. Now that he's gone, I feel lost. We were always close. My family was unique. My parents never made us compete, just encouraged us to be friends with each other. Which was easy. Edmund was so nice. The best brother to have." Kaiden pinched the bridge of his nose as he finished. Trying to hide his tears, or so I assumed.

Silence enveloped us once again. I made no effort to continue the conversation. Not wanting to think of my family and how much I missed them despite, well, despite everything. Kaiden seemed to pick up on my lack of desire to talk and thankfully listened to his instincts.

It was nice to walk through the town and watch everyone going about their day-to-day life. I felt like I was becoming part of the community in some ways. When I rode my steamer bike to see the professor, there were people who waved at me, some smiled, and some just shook their heads. Even people thinking I was crazy made me feel like I belonged.

"Pippa," Kaiden said, interrupting my musings.

"Yes."

"I, er, never mind." Our eyes met briefly, then Kaiden looked away.

"Now I have to know what you were going to say. Let me guess, you're finally going to divulge all the secrets of the mysterious society you're a part of? No, not that. Darn, I'll have to continue to live with my curiosity. Or maybe regale you with the importance of crop rotation." I was being quite flippant at this point.

"No, I was going to ask—" Kaiden stopped, his face horrified by whatever had caught his attention.

"What is it?" I turned to look and saw flames licking and smoke billowing out of the upstairs windows of my dormitory.

Chapter Twelve

I broke into a run as soon as my brain registered what I was looking at. The fire was definitely in my room. The flames caressed the window frame over and over again. All I wanted was for the fire to stop, the smoke to go from grey and dingy to white and steamy. There was a bucket brigade already started, buckets of water being passed from person to person until water could be thrown on the fire. And then the last person with the bucket would run back down to start the process all over again. It was drudgery at its finest.

I took my place in line, helping in the only way I knew how. As I handed the filled bucket to Kaiden, I was shocked to see him there with me. I forgot all about whatever he was trying to say because, well, because my home was on fire.

"Where's Pippa, has anyone seen her? Did she make it out of the building? Does anyone know?" Georgi said, her voice frantic with concern. This was the first time I had ever seen Georgi rumpled. Her hair tumbled out of its intricate style, and soot streaked her face and dress.

"Georgi!" I yelled. I didn't want anyone thinking I was inside the building. "Over here!"

"Pippa!" Georgi engulfed me in her embrace, then took a step back, taking in my attire and my companion. "You haven't been home, have you?"

"No, I had my class this morning, and then I had to take my bike to a mechanic. I just made it back."

"Well, somebody started a fire in your room. We kinda thought it was you, since it was just the other day you tried to burn the place down."

"Wait. I did *not* try to burn the place down. It was an accident."

"I know, Pippa, I'm teasing. It's what I do with friends, and when I'm incredibly worried. First, I was worried you accidentally started the fire and injured yourself and were trapped in the fire. But now you're here, safe and sound." Georgi glanced over at Kaiden, then winked at me. "And now, I'm worried because, if you didn't start the fire, then someone who wishes you harm managed to get into the dormitory without anyone the wiser, go to your room, and start a fire. Which is almost as scary as you being trapped in there."

"Oh Georgi, that's the nicest thing anyone has ever said to me," I said, throwing my arms around her. Neither of us was known for giving hugs, but if there was ever a time for it, this was it. Tears sprung to my eyes, threatening to spill over.

The smoke billowing out of my room finally turned from an ominous grey to white, and then to nothing at all. The fire was out. I ran into the building, where everything looked even more monotonous than before. Other than that, there was no indication there had been a fire. That was, until you made it to my room. My room was destroyed. I could barely make myself look at it.

The curtains behind my worktable were charred, water soaked, filled with burn holes, and covered in ash. My books were thrown on the floor, burned. All my papers were piles of ash on the floor. My bed was no longer usable, and my clothes, well, they had definitely seen better days.

At least I'm wearing my biking clothes, I thought. And then that seemed like such a weird thought to have right now. I almost wanted to take it back.

"Where am I supposed to sleep?" I asked no one in particular. I know I joked about someone trying to rain on the Pippa Parade, but this felt like someone was really out to get me, and I had no idea who, and no idea why. I also didn't know where I was going to sleep tonight.

I turned to my friends, then back to my room, at a loss. I didn't know what to say. I felt someone walk up behind me and lightly touch my shoulder. I turned, Kaiden was there. Without thinking, I threw myself at him, grabbed his waistcoat, and cried. So much for me not crying anymore today. I felt his arms slip around my waist, and I stood there accepting his comfort. I didn't want to face what was happening.

"I'm sorry," I said, backing away. "I didn't mean to soak you for a second time today."

"It's nothing. You've had a hard day. If anyone deserves to cry copious amounts of tears today, it's you."

* * *

The fire was out and everyone had left the dormitory, including Kaiden. He looked at me like he wanted to say something to me as he left, but he refrained, going on his way with only a brief glance back and a curt nod.

Georgi let me move into her room. Normally, that would have taken some time, but since all my belongings were either piles of ash or coated in ash, it took no time at all. When the two of us settled into her bed, I told her about all that had happened during the day, from the strange conversation Professor Aneurin had with Professor Gates; to Lord Middleton being an insulting, pompous arse; the damage to my bike; reconnecting with Colin and getting a new workshop; and the moments spent with Kaiden. The last topic would have probably involved massive blushing and fits of giggles. Instead, it was subdued, overshadowed by the amount of destruction targeting me throughout the day.

It was strange. I had only known Georgi for a week, but we were already closer than Penelope and I had ever been. Georgi and I had the relationship I actually always wanted with my sister. The two of us were quite different, but deep down we shared similar beliefs, whereas Penelope and I didn't share any common ground.

"Oh Pippa, I forgot to tell you. We've been invited to a soirée with other students and professors here at University. It's supposed to be a welcome of sorts. Isn't that exciting?" Georgi said, sitting up. As much as I wanted to be done with today, my friend still had things to share, and I knew the right thing to do was listen. Even if all I wanted to do was sleep and forget about everything. I sighed, turning towards her as I sat up.

"I don't know, Georgi, things have been so crazy lately. I don't know if I have it in me to smile and act like everything isn't falling apart. And I don't have anything to wear now because of the fire. Not that I had very much before."

"I'm sure we can find something. This will be a great chance to show everyone at the University that we're not only here, but here to stay." I swear Georgi wanted to rub her hands together like a villain hatching a plan.

"Do you really think going to a soirée will make a difference? With everything that's happened so far, I really don't think one event is going to change anything." I flopped back down in the bed.

"You never know, Pippa. It's worth a shot. We need to do something to get more people to believe we belong here. Hiding in the shadows isn't going to convince anyone."

I snuggled down farther under the blankets, not wanting to think about tomorrow, or anything else after today.

"Okay, Pippa, let's talk about it tomorrow. Get some rest." She rolled over and turned off the light, leaving me with my thoughts until I fell asleep to the sound of her even breathing.

* * *

I woke up, unaware of where I was. The light coming in through the window was brighter than I was used to and in the wrong spot. I rolled away from it, burying my head in the pillows, unconcerned that I didn't recognize the room. Didn't recognize the room—suddenly, it all came rushing back. My bike, the fire, all my research, books, and clothes, everything broken or burned. I burrowed even farther into the bed, wanting nothing more than to stay here and hide from all the crap that happened yesterday.

“Pippa, are you awake?” Georgi asked. She sounded cheerful. How dare she sound cheerful this early, or in the morning. I wasn’t really sure if it was early.

I threw the cover over my head. “No.”

“Come on, Pippa, we have a lot to do today.”

“I don’t want to do anything today. I’ll stay here all day, and the rest of you can go do whatever needs to be done today.” My voice was muffled. I hadn’t left the safe embrace of the covers.

“Don’t tell me you’re just going to hide in here all day letting our arch nemesis win?” The safety of the covers was torn away from me. I stared at Georgi, accusation in my eyes, then grabbed the covers and pulled them back over me.

“Arch nemesis, who is our arch nemesis?” I muttered.

“I don’t know, but we clearly have one. And we need to figure out who it is. What better way than involving ourselves in different university activities.”

“Okay, Okay.” I threw the covers back. “What do you have planned for today? How are we going to prepare for our arch nemesis?”

“By shopping, of course. You need a dress for the soirée, and clothing for every other day.”

“Shopping? No. No. No. I didn’t know you wanted to torture me. I thought we’d be doing something like investigating, not wasting time with fripperies.”

“Of course shopping. Whether you like it or not, Pippa, fripperies are not a waste of time. A soldier wouldn’t go into battle without armor, and no matter how much you dislike it, clothing is our armor. When we look like a lady, we’re treated with a modicum of respect. If we completely flout convention, then we’re hysterical, not worth listening to.” Georgi had a point, whether I liked it or not. And my pants just were not the right armor for this battle.

“Fine, Georgi, you win. Let’s get this over with.” I threw off the covers and stood.

“Here, try these on.” Georgi threw a corset and about a million petticoats onto the bed.

“Georgi, you’re so much taller than me, none of these are going to work. I’ll spend all day tripping over your skirts and dragging them through the dirt.” Georgi was at least five inches taller than me; there was no way this was going to work.

“Pippa, I know what I’m doing when it comes to fashion. Stop arguing with me and trust me. And put those on.”

Reluctantly, I got dressed and was shocked when the pale green dress fit, and actually complemented, my complexion. There was only one pleated ruffle at the bottom, a fitted bodice, and lace at the neckline. It actually looked good on me, unlike everything that my mother had made me wear.

“Okay Georgi, you’ve made your point. You know what you’re talking about. Let’s get this shopping trip over with. Although I don’t understand why the skirt isn’t too long.”

“I was trying out this fashion trend where your skirts were short enough to show off your boots. I ended up not liking it. The hems just looked too short to me, but I kept this dress because of the fabric. I adore the color, even if it’s not quite right for my complexion.”

“Well, it does suit my complexion and the length is just right. I don’t know how you do it?”

Georgi clapped her hands with glee. Grabbing my arm, we ran down the stairs. Her enthusiasm was contagious. I couldn’t help but feel excited as we made our way to the dressmaker’s.

Our walk through town was brief. Georgi on a mission didn’t stop on the bridge that crossed Grantabridge river like I always did. It felt like only moments before we were walking into the modiste, the bell above the door jangling, alerting the shop owner to our presence.

The shop was delicately appointed with cream walls accented with pink and gold. Delicate chairs matched the walls, and a screen of cream and pink blocked the area where fittings happened from any roving eyes. A petite woman entered the room from the back, her look complementing the decor.

“Bonjour, I am Madame Cosette Toussaint,” thc petite woman said.

“My dear friend here is in dire need of clothing. Her room

caught on fire, and all of her clothes are gone. We need one gown for a soirée, at least three day dresses for classes, a travel suit, and all the unmentionables. She likes to wear a short corset most of the time, and while I tell her it ruins the lines of the dress she insists it's worth the comfort," Georgi said, rattling off way too many things.

"Ah, c'est bon." Madame Toussaint left to gather fabric samples.

I tried to tell Georgi I couldn't afford this, it was too extravagant, but she waved it off. Madame Toussaint came back into the room carrying fabrics in differing shades of blues and greens. I was taken behind the screen and measured while Georgi pointed to fabrics and designs. Every time I tried to speak, Georgi waved her hand dismissively.

By the time we were done, Georgi had ordered me more clothes than I thought was humanly possible. I told her my financial limitations, which she waved off like that didn't even matter. The clothing would be delivered in a matter of days. Just in time for the University soirée.

"Georgi, do you have time to stop by the workshop."

"Of course!"

We walked through town, crossing over the river. It was such a lovely day.

"Knock, knock, Colin, are you here?"

"Pippa? Two days in a row, what a nice surprise. And look at you, wearing an actual dress! That's completely unexpected. I can't even remember the last time I saw you in a dress."

I hugged Colin.

"Georgi, this is Colin Finnegan. Colin, this is Georgiana Spencer. The ladylike attire is completely her doing."

"Hello, Miss Spencer, lovely to meet you," he said with a small bow.

"Thanks for providing Pippa with a workshop. Not that it stopped the building from nearly burning down. Not that Pippa had anything to do with it."

"What?" Colin gasped, whipping his head towards me.

"Are you okay?"

"I would say it was nothing, but it destroyed all my things, all the research I had done. Quite the inconvenience. But yes, I am fine. I was out when it happened."

"What a relief."

"Actually, Colin, I stopped by because it's going to take me a little longer to fix my steamer bike. With the fire, I feel like I'm starting over, and it's a bit much right now." I sniffed as I finished my thought. I would not cry.

"Of course, Pippa, take your time. I'll keep the steamer bike safe, covered in the corner," Colin said.

Chapter Thirteen

It was early in the morning, really too early for me to wake up Mads, who liked her sleep as much as I did, but I was desperate for her help. Grabbing the tray I had just filled with spicy-pepper pesto and scrambled-egg-and-cheese sandwiches, I made my way to her room. I was hoping the noise of the stairs and the creaking of the hall floor outside her room would wake her up before I got there.

Outside her door, I balanced the tray on one hip. I took a deep breath and knocked.

"Mads, are you awake? It's Pippa. I was hoping you had a moment to talk," I said. I heard some shuffling behind the door and sighed. At least she wasn't dead asleep.

"What is it, Pippa?" Mads said, opening the door. She stood there, wrapped in a velvet robe, her long black hair hanging loosely down her back. She crossed her arms and glared at me.

This was not good. "I, uh, that is . . . I made breakfast." I finally got some words out. Pasting a dopey grin on my face, I held up the tray, hoping she would accept my bribe.

"Did you say breakfast?" Mads sniffed the air, her mouth twitching into the beginnings of a smile. "And coffee? Puh-lease tell me that beautiful aroma is coffee." Arms still crossed, Mads stared at the food tray longingly.

"Of course it's coffee. I wouldn't dare wake you up this early without bringing your favorite Latikan coffee. Bold and slightly sweet, just the way you like it."

"Come in then, you brought all the correct tokens of affection." She stepped aside, letting me into her room.

I set the tray on her immaculate worktable. Precise piles of papers lined the top of it, and her pens laid next to each other in a perfect line. I turned around to speak, but the array of colors on her bed distracted me. She had decorated the tall posts with vibrant, sheer fabrics, creating the look of a canopy. A gorgeous abundance of colorful pillows was scattered across the bed. It looked divine.

"Oh my, your bed, it looks so sumptuous."

"Thank you, Pippa." Mads reached out greedily. "Now hand me that glorious cup of coffee and tell me what you want."

I passed her a cup of coffee.

"I need help budgeting. I've never had to even think about money, and now I'm here. All these things have happened. And I can't ask my aunt for any more money. She's already being so generous."

"Of course." Mads rubbed her hands together, her face lit with glee. "This will be fun."

"Did you say fun? I can't see this being any fun."

"Yes, fun. Budgets are my absolute favorite. And so important. I used to do this for my father when I lived at home. It was one of my tasks to keep the budgets for our family. My father never did have a head for numbers." Mads sat in her chair, leaning back, lost in thoughts of her past. "Then you have schedules. I love creating schedules for multiple people. I planned out my sisters and my schedules to the minute. I knew when each one woke up, how long it took for their lady's maid to get them ready, when they came down for breakfast, how long it would take each one to eat, and so on."

"I don't think I could ever keep track of so many details, especially if they weren't my dctails."

"Someone had to do it, and after *Maman* passed, there was no one else. After a while, it was the only time I had to myself. It became a relaxing time for me before bed, when no one would interrupt me, and I could exercise some control over our chaotic life."

"I remember you saying something like that after, well, the fire I started."

She pulled her chair over to her worktable, grabbed a paper and pen. "Okay Pippa, let's get started." She wrapped her hair atop her head and jabbed a pen in to hold it out of the way, rolled up her dressing gown sleeves, and gestured to me to grab a chair. Apparently, it was time to get serious.

Together, Mads and I went through my expenses and the funds I had to work with. She finished her breakfast sandwich while she worked. I nibbled on mine as I sat and watched, answering whatever questions she had. It wasn't long before Mads was done.

"It won't be hard to stay within your budget," Mads said with a satisfied sigh. Tossing her pen onto the table, which she instantly picked back up and placed back into her perfect line of writing instruments.

"Not if people keep burning all of my things." I let my head fall into my hands.

"At this point, there isn't much left to burn. So that's good."

I glanced up. "Well, that's one way of looking at it."

* * *

I made my way to Professor Aneurin's workshop—I didn't have any new ideas. Everything that had happened over the past few days overwhelmed me. I walked into the Professor's workroom. It was shocking how it hadn't changed at all, yet everything else around me was in constant flux.

Professor Aneurin was bent over his desk, intently studying a book I had seen before. This one was bound in red leather. Professor Aneurin shut the book and looked up at me. I noted the gilded sword intertwined with two letter *S*'s on the cover.

"Ah Pippa, how nice to see you again. What do you want to work on today?"

"I didn't come with any plans for today. I'm sorry."

"It's okay, Pippa, every now and then you need a break."

"What were you reading when I came in? You looked fascinated by it."

"More like completely puzzled. I've been trying to figure it out for so long. The code is beyond my skills."

"A code, Professor? One of my friends is studying cryptography. Perhaps she could help?"

"Perhaps. I'll definitely think about it."

"What is the book?"

"It's the journal my father kept during his years at school here."

"Your father studied here?"

"Yes, I hoped to follow in his footsteps, but the University has changed so much since he was here in the 1840s. When he attended, technology was changing faster than ever before. Everyone struggled to keep up. Universities admitted students from the wealthy merchant class with a penchant for inventing. Now, admitting more students is viewed more than a threat to the established hierarchy. All the more damning, because many of the peerage are no longer wealthy. My father used to talk about being a member of this secret society and how they met with men from all different stations. He talked about how the society exchanged ideas, constantly reaching for progress. Until progress became a threat."

"Of course, it was just men," I muttered.

"Well, yes, unfortunately, as welcoming as they were, it was still not welcoming towards women. Even now, so many people fought letting you and the others attend."

"I don't understand why, but I believe it. My family would have fought it."

"I was hoping going through these journals would help. At least give more arguments to support change. Reminding them this is more of a change back to values once held, not moving towards something foreign and unimaginable. But I can't even read them." Professor Aneurin tossed the journal onto his desk, frustration radiating from him. "I wanted to follow in my father's footsteps, but they wouldn't even let me study here. At least they let me teach here."

"You're a brilliant professor. I don't know where I would be if you weren't here to work with me."

"You are a delight to work with, Pippa. I've never seen a mind work quite the same way as yours does. It's quite exciting to watch you work."

"Thank you, Professor." I felt the heat in my cheeks. "What society did your father belong to?"

"A secret society on campus. I think you know a couple of its members."

"Me? But I barely know anyone here at all."

"You would be surprised, Pippa, you would be surprised." Professor Aneurin handed me a book on dirigibles and aether. I curled up into my normal chair.

* * *

Two days later, it was time for the soirée, and I was not ready for it. I don't know how the others were handling the event, but I was a ball of nerves. My clammy palms and riotous stomach indicated just how much I was dreading tonight. I dressed in my gown (or as I preferred to think of it, my armor) Georgi picked out for me with the assistance of Hannah, Georgi's lady's maid. It was an aqua gown of dupioni silk with minimal ruffles. The black velvet trim added to its exquisite detail. Not to mention, the jaunty aqua-and-black feathers adorned my red hair perfectly. Georgi spent hours this morning setting curls and placing them perfectly. Her finished product, me, was a masterpiece. Unfortunately, I didn't feel like myself. I brushed off the skirt with gloved hands and made my way downstairs.

The rest of the ladies were waiting in the drawing room. I walked in to see Georgi in a frothy yellow confection. Mads wore a gorgeous magenta silk dress with black-and-white roses embroidered along the hem of her square drape and the bottom of her skirt. Willa was subtle in a light violet dress with minimal pleated trim. Everyone looked gorgeous and together we were absolutely striking.

“Are we ready to take the University by storm then?” I asked.

“Of course we are, Pippa, just look at us. We look fabulous; no one will know what hit them,” Georgi said, pride emanating from her voice. Georgi grabbed her reticule and looked at us. Soldiers in her army and she had just ordered us to fall in. Like the obedient soldiers we were, we did as ordered.

The brief walk to the dean’s home was just that: brief. There was no time to come up with an argument why this was such a bad idea. Georgi marched directly up to the door and knocked. The butler, I assumed, answered the door and let us into the great hall, where the ornate marble-and-gold design forced me to look away. Its ostentatious design overwhelmed my vision. To me, the entryway was cold and uninviting, lacking the warmth that made a house, or in this case, a mansion, a home. One of the liveried servants escorted the four of us to the parlor. The room was decorated with red-damask-covered walls and delicate mahogany furnishings. It was in this opulent room where several men and women had already gathered. The women were dressed in an array of colors with glittering jewels adorning their necks and arms. In stark contrast, the men were dressed in black and white. The crowd had naturally broken down into smaller sets, each set having its own conversations, causing the room to house an overwhelming murmur.

I excused myself from my friends and found a corner to occupy while they mingled. Disappearing in a room like this was what I did best. I had done it at all the parties Penelope insisted on hosting during her season. At each of them, I found a spot where I didn’t think anyone would bother me and watched the guests in their fancy clothes and made up stories about them. Most of the time, Percy would sneak in and join me in my little game.

Everything was going to plan until, out of nowhere, and for no apparent reason, Lord Middleton made his way directly towards me. I searched for my friends, willing them to come and walk me away from him as he approached to avoid any interaction with him. But I did not see them anywhere. Bloody hell.

“Ah, Miss Stanhope, how are you enjoying the evening?”

Lord Middleton asked.

“About as well as can be expected, considering.” One day, I would learn to keep my mouth shut. Apparently, today was not the day.

“Considering?”

“Your apparent need to come speak with me.”

“I am nothing if I am not well mannered.” Lord Middleton smirked.

“You could have fooled me,” I said, rolling my eyes.

“Whatever is that supposed to mean?”

“Lord Middleton, is this the first you’ve heard? Women have ears and are able to actually hear the words that come forth from your mouth, while many might choose to ignore those harsh words because you are a young, wealthy duke. However, I don’t give two figs. In fact, after all you’ve said in my presence, I’m shocked you even know my name.”

“How could I not know your name when you are all that Professor Aneurin talks about? Your brilliant ideas and brilliant drawings and brilliant ideas. I just wanted a chance to speak to the infamous Miss Stanhope.”

“And yet, you could have spoken to me on many other occasions, instead of just insulting me.”

“What can I say? You took the spot of a man at University. A spot that should have gone to someone who would have actually used the education they received here. You studying here is nothing more than a waste: a waste of your time, a waste of the professor’s time, and a waste of resources.”

“My studies aren’t a waste. In fact, if it wasn’t for men like you, I could work in steam engineering and design.”

“Men like me?”

“Men who don’t believe women have the skills or talents to attend university, much less do anything with the knowledge we could get while we’re here.”

“It’s not unreasonable to think that women shouldn’t study here. What is a lady going to do with the information once she is married? It’s not like she’ll use the information to run a household.

She'll not be pursuing a profession. A lady has no need for any of the knowledge obtained here. And if they have no use for the education, why should they take the space that a man could fill?"

"Who says a lady must marry? Or that if she did, she would marry someone as close-minded as you." I could feel the rant coming and there was no stopping it. Even if I knew it would do no good. "You don't even realize how much you contradict yourself in your statements. First, you act as if there is limited space here at the University. When in truth, there's no limit on space other than time. There are no classrooms we sit in, so there is no limit on space. I'm the only student that meets with the professor other than you. Most of the gentlemen here spend their time on anything and everything other than studying.

"Second, you don't actually mean I'm taking up the space a man could fill; you mean a space a gentleman could fill. If my old stable lad applied here, he would never be admitted because he is not a peer.

"Third, and finally, none of the peers are going to do anything with their education either. They might remember the time fondly, frame a piece of paper, and put it up on the walls of their office. But it's not like you're working to invent something, to change the future, to make life easier for the common man. Unless, of course, I have misjudged you." I waited a few seconds. "No, I didn't think so."

With that, I lifted my skirts and stepped around Lord Middleton to walk away, only to be stopped midstep and spun around. I looked at Lord Middleton's hand on my arm, his fingers digging into my skin.

"Unhand me."

He did no such thing. His hand stayed right where it was, his fingers vicelike around my arm. So tight I knew it would leave a mark. His icy blue eyes looked down at me, his mouth twisted into a sneer.

"You think because you are here, you can speak to me like that? Without respect or decorum. I am a duke and you will treat me as such."

"If you do not let go, you will find out just how little I care about your title. Or have you forgotten the people in my family? I will cause a scene you cannot even begin to comprehend. My reputation may end up in tatters, but you'll find out I do not care because my reputation is already ruined by attending university."

Hatred glinted in his icy eyes. Slowly, he released me. "You may think you have nothing to lose, but I'm sure I can find something."

I turned and walked away, my heels clicking on the floor with each step. Each click drew me farther away from him and closer to my friends. I definitely did not want to be caught alone again this evening. In my search for a friendly face, a safe haven in the crowd, I ran directly into Professor Aneurin. He grabbed my arms, ensuring I did not fall to the floor, although I tried not to. I winced as he did so.

"Are you okay, Miss Stanhope?" he asked.

"I'm as well as can be after having to deal with an insufferable brute. I was happier when he just ignored me and insulted me to others rather than to my face."

"Who . . ." Aneurin glanced around, and I could see the moment realization hit. "Was Lord Middleton bothering you?"

"That would be putting it mildly," I said. "Well, it started as somewhat of a conversation. But he was most displeased when I went to leave without showing him the proper respect and asking his permission. He insisted on letting me know just how unhappy he was with my behavior."

"Let's find somewhere for you to sit and take a moment for yourself." Aneurin led me away from the crowded room. I went with him, thankful for a moment away. All I wanted to do was leave, but I doubted Georgi would let us yet.

"Here," Aneurin said, leading me into a study. He sat me down on an oversized leather sofa and continued to walk around the room. Finding what he must have been looking for, he grabbed the decanter and poured two glasses of the amber liquid. "This should help a bit, but drink it slowly; it's strong whiskey."

I took a sip and gasped; it wasn't so much the flavor, but the fire burning all the way down my throat and into my stomach. I set the glass down, not intending to pick it up again. Apparently, I didn't know my own intentions, because before long, I was taking another sip of the burning liquid.

"What did Lord Middleton say to you?"

"More of the same really, just that I don't belong here, that I am taking up a space a man could use, and that he would find some way to ruin my life." I failed miserably at my attempt to sound flippant. "I don't know why he is so bothered with my person taking up space here. He has no need to see me if he doesn't want to. It's not like he wants a commoner to come and study here. They won't use what they learn, either. His arguments were convoluted at best and irrational at worst."

"I don't know what to tell you, Miss Stanhope. He's part of a society that fears progress and change. It's his belief that he will lose his wealth and power if others are allowed things like an education. Which may be true in some ways, but not in the way he fears. I'm honestly surprised this is the first time the two of you have interacted."

"Oh, well, I always leave when he comes around. I don't like the way I feel around him. It's like his beliefs create a seed of doubt as to my own worth and talent. And I don't want to be around that anymore, especially when it's based on broad assumptions and not talking to me."

"I see intelligence in who you interact with as well as all of your fantastic designs."

I blushed at his words. I really wished I blushed as prettily as Willa. Instead, I turned beet red and my skin ended up the same color as my hair, my freckles standing at attention.

"I think I'm ready to go back, Professor. At least I won't barrel anyone else over at this point. Thank you for taking the time to help me."

"Of course. I should be going anyway. I have some things I want to take care of at the lab tonight."

"This late?"

"The better to remain undisturbed. I will see you tomorrow, Miss Stanhope."

Leaving the study, I once again looked around for my

friends. Over there, by the champagne. I carefully made my way over to them, weaving in and out of the crowd. Careful to not make contact with anyone.

“Georgi, c-c-c-can we leave yet?”

I turned, hearing Willa, and made my way towards them.

“I second leaving, I just had the most arduous discussion with Lord Middleton,” I said, rubbing my arm. I was definitely going to have a bruise from that arse.

“Not yet. We have to make our presence felt and appreciated. And so far, both of you have been hiding in corners.” Georgi did have a point, I thought.

Thankfully, the rest of the evening went on without further confrontation. We heard the string quartet play some hauntingly beautiful music. Others milled about happily. The dean spoke about coming together, and just because things were changing, it didn’t mean we couldn’t support each other in our higher-learning endeavors.

Finally, Georgi decided we had mingled enough. Once again, I had the thought that the four of us together in our finery were quite the sight to see. Maybe Georgi was right, and the proper attire was like wearing armor to war. Which made me think of the arrogant Lord Middleton.

As if just thinking of him conjured him into existence, Lord Middleton and I made eye contact across the room. It didn’t seem possible, but I could feel his hatred. I shivered in response.

Chapter Fourteen

I felt so much better in the morning, despite the finger marks on my arm serving as a reminder of last night's unpleasantness. I was still in Georgi's room and probably would be for the rest of the year. But today felt hopeful. I didn't have any new ideas for my steamer bike, but I was looking forward to being able to discuss it with someone that understood.

I walked across the bridge, wishing I had my bike, but with the fire, and then the soirée, I hadn't had any time to fix it. I really needed to. Right now, it was just taking up space in Colin's workshop.

I waved to the owner of the bakery as I walked by, contemplating stopping and getting a croissant. But I was too excited to work with the professor this morning. Walking through the courtyard to Professor Aneurin's workshop, I tried to think of something to focus on, but nothing was sticking. Hopefully, the professor would have some ideas.

"Professor, what do you want to work on today?" I asked as I pushed the door open. "Professor?"

I looked around. The silence was unreal and papers were more scattered than normal and books were dumped on the floor. Professor Aneurin was messy, but this seemed unusual even for him. I noticed there were two snifters on his desk and an empty decanter on its side. Fear rolled through my body, sending a chill up my spine. The hopeful morning skirted away, and a general sense of foreboding took its place. It was at that moment my foot hit something solid.

"Oh, please no."

I looked down.

It couldn't be.

But it was. My foot had just hit Professor Aneurin. And he didn't look okay. He had a hand to his heart, and his fingertips were blue. I dropped to my knees. In fact, he was not okay; he was very, very much not okay. His lips were blue, and he stared glassy-eyed at me. He was dead.

I didn't know how long I sat there on my knees, staring at my mentor's lifeless body. I wanted to get help. I wanted to wake up and find out this was all a dream. I wanted . . . but all I could do was sit there, staring at the body of the most encouraging person I had ever known.

"Pippa, are you . . . Dear lord. Is that Professor Aneurin?" I looked up to see Kaiden rushing towards me. I tried to nod my head. I tried to say something, anything. But I couldn't make a sound. I was frozen. Frozen in this spot, frozen in time. I didn't know. Nothing seemed real at the moment.

"We spoke last night," I said. "We spoke last night. He . . . I . . . He's dead. Kaiden, he's dead." I looked up into his amber eyes, waiting—for what, I didn't know. Maybe to be told I was wrong. That this was a dream. But why, why would I dream this? Nothing made sense.

"I don't know what to do, Kaiden. I don't want to leave him on the floor alone, but we need to tell someone, the police, I assume. Right, we should contact the police. How does one contact the police? I've never had to do such a thing. But I don't want to leave him. He's so alone on the floor, it isn't right. None of this is right." I felt wetness on my face, tears. I must be crying. It made sense to cry right now. I made no effort to stop the tears or wipe them away.

"Pippa, look at me, that's it. Deep breaths now. Breathe in and let it out." The two of us stayed there for a moment, breathing together.

"I'm going to find someone to get an inspector. I'll be right back. Okay?"

I nodded my head ever so slightly, not wanting him to leave, but what choice was there? Professor Aneurin was . . . was dead, and nothing made sense. He told me to meet him here this morning. How long had he been on the floor like this? He should be made more comfortable. Wait, that made no sense. He couldn't be comfortable, or uncomfortable, anymore.

"Kaiden, is that you?" I asked.

"Sorry to disappoint, Miss Stanhope. My, it seems like you've been busy," Lord Middleton said, walking into the room, finding me on the floor. He was impeccably dressed, as always. However, it did not stop him from flicking imaginary lint from his coat.

"Been busy . . . What do . . . Oh . . . You can't believe I had something to do with the professor's death! He was . . . There's no way I would ever, I mean without him I . . ." At that moment, I felt the tears course down my cheeks again. They were hot against my frozen cheeks. And while I did not want to cry in front of this horrendous man, the reaction was so normal under the circumstances, I did not attempt to stop the tears from coming. It was pointless to try to stop them, anyway. I concentrated on my breathing. Doing what I could to not let the emotions overwhelm me more than they already had.

"You were just found alone with a dead body. What am I supposed to think?" Lord Middleton sneered.

At that moment, I learned two things about myself. One, if it came down to it, I probably could murder a person. Two, I had incredible willpower, because I did not attack Lord Middleton in an attempt to wipe the sneer off his face.

* * *

"I'm Detective Inspector Devon Radcliffe. You must be Miss Stanhope. Lord Fremont told me you found the body. I know this is difficult, but I'm going to need to ask you some questions."

Detective Inspector Devon Radcliffe was rather imposing. Not as tall as Kaiden, but what he lacked in height he made up for with broad shoulders and muscles I could see move beneath his layers of clothing. His piercing eyes made contact with mine, and I realized I had only answered in my head, not aloud.

"Yes, sir, anything to help. Professor Aneurin was my mentor, and his death is a significant loss. I want to find out what happened." I rattled off any words that came into my head.

"That's good to know, Miss Stanhope." The detective inspector nodded. "When was the last time you saw Professor Aneurin, before this morning?"

"Last night. The University held a soirée to introduce us as new students. I had an unfortunate encounter with, well, with a fellow classmate and, quite literally, ran into Professor Aneurin. He took me to the study in the dean's home and waited with me until I was able to compose myself. He mentioned he had to leave to get some work done here. Then said he would . . . would see me tomorrow." I sniffed, wiping tears from my eyes.

"Did you see him at anytime after that?"

"No, my friends and I left after the dean's speech and went straight back to our dormitory. And then I walked here this morning and, well, you know the rest."

"Thank you, Miss Stanhope. Was the room like this when you arrived? Did you notice anything else out of the ordinary? Anyone else around?"

There were so many questions, and I tried to answer them the best I could. But it was all so much. The body was still right there, not moving. More police arrived, and then the coroner. They all had notepads, jotting down something here and there. The coroner moved the body, and then I saw his face. I couldn't be here anymore. Anywhere else, but right here. I took a step towards the other side of the room, moving away from the professor's lifeless body, but no one followed. The detective inspector, Lord Middleton, and Kaiden just stared at me. What had I done?

"I'm sorry, I just can't be there, right there, while the coroner moves his body."

"What, you don't want to admire your own handiwork any longer?" Lord Middleton muttered.

"Excuse me," I said, turning to face the obnoxious, entitled arse.

"I heard your account of last night. You forgot to mention your argument with Professor Aneurin," Lord Middleton said.

"Miss Stanhope, you argued with the deceased last night?" Radcliffe asked.

"No, Detective Inspector, we did not argue at all. He was looking out for me after I had an argument with someone else entirely. Someone who didn't know how to keep his hands to himself." I glared at Lord Middleton. Why was he lying?

"Are you referring to the bruises that the professor left on your arm, Miss Stanhope? We were all there last night. We heard you tell him to unhand you." I watched as Lord Middleton's normal smirk settled on his face.

"That wasn't Professor Aneurin, that was y—"

"Miss Stanhope, let me see the bruises in question."

"But detective Inspector, they are irrelevant. Professor Aneurin would never lay a hand on me."

"Miss Stanhope, quit with this charade. We all know you were accepted here because Aneurin was fascinated by you. I'm sure his behavior was not that of a gentleman and you did the only thing you could. I mean, he already gave you whiskey last evening. Is that the behavior of a gentleman?" I had never wanted to harm another human being so badly in my life.

"Detective Inspector, none of what Lord Middleton is saying is true. Well, other than the whiskey, but that was to help me recover from an argument I had with, well, Lord Middleton. The bruises are from that incident and have nothing to do with the professor. You have to believe me. The professor would never do something like that."

I looked around frantically. Someone had to believe me. I saw Kaiden swing his head towards Lord Middleton. The look on his face was anything but friendly. Lord Middleton seemed unaware of it all while he stood there examining the bookshelf. The coroner and his crew chose that moment to lift the body on the stretcher and carry it out. My stomach rolled as I turned away. I wanted out of here but also wanted to stay for a while and see what I could find. The detective inspector's questions did not give me much hope that he would solve this crime. He was too quick to believe Lord Middleton.

"Where did you say you went after the soirée last night, Miss Stanhope?" Detective Radcliffe asked again.

"To my dormitory. You can ask anyone there what time we got home. And I'm sharing a room with Georgiana Spencer since there was a fire in my room a few days ago."

"And who did you speak to at the soirée?"

"Lord Middleton, Professor Aneurin, and my friends, Georgiana Spencer, Wilhelmina Schulz, and Madeleine Cavendish. Other than that, I tried to keep to myself. I don't much like events like that. I find them overwhelming."

"Thank you, Miss Stanhope. That's it for now. But don't leave town until this investigation is over."

"Thank you, Detective Inspector."

I had been summarily dismissed, but I still didn't feel right leaving. I went outside and did what I did best. I listened at the door.

"Inspector, are you just going to let her walk out of here? She is clearly up to something. Normal people don't just find dead bodies."

I almost walked back in. Was Lord Middleton trying to say I murdered the professor? Why? I would never murder him. He was the best part of being here in Grantabridge. I stopped myself as I heard the detective inspector.

"I have no reason to hold her, as there's no evidence of foul play. After the coroner examines the body, I'll know more."

* * *

I moved away from the door, slightly worried Detective Inspector Radcliffe was automatically going to think the worst of me based on the lies told about me moments ago. I was terrified Simon Middleton was going to succeed at whatever he was trying to do. Frame me for murder was my best guess, but I didn't understand why he would do such a thing. I felt lost and confused and this turn of events wasn't helping at all. I didn't want to worry about Simon Middleton when one of my favorite people here was dead. Probably murdered.

I wanted to get back into the room to look around again. I didn't know why I thought I could figure out what happened to the professor. The detective inspector seemed perfectly capable, I guessed. Not arresting me was at least something. But some part of me believed I owed it to Professor Aneurin to make sure his death didn't go unsolved. Too often, our society let those in power decide how things that had nothing to do with them would end. I was worried that the University would find it bad form for a professor's death to be investigated, and somehow it would be pushed under the rug. In the end, a good man's life would be forgotten.

I sat on the bench outside the professor's workshop for what seemed like hours on end, waiting for everyone to leave, twisting my red hair around my fingers. I hoped I would make it inside before a university official came by to lock it up. Finally, Lord Middleton left. I shrunk down in the corner, hoping he wouldn't see me. I couldn't take another one of his diatribes implying I was the guilty party. Thankfully, he strode on by. He did not look pleased, which made me the slightest bit happy. I thought his pleasure would be to see me locked away in shackles, which I was vehemently opposed to. Finally, the detective inspector left. I watched as he walked out of sight, then pushed myself off the bench.

I laid my hand on the doorknob but did not enter. Did I really want to go back in? What did I think I could do? Then I remembered Aneurin telling me how talented I was last night and not to let anyone take that away. I pushed the door open and ran directly into Kaiden's chest. I seemed to do that a lot. His hands reached out, grabbing me around the waist to steady me. I stood there a moment, stunned he was still here.

"Pippa, I thought you went home," Kaiden said.

"I couldn't. I think he was . . . he . . . The professor was . . . murdered. I need to do something. I can't let it alone." My tone was frantic but also belayed the point. "I'm stronger than I look, so don't ask me to step aside."

Kaiden eyed me like he was looking for an excuse to take me home. "You know that's what the police are for?"

"But who else knew him like I did? At least I'm one of his students. I spent so much time with him since the semester started." I looked at Kaiden, pleading.

Kaiden abruptly gestured towards the door. "Get in here, but look quickly. What are you looking for, anyway?"

"I don't know. Last time I was here, the professor was looking through some encrypted journals. I'd like to find them. They seemed important to him. Something to do with his father, if I remember correctly. And I would kinda like to take the whiskey snifters to see if Willa can find anything, can find out if there is poison in one of them."

"And that's all?" Kaiden rolled his eyes.

"Yes, Kaiden, that's all," I said, deadpanned. "Are you going to help, or not?"

Kaiden started to shift through the books on the shelf. "I hope this doesn't come back to bite us in the arse, Pippa."

With that, I shuffled through the papers on his desk. The majority had to do with what we were working on together. Or . . . what we had been working on. But there were some that reminded me of the symbols and formulas in my alchemy book. I set the journals beside me.

"Kaiden, come look at this. There are pages missing." I searched for a pencil. Finding one, I grabbed another paper and rubbed the graphite over the paper. A formula appeared.

"Is that what I think it is?" I asked.

"If you think it's the formula to turn certain metals to gold, then yes, it is exactly what you think it is," Kaiden said.

"Do you think this is why he's dead? Someone killed him for this formula?" It seemed as good a reason as any. Greed was always a powerful motivator. The conversation I overheard between Professor Gates and Aneurin flitted through my mind, but I couldn't grab onto it to analyze it further.

"Men and women have killed for less."

I went to grab the journals, but Kaiden stopped me.

"Where did you get these?"

"The professor was looking at them the other day. He said they were his father's. Why?"

"That emblem, it's the one for the Shadowed Sword."

"Oh, is that the secret society you're part of? Why would he have encrypted journals from a secret society?"

"I don't know, Pippa, I truly don't know. But you should be careful."

With that warning, I quickly grabbed the two snifters, wrapped them carefully, and put them in my pockets. I took my scrap paper and the journals from the bookshelf, then stopped and looked around. I couldn't think of anything else to take other than my work.

I started shoving my papers, some with his notes and others without, into the journals. I noticed one had a corner ripped off, which was strange. Something to look at later.

"Did you hear that?" I asked. My eyes darted around, trying to ascertain where the noise came from.

"Yes, bloody hell, Pippa, you need to hide."

"What are you going to do?"

"I don't know. Act like I belong. And look down my nose at whoever is there, making them believe that they don't belong. Isn't that how dukes behave?"

"Just get them to go away." Kaiden shoved me into some sort of back room as the door opened.

"Professor Gates, I'm surprised to see you here."

"Ah, young Lord Fremont. I heard you were here after the body was found. I didn't expect anyone to still be around."

"I just wanted to secure everything as much as I could before leaving. It's so tragic. I would hate for his research to be lost on top of everything else."

"Ah yes, that's why I am here. Aneurin, may he rest in peace, and I were working together on a project. I wanted to grab his notes if I could before something happened to them during the investigation."

Well, that's not suspicious, I thought to myself, stuck in this room with no light, not making the connection that I had literally been doing the same thing.

"I believe most of his notes and current journals are on his bookshelves."

"Here it is. If anyone has any questions about where the journal went, please send them over to me."

I heard the door click and then rushed out of the room.

"Which journal did he take?"

"He took the alchemy one, Pippa. The one with the ripped-out pages."

Chapter Fifteen

Kaiden insisted on escorting me back to the dorm. Honestly, it felt nice. After the dormitory fire and now this, this–this loss, death, murder . . . I couldn't even think the words, and I didn't want to be alone. It was like my world was crumbling down around me and I was the only one around to attempt to clean up the mess. I wanted to prevent the destruction.

The farther Kaiden and I walked into town, the more I noticed a change. This morning, it was bright and happy with shop owners coming out to wave good morning to me. Now, after this morning, the entire feel of Grantabridge was different. The people who waved at me just this morning now turned their heads and ignored me. Which made no sense. It's like they thought I did something to disturb the balance. It was like they already knew Professor Aneurin was dead, and they all thought it was my fault. Those thoughts whirled in my head. But that couldn't be the reason for the change. There had to be some other explanation. I wasn't sure why everything changed, but I didn't like it.

"Does it seem like everyone is looking at me weird?"

"Not really. Wait, maybe a little. It's more like they won't look at you."

"Do you think Lord Middleton did something to start the

rumor that I killed Professor Aneurin?"

"Simon, speak to a commoner? He would never demean himself to do so. I can't imagine him doing it now." Kaiden rolled his eyes at the thought of it.

"Okay," I said, but I was doubtful. No one was looking at me, and that was strange.

We continued our way through town, crossing the bridge, which was my favorite spot in town. But the day had turned grey and foreboding. So different from when I crossed the bridge this morning, feeling like anything was possible.

Kaiden and I walked on in silence. I had no idea what to say, but I wanted to know what was going through his mind. Especially since he was the one that found me this morning.

"Thank you for getting the police this morning," I said. "I don't think I've ever been in a situation where I did not know what to do. If it had been Simon who showed up first, I don't know what would have happened."

"Is any of what he said about last night true?" Kaiden asked. I looked at him, trying to determine whether he already believed Simon.

"What? None of it. I argued with Lord Middleton last night. He grabbed my arm." I subconsciously rubbed the bruises he left. "He's the one who threatened me. I ran into Aneurin after that incident. Aneurin took me to the study and encouraged me to calm myself before going back to the party. He is . . . was always so kind to me."

Kaiden took my arm and slowly rolled up my sleeve. His fingers brushed over the five distinct bruises on my arm. I shivered in response. I looked up at Kaiden and thought I saw his lips move, but I couldn't make out what he said. Our eyes met as he slowly lowered my sleeve.

I felt the tears coming; I didn't think I could cry anymore today. Once again, I was wrong. These weren't loud tears, but the ones that ran down your face silently, the ones that escaped when you wanted to scream at the universe for what happened. If I let myself scream, the tears would turn to ugly, loud tears. These were the precursors. The ones that escaped, letting you know that every bit of control you thought you had was just an illusion. And the illusion was cracking.

"Pippa." He stopped and wiped the tears from my face with his sleeve. He didn't say anything more to me. Just took my hand as we walked back to the building I currently called home.

"What am I going to tell them?" I asked myself. But Kaiden heard me.

"The truth. Your friends will know how to help you. They'll help you through the loss, and then, when you're ready, they'll help you figure out what to do next."

"Next?" I hadn't thought about a next. But with that one word I realized I needed a next. The one person who would work with me here at the University was dead. A peer was insinuating I had murdered him. There was no one else here that worked with steam engineering. There was no one else here who would fight to make sure I could stay.

"Oh my god, I have to figure out what I'm going to do next!"

"Worry about that another day, Pippa. Today let yourself grieve. There will be plenty of time and help from those around you to determine what's next."

* * *

Kaiden left as soon as we arrived at the dormitory. There was a part of me that wanted to turn and ask him to stay, but a larger part was ready to talk things over with my friends. Having their perspective was more imperative than keeping Kaiden here.

I took a deep breath and walked through the heavy door. Everything felt different. The door screeched louder than I had ever heard it. The greys looked gloomier. It was like what tethered me to this place had snapped and I was adrift. Yet everything here was the same. The walls were still dull, everything in shades of grey. They weren't actually any gloomier than before. The door wasn't actually louder. The difference was that my world had changed at its very foundation.

My heels clicked on the floor. The noise echoed through my head, or maybe it was the hall. I was in a fog; at times it seemed to clear, but then it was thicker, and I felt lost.

"Pippa, are you okay?" I looked up as Georgi walked down the stairs. How long had I been standing there?

"He's dead," I said.

"Dead? Who's dead?" Georgi rushed down the rest of the stairs.

"Professor Aneurin. I think he was murdered."

"Wait . . . what?" I could see the shock on her face.

"I found his body this morning. When I went to class, I stumbled upon his body. I don't think he died from natural causes."

Georgi took my arm and led me to the parlor. I felt her lightly push me down onto the settee. I could feel the springs poking through all my petticoats. The settee was so uncomfortable. I tried to adjust myself and realized I still held my bag with the notebooks from the professor's office in my arms.

"Tea, we need a cup of tea," Georgi said. "Willa, Mads, can you come to the parlor, and bring some tea, or something stronger, if you can find it."

Georgi sat down beside me, took my bag of notebooks from my arms, and just held my hands, waiting for the others to come to the room. I barely noticed Willa and Mads come into the room, but Georgi's hands were replaced with a hot cup of tea and a plate of cucumber sandwiches. I didn't know if I could eat right now, but I appreciated how thoughtful my friends were to bring me my favorites.

"Okay, now that we are settled, start at the beginning and tell us what happened," Georgi said. I noticed she had a pen and paper in front of her. She was taking notes? Why was she taking notes?

"The beginning really starts at the soirée last night. Lord Middleton had just accosted me when I quite literally ran into Professor Aneurin. I was out of sorts after the argument with Lord Middleton." I went to rub the bruises on my arm and almost spilt the tea instead. "Aneurin took me to the study and poured each of us some whiskey. And we talked, he said . . ."

I gulped, but it was no use. These weren't the soft, streaming tears from before. These took over my entire body. I felt myself shake, sobbing, each wave coursing through me more violently than the one before. I felt Willa, Mads, and Georgi all surrounding me on the sofa, holding me, murmuring words, words that made no sense at the moment. They must have been words of comfort, but I was in such a haze, I couldn't understand them. Words that would have made sense if they could get through the fog in my head.

Finally, I was able to draw a shaky breath in and let it out slowly. My sobs slowed to tears.

"Can you continue?" Mads asked.

"I think so." I took another deep breath and wiped my eyes. "He said he needed to go to the workshop last night, and that he would see me today, which was still tomorrow when we talked. Do you think I was the last person to see him alive other than the killer?"

"It's imp-p-p-possible to know, but if you were, at least it was a favorable moment in time."

"What a lovely thought Willa, let's definitely think of it like that," Georgi said. "Pippa, do you know what time the professor left the soirée last night?"

"Sometime before the dean's speech. I met back up with you, and both Willa and I wanted to leave. You wouldn't let us. So we mingled for a bit, and then there was the speech. That's when we left. I'm sure Aneurin was at his workshop by then."

"Did you see anyone else at the soirée last night?" Georgi already sounded like a solicitor.

"I saw Lord Middleton. He was still there when we left. I don't remember seeing Kaiden there." I gasped and looked up sharply, my eyes wide. "You don't think it could have been Kaiden, do you?"

"First, Kaiden and you are getting rather close. Is there something you need to tell us? Second, does Lord Fremont have a reason to murder the professor?"

"Is there a third?"

"I don't know," Georgi said. "I'll think of one, eventually."

"Kaiden and I are friends, at least I think we are. I can't think of any reason he would want Professor Aneurin dead. He seemed to like the professor."

"What time did you head out to work with Aneurin this morning?" Mads asked.

"I don't know. I woke up in such a good mood this morning. Refreshed after everything. Then it all came crashing down." I let out an uneven breath.

"It'll be okay, Pippa, we will do everything we can to make it better. When you arrived at the workshop, tell us what you felt."

"It was so silent. The room was more of a mess than normal. Aneurin always left things out, but he knew exactly where everything was. But today there were designs on the floor, everything was scattered, and quiet. There were two glasses and an empty decanter on the work desk." I described the rest of the room to the ladies, finding Professor Aneurin's body, and then the arrival of Kaiden, Lord Middleton, and Detective Inspector Radcliffe.

"Oh, I forgot, I took the two whiskey snifters," I said. I pulled the two glasses from my pocket and put them on the table to the left of me. "I was hoping Willa could see if there was poison in one of these glasses."

The discussion continued like this for what felt like forever. By the time we were done talking about what I saw, I felt like I had re-walked the room at least eight times. I was numb, I was tired, and I wanted to see if I could close my eyes without seeing the body over and over again as they moved it to examine the professor. That was something I never wanted to experience again.

* * *

After what felt like hours, if not days, of questioning, Willa convinced the others that I needed to lie down and took me upstairs to rest. She was a caretaker down to her very core. Whether she was looking out for her plants or her people, she was always looking out for someone. At the moment, it was me and I was very thankful for her. Not that I could actually rest. Every time I closed my eyes, I relived the most horrible moments of my life.

I made my way back downstairs, deciding I would rather be

with the others right now instead of stuck in my own head, seeing things no one should have to see over and over again.

"Pippa, you're up," Georgi said.

"Unfortunately, resting was not meant to happen. And I do not want to be alone with my thoughts."

"I understand completely," Mads said. She patted the seat next to her. I made my way through the room to sit on our sad little settee with her. I thought I had become immune to the dreariness of our dormitory home, but today the dullness stood out even more, as did the furniture that had seen better days. My mother would be horrified if she saw this place.

"I think we have a bit of a plan to help you out. Before you say anything, I do think you need our help. While the detective inspector wasn't swayed by Lord Middleton's accusation right away, I have no doubt that he will be back, and you are at risk." Georgi was in her take-charge mode. It was, after all, her favorite mode to be in.

"Bloody hell." My head fell into my hands. "I don't understand what Lord Middleton is trying to accomplish with lies."

"Oh Pippa, you have so little experience with the vagaries of spoiled, entitled men, even though you grew up around them. Lord Middleton never needed to target you until you decided to attend University. Then when you questioned Lord Middleton last night, you probably made him question himself, which is even worse, and then you had the audacity to walk away, making him feel insignificant. He wants revenge," Mads said. I had a feeling there was quite the story behind her statement. I wanted to know it, but I didn't have it in me to ask about it, at least not right now. Mads patted my hand like she understood my thoughts.

There was a knock at the door. I heard a collective, sharp intake of breath; I hope we hadn't just manifested the detective inspector showing up to take me in for murder.

"I'll get it," Georgi said. I watched her stand and smooth her sky-blue dress before walking out of the parlor, a clear sign she was worried. I listened as her heels clicked against the entryway floor, and as the front door opened with that terrible sound, I held my breath, waiting to hear who was at the door.

"Lord Fremont, what a pleasant surprise," I overheard Georgi say.

Willa, Mads, and I let out the collective breath we had been holding.

"What are you doing back so soon, Kaiden?" I asked. I saw Georgi mouth "Kaiden" towards Mads. I rolled my eyes at them.

"I wanted to come and warn you. Simon, that is, Lord Middleton, has been at the local clubs and is telling everyone about the fight you had with Professor Aneurin last night."

"You mean the fight that never actually happened."

"Yes, the fight that never happened. But, Pippa, do you think that's going to matter when it comes down to it? He's a duke and your family isn't even speaking to you now."

"That's incredibly unfair. I'm still the daughter of a viscount and a person who has no reason to lie about what happened last night."

"It is unfair; that being said, do you think the fact that it's unfair is going to stop society from spreading the rumors, true or not? I'm not telling this to you to hurt you. I wanted you to know so you could prepare. Maybe come up with a plan to counteract his attack on you. I don't want to see you hurt any more than you already have been," Kaiden said. Deep down, I knew he was right, and hated that he was right.

"Bloody hell, who's going to fall in with the disowned daughter of a viscount when a duke is telling his stories? He's such an arse. Why does he want to ruin me? I was doing that just fine on my own."

"Did you mention your fight with Lord Middleton to the detective inspector?" Georgi asked.

"I think I eventually did, but I was trying to avoid it. I didn't feel comfortable calling out Lord Middleton as he stood in front of me."

"So he is the one who left those bruises on your arm. I'm going to kill him," Kaiden said.

"Let's not throw around threats like that," Mads said.

"She has a p-p-p-point," Willa chimed in.

"I was hard pressed to not do more than walk away last night, but I was trying to avoid causing the dreaded 'scene.' If I had, it would have come down on me, anyway."

"It will not do us any good bemoaning the current state of society. The majority of us are at University to change society anyway, so let's start by ensuring Pippa comes out of this horrendous turn of events as unscathed as possible." Georgi took charge. I swear she should have been a general. "I have detailed notes from our conversation over tea. But we haven't gone over what you brought back from the crime scene."

"That probably wasn't the smartest move on my part, but I need to do something to figure out who killed him. I don't trust anyone else to care enough," I said, wringing my hands just thinking of the bad choices I was making.

"No use worrying over how it looks now. The items are here, so let's figure out why you thought they were important, if they are actually important, and what we should do with them next."

"Well, I told you about the snifters. I was hoping Willa could test them for poisons. Do you mind, Willa? I know it's not exactly your skill set, but I'm hoping there's some crossover with everything you do." I turned towards Willa.

"What is it you do, Willa?" Kaiden asked.

"I am st-st-st-studying to b-b-b-become an ap-p-p-apothecary. It's my dr-dr-dr-dream." Willa turned bright red under the stare of Kaiden's amber eyes. I hadn't heard her stutter this much for weeks.

"You sound like the perfect person to test it out. That's quite a skill to have. And here all Pippa does is set fire to workshops," Kaiden said, tapping his knee into mine as he spoke.

"Come on, I've only set fire to one workshop here. It's not like a daily habit," I replied.

"You are still sleeping in my room." Georgi laughed.

"Which gives me an alibi for last night. Okay, I also grabbed my notes and sketches. I don't think any of those are related to the case. I just couldn't leave them. Then I grabbed this formula I found in another notebook." I showed them the formula and the last of what I grabbed, the journals Aneurin's father left behind.

"Can I see those journals?" Kaiden asked.

I handed them to him. He looked at the cover for a bit, taking in the sword wrapped in shadows embossed on the front. Then opened the first journal.

"These are all in code. Did Professor Aneurin know how to read them?" Kaiden asked.

"No, he told me he spent quite some time trying to break the code, but never succeeded, as far as I know. His father was part of some secret society back in the 1840s that's still here on campus. He implied I knew some members but wouldn't tell me what the society was."

Kaiden looked at me sharply. His long fingers tapped the cover of the book. "I'm probably going to get myself kicked out for saying anything. But it could be important. The society is the Shadowed Sword. Simon and I are both members, as was my brother before he was killed."

Georgi clapped her hands in excitement. "A secret society, I love it."

"And it could actually be great if it was fulfilling its original charter. Instead, it is just another place for titled and wealthy men to get together to talk about their own importance. Simon is the president of the Shadowed Sword and has been since he started here. I think Edmund was going to run against him this fall. Edmund was always trying to institute change, whether or not anyone else wanted it."

"I wish I had met Edmund," Georgi said.

"Anyway, I can check around the club and see if there's any key to the code. It would have been impossible for Aneurin to figure it out if it required a key."

"I can also look at them. I'm quite talented at cryptography," Mads said.

"That's settled. Mads will look at the notebooks while Kaiden checks to see if there is a key to the code. Willa will see if there was poison in the professor's whiskey. I will go over the notes to see if there are any further clues, and Pippa, I think you need some rest." Georgi delineated the plan.

"I can't rest, I can't close my eyes without seeing . . ." I shuddered.

"Oh, and I have another idea to start to wear down Lord Middleton. We just need Hannah to start making more friends."

Chapter Sixteen

The next morning I woke up feeling like death—wait, not death, death was permanent and should not be joked about. Or maybe it should. I sighed.

"That's a heavy sigh for so early in the morning," Georgi said.

"Isn't that when sighing is best?"

"What's the matter, Pippa?"

"I just feel awful. Like death, as they say, but even thinking that seems wrong."

"Don't be so hard on yourself. That's a common saying, and it's not like you're dismissing the seriousness of death. Especially now." Georgi gestured for me to come over. "Here, can you help button the back of this for me? I sent Hannah into town to gather information for us, maybe see if she can start some ugly rumors about Lord Middleton."

"I will never understand why women's clothing has closures in the back. It baffles me. It makes us dependent on someone just to get dressed." With that said, I helped Georgi into her bodice with at least a thousand, maybe even two thousand, buttons up the back. "That's unnecessary, Georgi, I don't want to stoop to his level."

"I know you don't, darling, but this isn't a fight you win by playing aboveboard. If a rich, titled man is going to try to pin a murder on you out of spite, you better be ready to fight fire with fire. He already has lit the flame, and at the moment, you better believe he's winning."

"I'm sure you're right, I just don't have to like it."

"Like it or not, I hope you get used to it."

"All done. Do you think there are enough buttons on your bodice?" I stepped back, taking in my handiwork. "Although it is absolutely stunning on you."

Georgi was decked out in blue and white with red accents. The combination reminded me of the Brythion flag and made her look quite patriotic, for lack of a better term. However, it was subtle. She wore a bright blue top with a red ribbon accenting the white trim. The bustled apron and underskirt were also blue with alternating white and red ruffles. I watched as she put on a delectable blue hat with red-and-white feathers and couldn't help but laugh.

"Are you visiting the queen today? Trying to give off subliminal messages of 'I live for Queen and Country'? Not that it isn't absolutely stunning on you, it just has that certain feel."

"It's not too over the top, is it? I want people to sing 'For Queen and Country' after they see me, but not know why."

"No, it's not too over the top. I think you've perfected clothing as armor. You always give the right impression."

"Perfect. I'm off to see the detective inspector and maybe the coroner." With that, Georgi flounced out of the room.

My dress this morning wasn't nearly as complicated. I grabbed my jodhpurs, wide leather belt, white top, side pack, and boots, threw them on, and quickly braided my hair.

I was out the door in no time flat, ready to . . . Well, I was at least ready to fix my steamer bike. I definitely missed riding her and experiencing the freedom the steamer bike gave me. I laughed at myself missing an inanimate object. And then stopped. Sadness crashing in all at once. I had to remind myself that everyone grieves differently. A little laughter was not a bad thing.

It didn't take long to get to Colin's shop. Thankfully, he was open. I wanted to get right into the mindset where you spend a while working on a mind-numbingly boring task, like the pounding of metal, until it becomes what I want.

"Colin, how are you this morning?"

"Here and working on what I love. What could be better?" Tears immediately picked at my eyes. I tried to stop them, which only caused me to hiccup in despair. The flood gates opened and once again I was bawling. I hated being unable to control my emotions. I also hated crying in public. It was so unfair that I always looked so red, puffy, and splotchy when I cried, and I spent so much time crying.

"Oh, I didn't mean to make you cry." Colin awkwardly patted me on the shoulder.

"You didn't," I sniffed, "Professor Aneurin, he's, he's dead."

"I read about it in the paper this morning. Shocking news. I didn't realize you were close."

"He was my professor and mentor. We met a few times a week to work on my ideas, trying to work through the flaws in my designs. He was so helpful and encouraging. I think he's one of the reasons I was accepted here. He implied he was impressed by my drawings and pushed to get me here."

"I'm so sorry. That's quite a loss. I was hoping to get into University here and get to work with him. But it never worked out, not that I would have been able to afford it on my meager earnings," Colin said dismissively.

"Oh." I really didn't know what to say. It was like the conversation I had with Lord Middleton coming back to haunt me. Although, my guess was that his status kept him out of University, and not that I was accepted. "It's a shame they didn't accept you. The university needs more people like you attending."

"It is what it is. I have this shop now, which has been quite successful here in town. We're the perfect distance from Fintan. It means all the gentlemen attending University want a steam carriage to get to and from Fintan faster. By the way, your beau's steam carriage is done."

"My beau?" I said, confused.

"Lord Fremont. You two are always seen out strolling together. I assumed he was courting you."

"Oh, really, well, we, I . . . I should get to work." My face was red once again, but this time it had nothing to do with tears.

I put on my safety goggles, waxed leather apron, and gloves, then tied my braids together on the back of my head, all to prepare for working with the high heat needed to patch the hole in the tank. I put my patch into the fire until it was hot enough to meld and mold, but not so hot it was a complete liquid. Then I started hammering. At first, it was just a nice, peaceful rhythm. It felt good to be here and working on an actual project instead of theorizing. But the world crept in. Especially Lord Middleton. Next thing I knew, I wasn't swinging the hammer in a nice, peaceful rhythm. I was swinging with vengeance. Just beating the living daylight out of the metal as I pictured Lord Middleton's face on it. Again, and again, and again, I felt the hammer come down and crack into the metal. And I did it over, and over, and over again.

"Pippa."

I kept hammering as hard as I could.

"Pippa!" Colin grabbed the hammer from my hand. "You have to stop, you're going to ruin the tank."

I looked at the tank and saw exactly what he meant. While I had managed to fix the damage, I also created enough divots in the metal to give it a whole new texture around that spot.

"Thank you. I don't know what's wrong with me. That's not like me at all."

"I would guess it has to do with someone you were close to dying. Why don't you let me finish it?"

Colin took the tank away from me and brought it over to his workstation. I watched as he hammered out the dents I put in. At least I did the patch right. I hated that I let myself get distracted by all my frustrations, but it did feel good to imagine pounding Simon Middleton's face into oblivion.

I couldn't sit still anymore. I hoped Colin would be done

soon, but he was much more of a perfectionist than me, if I remembered correctly, and it could take him a while to fix the damage I had done to the tank. To stay busy, I looked at Kaiden's steam carriage. It was a piece of art, that's for sure. It only sat two people, with room to tie trunks on the back behind the seats. There was a steering column just to the right of the center of the seating area. The tank was in front of the sitting area, with the escape pipe in the back. The driver had a pedal that engaged the brakes and a hand throttle similar to my bike that controlled the steam flow to the pistons that would then move the wheels. Colin painted all the wood a beautiful red and added a thick coat of varnish that glistened like glass.

"This is beautiful, Colin. Have you thought about trying to recycle the steam that would normally be released? That's what I want to do on my bike. Create a way for the steam to condense and end up back in the water tank. There will be some loss, but you could travel farther."

I sat down and drew out a steam catcher and a retrieval pipe alongside the passenger side of the car. It sloped downward into the water tank using gravity to help with the return.

"Something like this. What do you think?"

* * *

"Is that for my steam carriage?" Kaiden Fremont asked as he walked up behind me, glancing over my shoulder.

"I don't know, Kaiden. This idea popped into my head while Colin and I were working. I haven't been able to test it to see if it would work." I hadn't expected him to walk in while I was tinkering. I tried to block my mother's discouraging words from entering my thoughts, but some managed to make it in anyway, all telling me that Colin had to be wrong. There was no way a gentleman of any status would be interested in a lady with my interests.

"It's a great idea, Pippa. I'm sad I didn't think of it myself. You always have been ahead of me on the practical design of steam engineering. Actually making it was another matter." Colin bumped my shoulder, letting me know he was teasing. "Here's the fixed tank. Almost dentless."

Kaiden looked over and raised an eyebrow. Clearly, he wanted to know what happened.

"I was a little too exuberant in my hammering. Lord Middleton's face might have taken the place of the tank as I was hammering. I'm thankful Colin stopped me before I destroyed it. Have you seen the work Colin did on the steam carriage?" I walked back to the vehicle. "It's like a piece of art. But something useful and pretty."

Kaiden looked at the vehicle thoroughly, looking quite handsome as he did so. His crisp, white shirt and cravat contrasted with his dark skin, and his waistcoat was almost a perfect match to the red of the car. He still was wearing black gloves and a black hatband.

"You know what, Colin? I like the idea of capturing and recycling the steam for longer trips. Is that something you think can be added with how the vehicle is designed now?" Kaiden looked over at Colin.

"Looking at Pippa's drawing, I think it can be done with minor alterations to the steam carriage. It'll take me a couple of days to add. It's also experimental. None of us knows how well it's going to work. But Pippa's ideas normally work, maybe just not the first time. She likes to blow stuff up first."

"That's a good point. I don't think this should cause anything to explode. But you will probably want to have some kinda pressure release. A fail-safe, if you will, so nobody gets hurt," I said.

"That's a great idea, Pippa," Colin said. "If you want me to start working on this, I can have it done in two to three days."

"I think that would be a great addition to the steam carriage. I'll be back in a few days then." Kaiden turned to leave.

"Kaiden, wait!" I said. He stopped, waiting for me. "I had an idea for some further investigation, if you want to come with me."

"Someone needs to come with you, or you're likely to get yourself in trouble you can't get out of."

"I need a moment." I took off my safety gear and grabbed

my bag. "Colin, can I pick up my bike on my way back? I know I'm taking up too much space, but I will have it off your hands today."

"Don't even worry about it. I'll get the tank installed for you. It'll be ready by the time you get back. I might ride it around for a bit beforehand, but it'll be ready for you to take home by the time I close up shop."

"Perfect." I stood on tiptoes and gave him a kiss on his cheek. "Let's talk about what else you are working on, specifically what's in the corner, covered." I nodded towards the project in question. With that, Kaiden and I left.

* * *

Strolling around Grantabridge didn't feel as welcoming as it had the past few days. I was pretty sure that had to do with Lord Middleton spreading his rumors about me. Hopefully, the judgment wouldn't last long. I just needed to prove I wasn't the one who killed the professor.

"Kaiden, I was thinking we should go to the professor's office. Look around there. Maybe there's something else that can help us determine what happened. I also think we should talk to Professor Gates. He argued with Aneurin the other day."

"Both sound like solid investigative ideas that should probably be left to, oh, I don't know, the police. You and me investigating is just a little crazy. So let's get to his office before things get too crowded on the streets and someone realizes what we are up to." I almost threw my arms around Kaiden's neck when he acquiesced to my plan.

On a normal day, this would be a peaceful walk through town. Kaiden and I had walked together many times since we met, but this was anything but peaceful. I was worried about being accused of murder. I was terrified I no longer had a place at the University anymore. My mentor was dead, and I didn't know who else could teach me. And now, thanks to Colin, I had uncomfortable thoughts about Kaiden running through my mind. I know my friends teased me endlessly, but I never took them seriously. It was, after all, just normal teasing. But Colin didn't treat me like that. Peering over at Kaiden, I thought again about how he really was quite handsome. I had noticed before; I had actually noticed quite often, but now it felt different. Every time I saw him, I became more aware.

"Did you know Colin applied to go to Grantabridge and was denied? He wanted to study under Professor Aneurin, but it didn't work out."

"I had no idea. It is quite unfair that he wasn't accepted. If you think of it, he would be the most likely student to use it in his life to create a living."

"Education shouldn't just be for the elite. The ways in which society insists on keeping people in their place is outrageous. I don't see how letting someone study their craft in a formal setting is ever a bad thing."

"I agree, Pippa. Colin should have been able to work with the professor. In a lot of ways, he should have been admitted before you were, because it really affects his daily life."

"As much as I don't want to agree, it's true. Here he is, a local mechanic, building things most people couldn't even imagine. I'm here, but I feel like everything is a challenge because no one really wants me here. But who knows what I will do with this information. I want to change the world with my designs, but if no one listens to me because I'm a woman, it won't happen."

"There are people who want you here, Pippa. I want you here. The professor wanted you here. Don't be deterred by those who are the loudest about what they want. There are plenty who think you and your friends should be here."

I looked away, blushing. Accepting a compliment was not one of my skills. We continued walking, crossing over one of my favorite bridges. I loved the stonework and the arches and the way it reflected off the water. Today was so different from yesterday. Not a single shop owner waved at me as we walked by. The sun was hidden by the ever-present grey gloom in Brythion. Colorful leaves lined the street, leaving the trees bare. It appeared autumn was on its way out, and winter was rearing its head. I shivered as the breeze turned into a gust of wind.

"You're cold. Do you not have a coat?" Kaiden asked.

"Honestly, I didn't even think of it this morning. I just needed to be out doing something, anything but sitting in that sad dormitory thinking about yesterday."

"Would you like my coat?"

"No, it isn't that bad, and I already look ridiculous enough. I don't want to add to it," I said.

"You look perfect, Pippa, like you are completely comfortable with who you are."

"Stop it."

"Stop what?"

"Stop saying the perfect things at the perfect moment. I don't know how to respond to you."

"I don't think I want to make that promise. I think saying the perfect thing at the right moment could continue to be useful. Ah, here we are, the professors' offices."

I looked up at the three-story brick building.

"Into the fire, as they say," I said, and I walked through the door. I entered a small atrium, looking around for a sign that would point me in the right direction. Nothing helped, so I just started walking down hallways. There were brass plaques on each of the doors with professors' names on them. Most I had never heard of. Who knew there were so many professors here? I wonder what they did while they were here, especially since there were no classes, just tutoring. And it didn't seem like most of the men here took advantage of it until it was time for their exams.

"Kaiden, are any of these professors ones you are working with?"

"Professor Coates teaches advanced farming techniques. I'm hoping to bring those back to my tenants. My tenants, that still doesn't sound right." Kaiden shook his head, almost like he was trying to shake away the weight of the title. "And I believe I saw Professor Smythe's office. I work with him on learning about the laws that affect the tenants. I think Miss Spencer studies with him as well."

"The name sounds familiar. I hope he realizes he's teaching Georgi how to rule the world. I'm sure she has a step-by-step plan that starts with wearing the correct clothing."

"She is quite the force. It's amazing how focused she is."

"Oh, here it is! It's his office." I turned the knob and almost fell when the door opened. I don't know why, but I expected the door to be locked. Professor Aneurin would never remember to lock a door. "Where to start? Why don't you look through the books, and I'll look at his desk."

The professor's office looked so much like his workshop. A mess. Papers were everywhere except on the floor. I assumed no one else had searched here because of the clean floor. Along the wall were stunning mahogany bookshelves stuffed to overflowing with different books, some shelves even two books deep. Papers stuck out of various books and piled on top of others. The desk matched the mahogany of the bookshelves—what you could see of it, that is. The entire top of the desk was littered with papers and books, some in a semblance of a pile, while others merged together in one enormous pile. I started picking up papers. There were designs for different types of steam-powered vehicles. I saw an airship, a steam carriage, and a railway engine. All of them were drawn with the condensation trap we had been working on together. It was unreal seeing someone else try to draw my ideas and make them into something practical. There were also all sorts of different transmutation equations. I wasn't as familiar with alchemy, but it looked like he was working on something that created a massive amount of heat. There were notebooks dedicated to experiments turning iron into gold. It didn't look like any of these had worked, but again, I couldn't be sure. I set those notebooks aside to compare them to the paper I took yesterday.

I started opening drawers, trying to find anything I thought might help. He had a drawer of student files. I saw my file, Lord Middleton's, and one labeled C. Finnigan. I grabbed them all and set them in my pile to take back. The next drawer was, well, daunting, to say the least. Unlike the student files, this one was an absolute mess of papers. There were invitations, calling cards, newspaper articles, and letters. The letters, at least, were neatly tied together, so I grabbed those. Looking through them, they were all from an Adelaide Wetherly. I opened one and immediately wanted to put it back. It seemed so personal. I had come across love letters the professor kept buried in his desk.

"Kaiden, do you think these love letters are important?" I asked.

"They could be. Most people say poison is a woman's method. Maybe the professor left her, or had a mistress, and she did something about it."

"That seems a little fanciful, but you could be right. I guess it won't hurt to read them. I don't know why I'm worried about the professor's privacy when he's dead. Have you found anything?"

"Just some theory books on alchemy and some steam engineering books. Nothing exciting," Kaiden said.

"I would love to find a calendar, see who he was meeting last night."

The doorknob started to turn. I looked up at Kaiden, panic in my eyes. We couldn't be caught here.

Chapter Seventeen

"Quick, through the window," Kaiden said.

It was like time slowed as I grabbed the pile of files I wanted to take with me and ran over to the window. I could hear the doorknob rattling. Thankfully, we had remembered to lock it behind us. I saw Kaiden throw open the sash.

"Go, go, go," I whispered.

I watched his feet hit the ground, and he looked back up at me. I tossed the files down, hoping he would catch most of them. Then I climbed through the window, hanging a moment by my fingertips before dropping to the soft, grass-covered ground.

"Hello? Is anyone here?" I heard Professor Gates as we crept along the side of the brick building and escaped around the corner, out of sight. If anyone looked out the window we just escaped from, they would not see us. It was also the exact moment I burst out laughing. I have no idea what came over me, but I couldn't seem to stop. Holding my stomach, I fell to the ground laughing, tears streaming down my face. I kept picturing the two of us jumping out the window like the characters in the dramatic novels I read. It was so ridiculous.

"Pippa?" Kaiden asked, stifling laughter of his own. Which didn't last long. He chuckled as he helped me off the ground with one hand, carefully balancing the files and papers I had taken in the other. His chuckle was a deep, warm laugh that reminded me of running through the hills near my home, carefree in the summertime. A very nice laugh.

"What's come over you?" Kaiden asked, mirth making his amber eyes sparkle.

"I really don't know. Everything that just happened reminds me of the serials I read. All the sneaking and lurking. Then the window escape. It was like something right out of fiction. It made me laugh. And once I started, I pictured us in the novels and couldn't stop laughing. By the way, it was Professor Gates that was in the office. I recognized his voice."

"Curious. I wonder what he was doing there? It seems odd he would enter a locked room that wasn't his office," Kaiden said, his smile acknowledging the ridiculousness of what had just happened, even though his words stayed on topic.

"I think we should speak to him, or I should speak to him. I could go under the guise of needing a new alchemy professor. And hopefully get a little more information out of him. I think he's suspicious. First, I heard him arguing with Professor Aneurin about the time he was spending with me instead of on their project. And now he's breaking into Aneurin's office."

"Take me with you. I'm really not comfortable with you going to speak to someone who could be a potential killer on your own."

"I would love for you to come with me, but do you think it would seem strange? I mean, you aren't taking alchemy. Why would you want to speak to Professor Gates?" I was oddly touched that Kaiden would worry about me at all.

"I could be your escort for the day. I know you have been here on your own, but it's still not common for women to go about without at least a lady's maid or some other company. That way, I can stand back while you talk and just observe. Because my presence isn't necessary to the conversation, I'll be another set of eyes and ears, which is always useful."

It would be beneficial to have an extra set of eyes, I

thought. And while I was used to doing things on my own now, it really wasn't the norm for society. I doubt Professor Gates would be suspicious if Kaiden were to come with me.

"That's a fantastic idea. Working on this together can only help us solve it faster. Do you think Professor Aneurin's death and your brother's could be related? Your brother was a member of the same society as Aneurin's father, wasn't he?" I don't know why I kept making those connections in my head when what tied them together was happenstance.

"I don't really see why they would be related. Aneurin wasn't part of the society. Why would anyone care that his father was in the society?" Kaiden asked.

"I'm not sure, but there's the society tie, which I get is tenuous at best. Aneurin and Edmund were both highly involved in getting women into the University. They have more in common than at first glance."

"Maybe, I guess we shouldn't rule out the possibility," Kaiden said, but he looked quite skeptical.

* * *

Back at the dormitory, steamer bike in tow, I was excited to see if anything had been discovered by the ladies of WACK. I put my bike in the dilapidated carriage house, where I had taken to storing it, before leading Kaiden into the house through the servant's entrance in the back. It was completely improper to take a future duke in through the service entrance, but it was so much easier than walking around to the front. Plus, I'm pretty sure Kaiden wouldn't care or even see it as an insult to his station.

"Oh P-P-P-Pippa, I don't know what happened, but it's all d-d-d-destroyed," Willa said. Her normally very prim hair knot was askew, with curly wisps surrounding her pale face, and her blue eyes were wide with anxiety.

"Why don't we have a seat in the parlor and you can tell us what happened," I said, taking her by the arm and gently leading the distraught Willa out of the kitchen.

I pushed her into a chair and sat beside her. Willa was wringing her hands constantly. I tried to place my hand on hers to calm her. Instead, she leapt up and began pacing the length of the parlor.

"I finished the tests on the snifters this morning. It wasn't hard. The professor's b-b-blue fingertips and lips made me think he had a heart aneurysm. There aren't that many p-p-p-plants that present as a heart aneurysm. So I tested those first. And one glass had traces of Wolfsbane."

"You mean he really was poisoned?" I asked. I was shocked. I really hadn't expected to be right. Someone had murdered Professor Aneurin.

"I'm afraid so, and by a very p-p-p-potent substance. Wolfsbane, also known as the purple poison, is one of the deadliest plants here. The plant is quite pretty to look at, if you can forget just how t-t-t-toxic it is. You can actually die just by touching the plant because your body absorbs the toxins. Plus, this plant and its toxicity has been known about for quite some time. Soldiers used to coat their arrowheads in the toxin to ensure a kill, even if the arrow itself did little-to-no damage."

"Did you say Wolfsbane?" Kaiden asked. I looked over at him, surprised he had a question. He looked confused.

"Yes, wh-wh-why?"

"Does Wolfsbane have any other uses?"

"Not any I would recommend. Some p-p-p-people insist it can be used as a treatment for l-l-l-lycanthropy, as well as a potential antidote for some poisons. However, it's my belief that it has no proper use, and is so toxic, it should not be allowed to be planted."

"There's Wolfsbane at the Shadowed Sword. I'm not sure why we have it, but there's a small, well-labeled patch of it growing in the garden, and some dried throughout the club, out of reach though."

"Sounds like someone is worried about werewolves," I said, trying not to laugh.

"That's exactly wh-wh-wh-what it sounds like. These are all things someone versed in witchcraft would do to protect a home. Ensuring that it was away from children and livestock, and out of reach of the c-c-c-curious minds who would want to touch it because it's there. Is anyone at the Shadowed Sword a suspicious lot?"

The turn in conversation calmed Willa tremendously. I watched as she stopped wringing her hands together, and her heart-shaped face returned to its normal, rosy color.

"Is there something else that happened?" I asked Willa.

"Oh y-y-y-yes, I took my notes and conclusions to Georgi's room. I f-f-f-figured that was the best place to gather everything. And I'm glad I did. I came back to my w-w-w-workshop, and everything was d-d-d-destroyed. There was g-g-g-glass everywhere, papers were torn and torched, and what was left of them were scattered everywhere. It looked like whoever was there left rather quickly. But everything is gone, all my equipment."

"I don't know how I'm going to do it, Willa, but I will fix it for you. I haven't forgotten how important your plants and that space are." My friends would not suffer because of me, or suffer more. I hugged Willa tightly, wishing I could make it all go away. She was too sweet to be part of this. "Do you mind sitting with Kaiden while I change? We are planning on interviewing Professor Gates, if we can find him."

I felt Willa nod her head against my shoulder. I stepped back, still holding her shoulders, looking at her, trying to determine her mood based on her appearance. She seemed calmer. I left the kitchen to change.

I climbed the stairs, mentally going through my closet and trying to think like Georgi. How would she dress me to meet a chauvinistic professor who might have murdered a man? In Georgi's room, I called for Hannah, hoping she was around to help. It was going to take a bit of work with very little time to make me look ladylike.

"Yes, Miss," Hannah said, entering the room.

"Oh, Hannah, I'm in desperate need of help. Kaiden and I are hoping to talk to a professor today, and he's a bit old-fashioned. I'm afraid my current dress would put him off and he would slam the door right in my face, so I need something more . . ." I trailed off.

"Demure, Miss?" Hannah said.

“Yes, that’s exactly it. I need to look demure. Which isn’t easy with my hair. Red hair tends to scream wild-child, not demure lady.”

“Ha, I can see what I can do. Do you have a dress picked out?”

“No, I’m not good at this. My mother always put me in pink ruffles, which made me look like an overdecorated cake. Georgi picked out some wonderful clothes for me when all mine burned up. But I don’t know how to outfit myself appropriately, like she does.”

Hannah looked through the wardrobe, her hand pausing on a pale minty green, dotted-Swiss confection.

“I think this is the one,” she said, pulling it out of the wardrobe. “Luckily, it still looks nicely pressed. Do you need help with your petticoats?”

I looked up at her, my clothes from earlier strewn about the room as I tried to button my petticoat over my bum roll.

“Pippa, let me help. It’ll go faster if you let me do it,” Hannah said, taking control. In moments, my undergarments were in place. The ruffled bottom skirt was on, with the apron over the top of it, and the bodice with its high neck and three-quarter sleeves was being buttoned.

“I can button it, see what you can do with my hair,” I said.

I don’t know how Hannah did it, but by the time I finished with those tiny buttons, she had whipped my braids into something that looked soft, feminine, and yet complex. She finished off my look by pinning the dress’s matching hat at a jaunty angle.

“How’s that, Pippa?” Hannah asked.

“You are a miracle worker. Where have you been all my life?” I said, giving her a quick hug. “Thank you!”

I rushed out of the room, leaving a perplexed Hannah behind. Thankfully, I didn’t fall down the stairs in my hurry. I always felt on the verge of falling with petticoats whirling around and between my legs.

“Kaiden, are you ready to go?” I asked as I walked into the parlor.

Kaiden turned towards me, and I swear I saw his jaw drop. It was only for a moment, but that moment made me want to giggle like a schoolgirl. He composed himself, rising from the sofa.

"Of course, Pippa." Kaiden's eyes met mine as he stood. He didn't look away, stopping right in front of me. We were so close that a deep breath on my part would have us touching. My eyes dropped to his mouth, licking my bottom lip. I wanted . . .

"You t-t-t-two should be off," Willa said, interrupting whatever was happening between Kaiden and me.

I took a step back and brushed my hands down the front of my dress, trying to compose myself.

"We should go back to the professors' offices before it's locked up for the day," I said.

"Of course," Kaiden replied, offering me his arm. With that, we walked out of the dormitory.

We walked through Grantabridge like we had done so many times before, but this felt different. I could feel Kaiden looking at me. I glanced over at him and our eyes caught. Then Kaiden looked away. This happened a few times until I was about to laugh, potentially inappropriately.

"Pippa, can I tell you something?" Kaiden asked, stopping on the bridge.

"Why ask? You can tell me anything?"

"Okay," he took a deep breath, "you look absolutely stunning." I blushed at his compliment. "You look lovely every day, no matter what you wear. I love how confident you are when you are at your most comfortable. But seeing you in this, it was so unexpected and elegant, my jaw dropped."

"You are too sweet. I could kiss you!" I stopped, realizing what had just come out of my mouth. Why did I always say things without thinking?

"I wouldn't mind that one bit."

My head shot up, and our eyes met. I looked away. I did not know what to do. As much as I wanted to kiss him standing right here at my favorite spot in town, on the bridge, I didn't know if I should be as impulsive with my actions as I was with my words. While I wasn't brave enough to kiss him on his lips I always stared at, I did get up on my tiptoes and gave him a peck on the cheek.

"Thank you," I said to Kaiden. I hope he knew how much I meant it. Meeting so many people that saw all the different parts of me and still liked me—it was all I had ever wanted. And here, I felt like so many people really saw me. It was eye opening.

Kaiden cleared his throat. "Do you have a plan for talking to Professor Gates?"

"Not really. I thought I would ask if he could help me with my alchemy studies since Professor Aneurin is gone, and just work in more questions from there."

"It might help to appeal to his ego," Kaiden suggested. I looked over at him quickly. "I mean, I'm sure you already knew that. I'm just thinking out loud, it helps sometimes."

"Of course, because you wouldn't be telling a lady that she needs to appeal to a man's ego to get him to pay attention to her. Like all ladies don't already know to do just that."

"I, erm, I . . ." Kaiden swiped his hand over his head and looked at his shoes.

"I am just teasing, I know you aren't like that."

Kaiden looked at me, nodded slightly, and we continued walking. The awkwardness I saw him feel released as I watched his shoulders relax. It felt like in that moment we understood each other, and it was right to just exist together instead of forcing conversation. As we walked, I mulled over what I would say to Professor Gates, not really sure how best to approach this meeting. I mean, it wasn't like I could just ask him if he poisoned Professor Aneurin.

We arrived at the offices, the brick building looming over me. It seemed more intimidating than it did earlier today. I took a deep breath to collect myself. I felt Kaiden look over at me.

"Pippa, you know you don't have to do this. We can call the detective inspector and see if he will handle it," Kaiden said.

"No, I need to do this. Professor Aneurin believed in me. I need to help figure this out."

Kaiden opened the door for me. I took a deep breath,

brushed my hands over my skirt, and walked through. I took Kaiden's proffered arm and continued down the hall, portraying more confidence than I felt until I got to the very last office. The door was open, and Professor Gates was sitting at his desk, holding his head in his hands. His grey hair was a mess, his cravat was askew; in other words, he looked completely disheveled. This was not the same man I had heard arguing with Aneurin the other day. This man was destroyed.

I lightly knocked on the door. "Professor Gates?"

He looked up and ran his hands through his hair, disheveling it even more. "Can I help you? It's Miss Stanhope, isn't it?"

"Yes, Professor Gates, we met briefly at Professor Aneurin's workshop the other day."

Dropping Kaiden's arm, I walked into the office. Kaiden followed me in, standing in the corner while I took a seat in a leather chair.

"Ah, yes. I remember now." He sighed. "What can I do for you?"

"I was hoping you would help me continue to study here. I was so happy studying with Professor Aneurin, and now he's . . . gone." Tears escaped at the thought of never working with Professor Aneurin again.

"I don't teach steam engineering like he did. I only teach alchemy."

"I know. I was supposed to be taking alchemy from Professor Aneurin. It just changed as we talked. I want to continue with alchemy. I was thinking if I learned about transmutation, I might find an additional heating source."

"I can continue with that if you are interested. It will differ from engineering, though. I can't stress that enough. My focus is vastly different from Professor Aneurin's. It was vastly different, that is." Professor Gates sighed once again, looking even more distraught with each passing moment.

"Oh, were you working with Professor Aneurin on an alchemy project?"

"We were, but all his notes disappeared." I looked at

Kaiden quickly. I had a lot of those notes. "We had worked together for a long time on our project, and now all our work, gone. All his work."

"Were you and Professor Aneurin close?"

"We were. I actually knew his father and worked with him for a while. And then watched Marcus grow up. When he decided to teach here I knew he would do great things. It was great to work with him. He just thought of things in this new and different way. We were so close to figuring it out," Professor Gates said.

"Figuring out what?" I asked.

"The ultimate in alchemy. Turning iron to gold."

"I wonder if that's what he went back to his workshop to do during the soirée."

"He worked that night?" Professor Gates asked.

"He told me he had something to work on when we talked that night, but he didn't tell me what he was going to be working on that night. Did you go to the soirée, Professor Gates?" I asked.

"What? . . . No, I was home all night with Mrs. Gates. We were supposed to go, but she was not feeling well."

"I'm sorry to hear that, Professor Gates. It was quite the event. Even though Professor Aneurin left to go work on something, I had thought, maybe, he was meeting you after the soirée."

"Where did all the notes go, then? Especially if he was working on them that night," Professor Gates muttered almost to himself.

"I'm sorry, Professor Gates, I wish I knew. Does alchemy ever include plants?"

"It's nothing. I would rather have Marcus back than have his notes." He wiped his eyes brusquely. "Did you say plants?"

"Yes, I just had a thought."

"Not normally. It's more about metals and minerals. Is there anything else I can help you with, Miss Stanhope?" He was quite clear in the fact that we were no longer welcome, even if those words never left his mouth.

"Thank you, Professor Gates. I'm so sorry for your loss."

With those last words, Kaiden and I left. Walking down the long hallway, all I could think about was how Professor Gates did not look like a man that would take another's life. He was so distressed. Maybe the distress was actually guilt, though. What did I actually know about the looks of a killer? The grief had felt like a tangible object in that room. Would a killer feel grief?

"Kaiden, do you think he did it?" Not waiting for a reply, I just rambled on. "I don't think the man we just met could have done it. The one I saw before probably could have, he was so angry and bitter. But this one was lost, desolate, grief-stricken even."

"I don't know. So many things can lead someone to do crazy things. But the man we saw there, he seemed to have lost someone he cared about. That doesn't mean he didn't do it, though. Maybe his 'grief' has more to do with the lost notes, and less to do with the lost life."

"I saw a man that was grieving the loss of someone he cared about. However, he mentioned the notes a lot."

The walk back to the dormitory was a silent one. I didn't know what else to say as I continued to think about the interview and how it had left me with more questions than answers.

"Excuse me, Miss Stanhope. I was hoping to have a word with you about Professor Aneurin's death," Detective Inspector Radcliffe said.

Chapter Eighteen

The sudden presence of the detective startled me from my thoughts. It took me a moment before I could process what he had said to me. Which probably meant I had stood there, looking at him blankly for way too long, before I could respond.

"Yes, Detective Inspector Radcliffe, I can answer whatever questions you have," I said. "If you'll come this way, we can sit in the parlor." I turned and started walking towards the front door.

"Actually, Miss Stanhope, I would like to go down to the station house for the interview."

"Is that necessary?" Kaiden said, stepping between me and the detective inspector, obviously creating a physical barrier to me. It was quite sweet and chivalrous, but I was sure it wasn't necessary.

"It's okay Kaiden, I'll be fine on my own, I'm sure." I was anything but sure. I wiped my hands down the front of my dress and stepped around Kaiden to follow the detective inspector. Kaiden gently grabbed my arm, stopping me. I looked up at him, trying to reassure him, even though I was anything but calm. His eyes bored into me. He must have seen something to calm him because before I could speak, he let go of me. I waved a small goodbye as I hurried to catch up.

I regretted my shoe choice as the detective inspector and I walked back into town. At least it wasn't too long of a walk, preventing me from saying anything I shouldn't. Before I knew it, we were there, the detective waiting for me to walk through the open door.

"Have a seat, Miss Stanhope," Detective Inspector Radcliffe said as we arrived at a large wooden desk with neatly stacked files across the top of it. I did as the detective inspector requested, trying not to let my emotions overwhelm me. I had never been to a police station before. Looking around, nothing was what I expected a police station to look like. There was so much wood and warm tones, I could almost describe much of the space as inviting. The room had wood paneling on the lower walls and molding around the ceiling. The detective inspector's desk was one of many large, wooden desks. I thought the desks were supposed to be imposing, but they reminded me of the large tables in Professor Aneurin's workshop. Then I looked into the detective inspector's eyes, and all the comfort the room gave off ran right out of the room. His eyes were cold and steely.

"Miss Stanhope, I need you to you to recount the argument you had with Professor Aneurin. What was that made you leave in such a rush?" he asked.

I looked at him, confused. None of those things had happened. I had already explained what happened, and it's like my words had meant absolutely nothing to the detective inspector, despite the fact he appeared to be completely reasonable yesterday.

"I don't understand. Professor Aneurin and I did not have an argument, and I did not leave in a rush. I can tell you what did happen that night, though."

He nodded his head, encouraging me to proceed.

"My friends and I arrived at the soirée at an appropriate time, neither too early nor too late. I'm not the most social at gatherings like that, so I split off from my friends and found what I had hoped was a nice secluded corner where I could enjoy my wallflower personality. It worked for a bit. But then, for some reason, Lord Middleton decided he needed to speak to me. I neither invited nor encouraged his attention, but he would not leave me alone. I tried to walk away at one point, and he grabbed my forearm and left bruises. When I finally was able to get away, I ran into Professor Aneurin. He escorted me to the study and poured a small amount of whiskey to help settle my nerves. We chatted about my designs for a bit. And when I was ready to face the crowds again, Professor Aneurin mentioned he needed to go work on something in his workshop, and he would see me tomorrow. I thanked him and found my friends. We stayed to hear the dean speak and then left. Miss Spencer and I currently share a room, so when we got back to the dormitory, we prepared for bed with the help of Hannah, Miss Spencer's lady's maid, and went to sleep."

"Did you notice who was still at the soirée as you were leaving?"

"I don't think so. Wait . . . Lord Middleton was still there when we left. I remember because he looked even more unhappy about my existence as we left."

"And that's it."

"Yes. That's it. What more could there be?"

"Did you go see Professor Aneurin in his workshop after Miss Spencer was asleep?"

"Good heavens no, why would I do that?"

"To kill him, of course."

"Why would I want to harm Professor Aneurin? He was my mentor. He had just told me my designs were going to change the world, that they would have already if men could've gotten over themselves. When I told him I gave up everything to come to University, he set aside time multiple days a week to work with me. In fact, he was on the committee that fought to have my friends and me admitted in the first place." I was trying so hard to stay calm, but sitting here was making me fidgety. Especially with these questions.

"There are quite a few people that saw you argue last night. Some even called it a lover's spat."

I guffawed at that. Me with the professor? Never.

"Detective Inspector, that is not the type of relationship the professor and I had, and to imply that it was is incomprehensible to me. I will say it again. Professor Aneurin was my mentor. I respected him immensely. That's as far as our relationship went. Anything else would have been completely inappropriate. I bet Lord Middleton and his cronies are the perpetrators of these ugly rumors."

I sat there, waiting for him to respond. This interview was not going well. It was clear the detective inspector believed nothing I was saying, despite the fact I was telling him the truth. I was doing all I could to not break down, or scream, or storm out of the station. I was sure I could provide just as many witnesses that would correspond with what I was saying as Lord Middleton had done to make his lies sound real, but I wasn't even being given the chance.

"Miss Stanhope, I really need you to tell me the truth," the detective inspector said. I knew it.

"Why are you so sure that I am not telling you the truth? I can provide witness names to confirm my account of the soirée and my relationship with the professor, if you would like."

"That won't be necessary." I knew it. The detective inspector wasn't even going to allow me to prove my innocence.

"Why? You're accusing me of lying to you, but not giving me an opportunity to prove that I am not. Why are you so ready to believe someone else, but are so sure that I'm deceitful?" I felt the tenuous grasp on my anger slip away from me.

"I need you to calm down, Miss Stanhope. And I need you to tell me what really happened."

Calm down. He wanted me to calm down!

I took a deep breath, and I looked at Detective Inspector Devon Radcliffe. It was like I was seeing the world for the first time. This man, for whatever reason, did not believe a word I was saying. No matter how many times I said it, he was not going to believe me. And for the life of me, I did not know why. What had been said that had destroyed my credibility so much that I automatically was lying?

"Miss Stanhope . . ."

I sat there and said nothing. Why bother at this point? I

could talk through the night, and he wouldn't believe anything I said.

"I need to know what happened, Miss Stanhope."

I said nothing. Just sat there, my hands folded in my lap, the bruises on my arm partly visible just below my three-quarter sleeves. I sat as still as I could. I tried to look as demure as I possibly could, all while I seethed on the inside.

"Miss Stanhope, I can't help you if you don't talk to me."

It's not like talking to him was helping me. Silence seemed like the best option, at least until he was actually willing to listen.

"Bloody hell," he muttered. "Miss Stanhope, you are under arrest for obstructing an investigation. Please follow me."

Well, that was not what I expected. I stood and followed Detective Inspector Radcliffe. He escorted me to the holding cell and locked me in.

"Just holler if you need anything."

I nodded. And he locked me into the cell and then left.

It was going to be a long night with just my own thoughts to keep me company. At least the room was clean, even if it offered absolutely no privacy. I took off my gloves and unpinned my hat and then my hair. No use getting a headache with the weight of my hair pulling on all those pins holding it in place. I looked down at my dress and really hoped Hannah could work miracles because it was going to be the worse for wear after spending the night in it. Oh god, what if I stayed here more than a night? At least I would have other clothes. I couldn't imagine Georgi and Kaiden leaving me here for more than a night without visiting.

Thoughts swirled around in my head, from Professor Gates and Aneurin arguing over how Aneurin was spending his time—too much steam engineering, not enough alchemy—to the man I spoke to today, who was clearly devastated at the loss of a dear friend, or maybe the loss of important research notes. And then to the notebooks from the Shadowed Sword, and the missing formula that might actually be the way to turn iron to gold. Could that formula be the reason he's dead?

But then there was the sabotage at the dormitory. So far there were the burning leaves, the loss of power, my room being burned down, the burned and stolen items, and the destruction of Willa's lab. It felt related, but that didn't make any sense.

Then Colin entered my mind. Could he be a suspect? Was his denial enough to get him to kill someone? I didn't think so, but everything felt so turned around. Maybe I was wrong about Colin.

And finally, Edmund's death, was it related somehow? Was this really just one case with lots of moving parts and not three separate crimes? I no longer could tell if there was any logic to my thinking. Everything I had always believed to be true somehow was called into question. I mean, I was sitting in a jail cell, a place I never thought I would end up.

My mind kept spinning through these thoughts, suspects, and potential connections between crimes. Professor Gates and his grief and his search for notes and the Shadowed Sword and Colin and the sabotage and Edmund, swirling around in my head over and over again. At some point, I must have drifted off to sleep.

Chapter Nineteen

I woke up to my name being called over and over again. My eyes felt dry and crusty. I rubbed them and nothing looked familiar. Where was I? Slowly, my eyes focused. The brick walls were completely foreign to me, and this bed was nothing like mine. Where was Georgi? Then it all came rushing back to me. I was in jail.

"Pippa darling, there you are. We absolutely must get you out of here right away. There is no reason that Viscount Stanhope's daughter should have spent the night in a cell." And just like that, Aunt Honoria was there. Her dark red hair was perfectly coiffed, the deep blue silk of her gown complimented her eyes, and the clicking of her heels on the ground could be heard as she strode into the room with purpose. She was saving me from this predicament the only way she knew how, with dramatic purpose. And I loved her for it.

Georgi and Kaiden ran in after her. Georgi watched Aunt Honoria with admiration, probably taking mental notes for future use. Kaiden was frantically looking for me, or so I assumed.

"Hello, Madame . . ." Radcliffe paused.

"Miss Honoria Porter," she responded, raising her chin just

enough to convey she was of some importance.

"Miss Porter, I arrested Miss Stanhope last night for obstructing justice. I am afraid she is not at liberty to leave until she answers my questions."

"Pippa, did you obstruct justice?" my aunt asked, turning towards me.

"No, Auntie, I didn't."

"Well, Mr. . . ." Aunt Honoria waited.

"Detective Inspector Radcliffe."

"Well, Mr. Radcliffe, how exactly did she obstruct the investigation?" Honoria ignored the detective inspector's correction.

"She refused to speak at all. And it's Detective Inspector Radcliffe."

"Pippa, did you refuse to speak to Mr. Radcliffe?"

"Of course not, Auntie, I told him exactly what happened at the soirée, the interaction I had with Professor Aneurin, and when I had left with Georgi and the others. He just didn't believe that I was telling the truth. After he refused to corroborate my account of the evening with any witnesses, and when insisted that I tell him what really happened, I stopped speaking. I figured it was better to say nothing at all, then repeat myself to someone that presumed I was a liar." I told Aunt Honoria about everything that had transpired the day before.

"I see, I see, now Mr. Rad—"

Radcliffe cut her off before she could finish her sentence. "It's Detective Inspector."

"I will use your title when you've earned it, Mr. Radcliffe. And so far you haven't. Arresting and throwing my niece into jail for telling you the truth. Inconceivable! Just because it wasn't the story that was convenient to whatever house of lies you have constructed to explain away this murder. Not only is that outrageous, it's the opposite of good detective work." Aunt Honoria gave the inspector a pointed look as she paused in her tirade.

The detective inspector opened his mouth to speak. Aunt Honoria looked at him sharply and held up her hand. The detective inspector closed his mouth immediately.

"So this is how I see it. My niece does not have a motive to have killed Professor Aneurin. She also did not have the means to have killed him. And she did not of have the opportunity. She has, in fact, provided an alibi. I'm sure she has tried to give you other information to assist you. And you refused to listen to her. Does that sound about right, Pippa?"

"Yes, Aunt Honoria. That is accurate." I was doing my best to act demure. I almost wanted to laugh at the scene unfolding but knew that would be a mistake. It was hard to contain my glee at the detective inspector being told what's what in front of me.

"Now, Mr. Radcliffe. You will release my dear niece, with no charges pending. Miss Georgiana Spencer has graciously agreed to speak with you, even though you refused to speak to her yesterday. I'm sure you will not continue to question the word of upstanding young ladies without reason. Lord Fremont is staying with Miss Spencer to ensure you don't dismiss her offhand. Once Pippa is released, we will bid you a good day, sir."

There was nothing about this day that I thought Detective Inspector Radcliffe was going to remember as good. Part of me knew I needed to stay quiet so I wouldn't always be on the detective inspector's bad side. The other, much more prevalent, part of me, the part that adored Aunt Honoria, could barely contain an 'it's over' harrumph as I walked by him after he opened the door of iron bars.

If I was ever back at the station, it would be too soon. I could think of worse things that could have happened to me. However, I'm pretty sure staying the night in jail would be on my top-ten-most-horrible-nights-ever list for a long time.

"Okay Pippa, explain what the bloody hell is happening here. University is supposed to be calm and, well, educational. This is outside what I would expect to happen, and I have a pretty vivid imagination. Getting arrested, Pippa? You know better. Your mother had a conniption when Georgi's letter got to the house, and it only said the police were speaking to you. She would lose her mind if she knew about last night." My aunt was in a dither, understandably so. Even though none of this was really my fault.

I explained everything to Aunt Honoria on the way back, from the random sabotage at the dormitory, the overall displeasure with ladies attending University, to Professor Aneurin's death and the following investigation.

Once I finished, I looked up at Aunt Honoria, worried about what I would see on her face, but she didn't look disappointed or distressed. In fact, I would say she almost looked impressed by what we knew so far.

"What's your next steps then?" she asked.

"I want to see if Mads has broken the code of the journals. I'm not positive the journals will help. Something keeps bringing me back to the Shadowed Sword, though. I also want to learn more about the love letters. See if anything leads to some actual suspects. I don't think the suspects I have did it. I just don't have other ones."

"That sounds like a good start. Are you doing anything to determine if sabotage is really happening, or if it is something else, potentially a lot of terrible luck? And what about Edmund? Are you looking into his death as well?"

"I actually think the murders and the sabotage are all related. But I don't know how or really why. It's just something I feel deep down, even if it doesn't make sense."

"I say you follow your gut, Pippa, in all things; it has never steered me wrong. Well, there was that one time in South Eletharis . . . but that is a tale for another day. Should we make some cheesy scrambled eggs with pepper pesto? I know it's your comfort breakfast, just like it is mine."

"Aunt, it's like you read my mind."

Chapter Twenty

Aunt Honoria and I arrived back at the dormitory. I looked at her as she saw the building, its faded exterior, and the small sign over the door. I continued to watch her as I opened the door and the door protested being used, and as we entered my current, muted home, with its many shades of grey, worn furniture, and faded wallpaper.

"Oh Pippa, is this really where the university put you? I've seen nicer tents traveling through Junhar. This is, well, this is pathetic and sad." Aunt Honoria looked around tsking.

"I know. It definitely wasn't what I expected when I first got here, but at least I have a roof over my head while I'm here to study." I shrugged as we entered the parlor. Aunt Honoria took a seat on the settee and grimaced. I only could assume the obnoxious spring had poked her through the multiple layers of her outfit.

"That's true, but it would be nice if it were a little more . . . colorful? And maybe some new furniture. The spring in this settee is literally poking my arse." She shifted a little, trying to find a comfortable way to sit, just like I did every time I sat in that exact spot.

"It's clear that the majority of the people here really didn't want us here. This place was not a warm welcome. And it seems every time I run into someone new, they have some theory or reason to believe I shouldn't be here." I flopped into one of the other chairs in the room.

"Has it really been that bad? Do you regret your decision to come?" Aunt Honoria looked worried.

"Of course not. My time here has also been wonderful. Working with Professor Aneurin was really the best. I'm not sure what I'm going to do now that he's gone. He was the only professor that worked in steam engineering at the university. I did talk to Professor Gates about learning alchemy. While the study is related, it's not the same as studying steam engineering. I want the university to hire a new steam engineering professor. But I also feel quite selfish for even thinking about that. He's dead and meant so much to me. How can I be worrying about my place here?"

"Oh darling, it's okay to think of your future and still be grieving. Thinking about your next steps doesn't lessen your grief. It's a lot to deal with right now. I know your mother said never to come back, and now you've lost the person who encouraged you the most while being here. Everything you're feeling is normal."

"Thank you. I needed to hear that, Aunt Honoria. I've been feeling guilty about worrying about what happens to me now. Not to mention so very sad. I mean, this encouraging person in my life was murdered. It's all I can do to not spend my days crying. Maybe I should get back to working on this investigation. I would love your help. It's at least something for me to focus on when everything else seems so up in the air."

"Sometimes that's the only thing to do, focus on what makes us feel in control when everything else seems to be spinning completely out of control. But try to remember that the control is an illusion. One that helps us handle what needs handling." Aunt Honoria stood. "Take me to the kitchen and let's see these letters you mentioned grabbing from the professor's office."

I showed Aunt Honoria to the kitchen and the stash of peppers she had sent me. She immediately started prepping everything for the pepper pesto and cheesy scrambled eggs. I ran up to the room I was sharing with Georgi and grabbed the stack of letters. Changing my clothes crossed my mind; I had slept in a jail cell last night in this outfit, but Aunt Honoria didn't seem to mind, so I didn't take the time. That being said, I felt the need for a hot bath, and one soon. There's only so much a girl can take before trying to soak away her troubles.

"These are the letters I borrowed. Do you know an Adelaide Wetherly?" I asked Aunt Honoria.

"Oh my, I haven't heard that name in ages. But she was part of the group of young ladies that came out with me. We didn't run in quite the same circles. I was quite the shameless flirt and, well, you know what happened with me. All of Brythion probably does. But Adelaide, she was a quiet sort, wonderful friends with Lady Corinne St. Gramflurri. I think Adelaide married a marquess, but I was in my own world at the time so I can't quite remember." Aunt Honoria seemed lost in reminiscing.

"These letters are not to a marquess, but to Professor Aneurin, and Adelaide is quite vocal in her love for him. I wonder what happened?"

"I bet Corinne happened. She has very clear ideas about what is, and is not, acceptable for a lady, including who to associate with and who to marry."

"I wonder where Adelaide lives now. It would be wonderful to stop by and have a spot of tea with her and then chat with her. I mean, she doesn't seem like much of a suspect, especially if she's the one that married someone else. But it couldn't hurt to have a chat, could it?"

"No Pippa, it can't hurt. Let's see what we can find out."

* * *

"We are in luck, Pippa. Adelaide settled here in Grantabridge. Her estate is actually within walking distance," Aunt Honoria said.

"That's perfect. I just need a bath and a change of clothes. I still feel like I smell like that jail cell. And I'm afraid this dress is crushed. I hope Hannah can bring it back to life. It really worked well as armor for the occasion."

Aunt Honoria shooed me away as she paced about the room. I left her wearing a hole in our already distressed carpet and ook the stairs two at a time, calling for Hannah at the top of them.

"Yes, Miss," Hannah said.

"I need a bath and a change of clothes," I said.

"I'll get started on that. And Miss, I hope you know I don't believe anything they are saying about you around town. I know you would never have killed Professor Aneurin," Hannah said.

I looked up sharply. "People are actually saying that I killed him? I would never do something like that."

"I'm sorry, Miss, I thought you knew. I was out for today and ran into one of the maids at Lord Bradbury's manor. She was interested in chatting about it, so it must be spreading through town."

Hannah continued to talk to me while I bathed. Everyone in town knew the professor was dead. There were so many rumors going around about the professor and me. That I killed him, that we were having an affair, that he had left me and I was a woman scorned. I lost track of all the things Hannah said she had heard and who she had heard them from.

"Hannah, you are amazing. How do you get so much information so quickly?" Everything she had told me was overwhelming. It was also a wealth of great information.

"The servants, Miss. We all talk about everything. And because no one cares what we think, we hear so much that people probably want to be kept private. But almost everyone will have private conversations with us in the room."

My mind started churning through the implications of what Hannah had just revealed. I wondered aloud if we could set up a network of servants to help us gather information and give them something in exchange that could help them out. Especially if we could include them in the salons. I shook my head. Why would I even think we needed a spy network in the future? I must be going a bit crazy with everything that had happened recently.

"Hannah, my aunt and I are going to go visit, or at least try to visit, Adelaide Wetherly. What do you think Georgi would suggest I wear?" While I was jumping into this clothing-as-armor thing with two feet, I had ignored fashion for so long I was always at a loss. The fact my mother always put me in clothing that I felt out of place in didn't help at all. Everything Georgi had picked out felt more me—not quite riding-on-my-bike me, but a more ladylike version of myself.

"Are you sure going to Lady Wetherly's is a good idea, Miss? Rumor has it she was quite enamored with the professor. Never got over the crush she developed when she first came out. If she's heard the rumors, she will not want to talk to you."

"Do you think that's going to be the case? Maybe she won't mind if she sees Aunt Honoria with me? They used to know each other."

"That might help, but prepare yourself for a chilly welcome," Hannah said as she grabbed one of the more severe outfits Georgi had picked out for me. The color was a deep green with some gold accents, but unlike the minty confection she had put me in just yesterday, I thought this one came across as stern and stuffy, with its high neckline, simple apron, and straight skirt.

"That's what you think I should wear, Hannah? It seems so, I don't know, severe?"

"Yes, Miss. Miss Spencer would say that, when going to an old lover of someone who might believe you replaced her, the more stuffy or severe you look, the better. Bringing more attention to your youth and beauty could backfire."

"Hannah, you are great at this. I should have you give me lessons in apparel." Hannah helped me don the outfit she had picked for me. Then I rushed downstairs to Aunt Honoria before she grew too impatient waiting for me.

"Well Pippa, don't you look ready to take on the world. We should go so we call on Adelaide at an appropriate time."

My aunt was always such an odd combination of what was proper and what was not. It's one of the things I've always found the most intriguing about her, that she would explore the world on her own, completely flouting convention, and still have concerns about whether or not we called on someone at the appropriate time of day.

We walked right to the more imposing side of town, and by more imposing, I definitely meant wealthier. Here all the homes were at least three stories high, and while you could stand in one and touch the home next to you, the insides made up for any lack of outdoor space. As did the convenient location close to parks, shopping, and local entertainment.

Aunt Honoria stopped in front of a large brick home with a bright blue door. She removed her card from her reticule before marching up to the door and knocking with authority. My aunt seemed to do everything with authority, another trait I hoped to mimic one day.

I watched the door to the townhouse open, and the butler stepped into view. He was lanky and seemed to look over his nose at us.

"May I help you?" he asked.

"Yes," Aunt Honoria held out her calling card, "please let Lady Adelaide know that Honoria Porter and her niece are here to see her."

The butler took the card with a pretentious sniff and scrutinized it. After a moment, he stepped aside, letting my aunt and me cross the threshold. I looked around, noting Lady Adelaide must have had quite refined taste. Her home was elegant, decorated in light blues and golds. The butler led us to the parlor, where the colors continued, making the space feel harmonious and welcoming. The furniture was quite delicate. Aunt Honoria sat herself down on a dainty cushioned chair. I sat on the coordinating settee. A parlor maid came in with tea and sandwiches and left without saying a word. I nibbled on a cucumber sandwich, waiting impatiently for Lady Adelaide to show up.

"Honoria Porter, it has been such a long time, too long, in fact." I looked up to see an incredibly stylish woman dressed in dark grey. Her brown hair was pulled back and piled on her head, and when she looked over at me, her eyes looked sad.

"Lady Adelaide, it's so good to see you. Let me introduce my niece, Miss Philippa Stanhope."

"Miss Stanhope, it's wonderful to finally meet you. Marcus has said so many wonderful things about working with you," Lady Adelaide said, and I'm pretty sure my jaw dropped. After everything Hannah had heard, I did not expect to be received with such grace and poise. Plus, I couldn't believe Professor Aneurin had talked about me with anyone.

"When did you reconnect with Marcus? I know you were close back during our season, but I assumed you drifted apart afterwards," my aunt asked.

"We met back up when he got the professorship here. I had moved to Grantabridge a bit before that, preferring the slower pace to the craziness of town."

"Is Lord Wetherly here with you?" Aunt Honoria asked. I sat there watching the exchange.

"No, Lord Wetherly has always preferred town. We've kept separate households for a while now."

"Oh Adelaide, I know that's not what you wanted when you married."

"I've made the best of my situation. It's been nice since Marcus moved here. At least I've had some wonderful friendships since I settled out here. And it is truly wonderful to meet you, Miss Stanhope. I've heard so much about you. Marcus raved about your ingenuity. I hope we can continue our acquaintance if you stay here."

"Oh, Lady Adelaide, that would be lovely. I was afraid that you had only heard the nasty rumors going around about me and nothing else, and might hate me on sight. Especially considering the content of those rumors," I said.

"Luckily, Marcus had already told me about you, and I'm no fool. Well, at least not anymore. Years ago I worried about rumors, based life decisions on avoiding them. And on the advice of a woman I thought was a friend. But now, I wish I hadn't cared then, and care very little for any of the rumors at the moment. The young lady Marcus described would never have hurt him. She loved working with him too much. And I can see the sadness in you, now that he's gone," Lady Adelaide said, giving me a quick once over.

"It has been truly devastating. He was fantastic to work with and I miss his disorganized ways so much."

"I know this is an indelicate question, but did you and

Marcus ever become more than friends? And maybe Lord Wetherly found out?" Aunt Honoria asked, changing the course of the conversation.

"No, we never crossed that line. As much as I know Lord Wetherly would not care, Marcus and I had too much honor, and look where that got us. He's dead, probably murdered, and I'm married to a man that doesn't want to be in the same room as me. I do not know why I listened to Lady Corinne. I should have followed your lead, Honoria, never caring what others thought. Especially when it had to do with matters of the heart."

Aunt Honoria and Lady Adelaide reminisced about their season and other madcap adventures they had when they were just coming out. It was apparent to me that Lady Adelaide would never have killed Professor Aneurin; she was still very much in love with him.

Chapter Twenty-One

Back at the dormitory, I sat on the floor with all the different pieces of evidence spread out in front of me. There were the letters from Lady Adelaide, the notes on alchemy equations, the secret society journals that still needed code breaking, and the student files, including one for Colin.

I was at a loss. I really didn't think anyone I had talked to had done it. Professor Gates had seemed to be truly mourning the loss of his friend, plus he had said he was home with his wife. I still was sad about the star-crossed lovers living apart. Lady Adelaide literally had no reason to kill the professor, especially since she didn't believe any of the rumors. Professor Aneurin's death was as much of a loss to her as it was to me. That left Colin, maybe, but I couldn't imagine my longtime friend doing something so dastardly. He had always been a good man, and he had found a good place for himself in this world. He was successful without the help of a university education and the connections he would have made while attending.

I reached over and grabbed the file with his name on it. Going through it, Professor Aneurin had notes on all of Colin's inventions. How they worked, what he thought could be improved upon. It was clear that the professor really respected what Colin could do. There was quite a bit of praise in his notes, not just on what Colin made but the speed with which he could get things done. At the very end of the file, there was a note to schedule a meeting with Colin to set up informal study. Professor Aneurin was annoyed at the close-mindedness of university officials and had wanted to work with Colin outside of the institution in his free time. If Colin knew about this, he had even less reason to want the professor dead and more reason to want those university officials out of the way.

I grabbed my hat and goggles and a bag to carry the file. I had already changed into my leggings after I saw Aunt Honoria off and headed back to the city. Dressing up was tiring, and I didn't think it necessary to talk to Colin. I hopped on my steamer bike, dropped in my heat stone, strapped on my safety gear, and rode into town, taking the road over my favorite bridge to Colin's shop. This was the first time I'd been on my bike since he fixed it. I don't think it had ever ridden so smoothly. I would have to ask him what he changed while I was there. Nothing like asking someone whether or not they were a murderer and what they did to your steamer bike to make it run so well.

I jumped off my bike, letting the steam disperse.

"Colin, are you here?" I called as I entered the workshop. "Colin?" There was a moment of fear as I looked around, as I imagined tripping over Colin's body like I had the professor's. I felt my body tremble just at the thought of experiencing that again over another person I cared about.

"Pippa, is that you?" I heard from somewhere below. I looked down just in time to see Colin push himself out from under the steam carriage.

"Oh, Colin, you gave me quite a start. After the last time I burst into a building and couldn't find who I was looking for, I didn't want a repeat." I brushed my hands down my legs, trying to expel the nervous energy that had built up in those few moments.

"Sorry, Pippa, just finishing up Kaiden's car. It should be done later today," Colin said.

"That's exciting. Is this the first time you've built

something like this?" I asked.

"It is, but I've had plans for a while. In fact, I showed some of them to Professor Aneurin." Maybe the questioning wouldn't be that hard if Colin was already talking about the professor.

"Oh really? I wonder if those were the designs he was talking about in his file?" I muttered.

"What was that, Pippa?"

"Oh Colin, did you know that Professor Aneurin wanted to work with you in his spare time?" I was so excited to tell him, even if it didn't matter now. In my mind, I could imagine us working together with the professor. It would have been so fun, each of us pushing the other to create new and better technology.

"He hadn't told me. After the university's rejection, I would never have expected him to come by and see me."

The thought again entered my head that maybe Colin could have killed the professor. I didn't think it was possible, but maybe I should ask him, in a roundabout way, of course.

"But it's true. I found this file in his office with your name on it. He was so upset that the university officials would not see reason, and how unfair it was to you. So he was going to do the only thing he could think of to make it right." I took the file out of my bag and handed it to Colin. Not that he took it from me. It was like he wanted nothing to do with it.

"That's quite upstanding of him. It would have been nice to know. I was upset when I was not admitted, but it is the way of the world. I don't know why I thought it would be any different here. And I found another way. It's too bad I couldn't have worked with him. Professor Aneurin seemed like a good man."

"Were you ever angry at him for not getting into University?" I looked down at my boots, kicking an invisible rock as I asked him.

"Of course not. It's not like he was in charge."

"Some people lay blame at the feet of the wrong people all the time." I looked up at Colin. He didn't seem angry. I was happy he didn't seem angry.

"I try not to do that. It can be difficult at times. But having seen the professor go all out for women and men like me . . . You can't hold someone like that at fault for not always winning the fight." Colin shrugged, dismissing the idea that he should have been mad at the professor.

"It really would have been so easy to blame him, since he's the only one that teaches steam engineering," I prodded.

"It may have been easy but it wouldn't have been right."

"Were you here working the other night?"

"Are you getting at something, Pippa? 'Cause it sounds like you want to know if I had anything to do with his death. Which one, of course I didn't, and two, I should be offended that you would even think such a thing." Colin crossed his arms and stared at me.

"I don't think you are capable, but I feel like I have to ask. I'm already the prime suspect, and there's all these rumors. And I know how disappointing it must have been to you. But, I don't want to ask because I don't want to upset you. You've always been such a dear friend," I stammered. This was so embarrassing. How could I even think of questioning my friend? I was so selfish. I didn't want him to know I was trying to ask that because I didn't want him to hate me if he didn't kill the professor.

"Pippa, I would never have killed him. I would never kill anybody. It would have been nice to know he wanted to work with me because then maybe we could have done something together. I know he wasn't ever truly in charge. He's just another servant, or was, working for the University. You have university officials deciding, and then secret societies like the Shadowed Sword, and I'm sure some other invisible hands, pulling the strings. It just wasn't meant to be." Colin ran his hand through his hair, looking back up at me, seeming to ask me to believe him.

"Did you say the Shadowed Sword?" I asked.

"You've heard of the Shadowed Sword?" Colin asked.

"Yes, I have. I believe Kaiden is a member, or at least his older brother was a member, and I believe Lord Middleton is a member as well."

"Ah yes, Lord Middleton. The arrogant cur."

"That's one way to describe him for sure. He yelled at me

the other day, saying I had taken your spot at University. Well, he didn't say that exactly, but if you worked it out, it's what he meant," I said. The reminder of that conversation made me want to rub the bruises on my arm.

"That's some tosh. They don't want me attending school any more than they want you there. It's just an excuse to be angry about any changes they don't approve of. Act like they support one thing instead of another, but really they don't support any change because they fear losing their power." This was Colin angry. He seemed more likely to take out Lord Middleton than the professor.

"Well, Colin, that's about as accurate of a description of Lord Middleton as I have ever heard. I don't know much about the society. It sounds like there are two ways of thinking at the Shadowed Sword, at least from what Kaiden has let slip. There are those that follow Lord Middleton, and then there are some that supported Edmund before he was murdered."

"That's probably accurate. I don't know much, other than they think they are secret and really aren't secret at all. Then there's the fact they are against letting more people into University. They want to keep it for the elite, specifically elite men."

"That does sound like Lord Middleton, and I told him such the other night at the soirée. He was not happy with me."

"Like Lord Middleton would be happy with an upstart young lady like yourself. You represent everything he opposes."

"That's the truth. In some ways, he reminds me of my mother. Why does the Shadowed Sword have any sway over what happens here at University? This isn't the first I've heard of them nosing their way in. I just don't understand why anyone would care what the members think."

"They are one of, if not the oldest, secret societies here on campus. Which means, a lot of the men that run or donate to the University at one point were part of the society. And when the society says to do something, anyone that was a member does that exact thing. I think it's actually how you were admitted to University. Edmund was such a proponent for it, and quite noisy about it; he actually convinced other members to go along with him. I had heard he was going to try to take Lord Middleton's spot as president this term. Which would have been huge. So many things could have changed around here. Unfortunately, Edmund was murdered."

"You have sure heard a lot about this secret society. Although, it's not the first time I've heard that Lord Middleton was losing control over his society. I could see him taking pretty drastic steps to stay in control." I lost myself in thought, thinking about my interactions with Lord Middleton, especially when he left bruises on my arm because I dared to disagree with him despite his title. Grabbing my arm seemed like such a small thing, but did it actually show a tendency towards violence?

"Did I get to tell you that Lord Middleton decided to have me build him a steam carriage? I should probably be nicer when I talk about him, but it's an arduous task," Colin asked, interrupting my thoughts.

"Really, Colin, that's fantastic. I bet you will be the premier steam carriage builder in no time, especially with patronage from Kaiden and Lord Middleton. Plus, they look so shiny, who wouldn't want to ride in one." I clapped my hands with glee.

"I admit, it shocked me when he came in. I showed him Kaiden's carriage, and he was quite impressed with it. But truly, it seems so beneath him to come to the shop at all. I even had to help someone else while he was here, and Lord Middleton didn't throw his weight around and insist I finish with him first. He just continued to examine Kaiden's carriage."

"He is supposed to be studying steam engineering. If it were me, I would be here every day. In fact, I would love to help here if I can. I know you already said I could in exchange for fixing my bike, but I want you to be really sure. Remember I can be a bit of a disaster at times. With the professor gone, I still can get an education, but there's no one here that actually teaches steam engineering. I'm stuck learning alchemy and the other tangential subjects. I bet I could learn so much more working here with you than I would anywhere else."

"I should say no, you were just accusing me of murder." Colin winked at me. "But really, how can I say no to such lovely help? Of course, you can work here. If business picks up, I might even pay you for the work you do."

"I would love to say I don't need the money, but ever since my parents cut me off, things have been tight. I'm thankful for Aunt Honoria, but with my room burning down and losing all my things, it has been rough. I would love to actually pay Georgi back, even if she would never let me."

"I think we can work something out. But I think you should solve this murder before you work here. I don't think you will focus right until this is all over."

"You're probably right, Colin. Thank you for not hating me," I yelled as I left his shop and got back on my steamer bike to head back to the dorm.

Chapter Twenty-Two

"Pippa! I finally cracked the code!" Mads said, running towards me as I entered our dorm. "It's a fascinating read once you can actually read it. I don't know if it will actually help us, even so, to read about this slice in time thirty years ago. So interesting." Mads looked lovely as always in a crimson dress, her cheeks flushed from excitement or exertion. I liked to think it was from excitement.

I pulled my goggles and leather hat off, shaking my head to let my braids fall, then walked into the parlor. If Miss Pierce saw me right now, she would surely disapprove, just as she had on my first day here. Strange, I hadn't actually seen Miss Pierce here for a bit; I wonder where she'd been.

"That's fantastic, Mads," I said. "It would be nice if it helped us solve the murder, but I would love to know more about the society, at least how it was back then. Colin and I were just talking about it, and it has quite a bit of power here at the University. Weighing in on admission decisions and the like. If Edmund hadn't been part of that society and supported our entry, we would never have been admitted."

Mads flopped down on the settee, grimaced, then adjusted. I assumed that spring was poking her. It really was quite obnoxious, that spring in the settee. I wished I could afford to replace it for our close-knit group, but it wouldn't happen on my meager funds. I sat in one of the more comfortable chairs, wanting to take off my boots and tuck my feet under me, but now was not the time to go change. Kicking off my boots in the parlor was beyond the pale, even for me.

"This fight over class verses intelligence has been going on for at least the past thirty, maybe even forty years, in the Shadowed Sword. Professor Aneurin's father, Michael Aneurin, was a member. He was the last inductee not from a titled family. And it annoyed him to no end."

"Really? Why is that?" I asked.

"Apparently, the motto is something like Seek Knowledge and Michael felt that the society was limiting itself by only letting in those that were titled. He really didn't believe the wealthy and titled were the only purveyors of knowledge, and everyone had something to offer no matter their status. In fact, he believed that those that lacked wealth and title probably had more to offer the society because of the different hardships they faced in life," Mads said.

"He wasn't wrong. You know, that's one area that I'm always going on about. I mean, why is Lord Middleton here studying steam engineering, when Colin would actually make use of the degree to better himself and potentially society?" The notebooks were another reminder of the conversation Colin and I had earlier today.

"Well, he ended up leaving the society when he married. He had always felt ostracized by its members, so when he married and got a job teaching at the University, he left. He was hoping things would change in the future, but he didn't think he could be the catalyst for the change that was needed."

"Sounds like the same arguments are being made now at the Shadowed Sword, but by men that have more authority than Michael did. I know Edmund was at the forefront of change, at least according to Kaiden. And if Edmund had lived, things might have been quite different here. Instead, Lord Middleton is still in charge. And nothing different is going to happen with him in charge. He's king of the status quo," I said.

"How intriguing, Pippa. In Michael's journals, he talks about Lord Middleton. I'm sure the senior. If Simon had to grow up with that man as his father, we are lucky he's as nice as he is."

"It could be his father's influence that created the Lord Middleton I've had to put up with." Once again, I fought the urge to rub my arm. "At least that's a reason, because I don't think I've ever seen anyone willing to be quite that nasty in public. I would hate to think that he was just born rotten. Although how sad is it to think his father made him so mean?"

"Interesting thought indeed, Pippa."

* * *

"Miss, I was wondering if I could talk to you about something?" Hannah asked as she undid my stays.

"What is it, Hannah?"

"I—"

Georgi burst through the door, interrupting Hannah. I watched as Georgi threw herself onto her bed in a huff, then immediately stood and began pacing.

"Georgi, is something bothering you?" I asked gently.

"Men, their worthless self-importance, their entitlement, and their overall mediocrity. Weeks . . . I spent weeks, weeks I tell you, writing this analysis of the works of certain legal—well, really religious, philosophers. I won't bother you with the names. I know those are details you don't want or care about. But basically it comes down to determining the mental state of the person performing the illegal act. My theories were automatically dismissed. The so-called professor of my class told me that if I wanted to make it in this male-dominated world, I would have to temper my opinion and keep it to myself."

"Oh Georgi, that's awful."

"Pippa, it gets worse! Then, Lord Bradbury, who we all know is not that sharp, presents my theory almost verbatim. And the professor acts like he's a bloody genius instead of the fool he is."

"I honestly don't know who I would be more mad at, the

professor or Lord Bradbury," I said.

Georgi stopped in front of me, hands resting on her hips. "The professor, of course: he's the one that's supposed to be teaching us. We already know Lord Bradbury is a bit of a fool. I want to know how he got his hands on my research, though. He doesn't have the wherewithal to listen to my presentation, remember it, and repeat it. He had to have it beforehand." Georgi flopped down on the bed again. "It has to have something to do with all the strange things happening here, the vandalism and the thefts."

I knew Georgi would stew on this affront for the rest of the night, or week, if we didn't start discussing something else. I figured it was time for a distraction.

"True, true." I paused. "Hannah was about to ask me something before you came in. Maybe it will cheer you up," I said.

"Oh, Miss, thank you. You see, the other day, Miss Stanhope and I were talking as I got her ready. She suggested it might be worthwhile to have an information-gathering team. I was telling her about the rumors around town that she killed Professor Aneurin because he broke off their illicit affair. Sorry, Miss Stanhope." I waved my hand, hopefully dismissing any concerns she had. Hannah continued, "I was thinkin' that this is actually something that I could organize for you. Especially if there were some sort of compensation."

I looked over at Georgi, who shrugged her shoulders. She was probably still fuming from earlier, but I didn't know what to say. This was exactly what I had thought of earlier today, but I couldn't see why we would need something like this, especially after the professor's and Edmund's murders were solved.

"You know, Hannah, you might be on to something. Maybe the ladies can help us determine who is spreading these ugly rumors and help us figure out why," Georgi said. "And we can keep it going in the future once we solve this murder. I have a feeling something strange is happening here, and things won't return to normal any time soon. There's the vandalism and thefts here to think about."

I looked over at Georgi in shock. Why would she think this was any more than what we were dealing with right now? Then again, Georgi was the schemer in our group, so was it really a surprise she would think schemes were everywhere?

"What would your friends want for helping us out?" I asked. Mads wasn't around to be super practical, so the task fell to me. None of us would count on Georgi for practicality. I was actually surprised she hadn't announced she was buying a university so she could run one just for women, especially on a day like today when she came home so frustrated.

"Miss, we hoped you could help teach us some things. Some ladies are interested in self-defense, especially those that work for lecherous old men, others would like to improve their reading and arithmetic skills, maybe work with herbs and botanicals that we could use if we wanted a job as a cook somewhere. Things that are practical for us but could help us improve our situation if we needed to," Hannah said.

"Hannah, that's such a fantastic idea. I would love to help you and your friends, even if it turns out we don't need information." The prospect of helping other women excited me. Maybe it could help give me a reason to stay.

"Hush, Pippa, information is power, and while I approve of the exchange very much, especially the self-defense—maids need all the skills they can if they are in a household that refuses to respect their autonomy—the information we could get could change things for us as well," Georgi said.

I watched Hannah watch Georgi and I discuss. Her face was so hopeful, and she was such a good person, I couldn't see denying her and her friends even if nothing came of it. I'm sure Georgi agreed, even if she wanted a bit more.

"Why don't we set something up and have our first salon? We had already talked of doing them, but with everything going on, it didn't happen. When do most of your friends have time off to meet? I know it's not always easy to get away when you are in service," I said.

"More like it's impossible to get away; even in households that say you have a day off, some people forget, and ask us to run errands or do other tasks on our day off," Hannah said.

"Oh Hannah, if I've ever done that to you, it was unintentional and you have to tell me," I said.

"I'm sorry, Miss, I didn't mean to imply that you did that. Even with working for four of you, I barely have any work to do at all unless you are getting ready for an event. I was thinking of my dear friend Francesca. She works over at Lord Middleton's and they always forget she has Sundays off."

"More like they just don't care," Georgi muttered.

"That's definitely more accurate," I said.

"Most of us are supposed to have time off on Sundays for church services. Maybe we can plan something for Sunday. A sort of test run."

"I think we can make something happen. It might be on the more simple side if you are okay with that. Like you said, it would be a test to see if we could do it, what works, what doesn't, what we could do to make it better," I said.

Georgi was much more animated. She was almost jumping up and down with her excitement. Apparently, a potential spy network was just the thing to make her forget her earlier anger.

"Hannah, you go spread the word and see how many ladies you can get here on Sunday. The rest of us will talk and plan something absolutely delightful.

* * *

The four of us convened down in the parlor at Georgi's request. Willa and Mads looked confused and also uncomfortable as they perched on the springy settee. I knew what was happening but really had no idea how this was going to go. This idea was not in my skill set, but I was looking forward to teaching some self-defense moves to a group other than my friends here. I could see that Georgi was in her general mode and was about to give off orders before explaining what was happening, so I hurried to step in.

"Earlier, Hannah approached us with this idea that she could help organize a kinda network of lady-spies for us, servants and shopkeepers, most likely. What they want from us is knowledge and skills. They would love self-defense training, to improve their reading and arithmetic, and Hannah mentioned some work with herbs for future jobs as a cook. We thought we could make this happen through some salons, and have our first one Sunday as a test run. What do you think?"

I looked at Mads and Willa, hoping to see them looking back with excitement. Which was at least partially what I saw. Mads looked thrilled. I thought sharing her love of math with anyone excited her to no end; it was so rare. Willa, on the other hand, looked terrified. Which probably had to do with her stutter, but she was so good with plants, we needed her to be on board.

"What do you two think? Would you be interested in doing something like this.?" I asked.

"I would love to be a part of this. To teach math to others. Especially those that have little opportunity to learn those types of skills." Mads looked ready to create a lesson plan at that very moment. She was on the edge of the settee, leaning forward, almost vibrating with her excitement.

"What about you, Willa?" I asked.

"It makes me really nervous, b-b-b-but I would like to p-p-p-participate. But I need more time to prepare. I hope that is okay." Willa refused to look up from the imaginary lint she was picking off her dress. I felt for her; her shyness made her the odd one out in some ways. The rest of us were ready to jump without looking, and she always seemed quite cautious.

"Of course that's okay, Willa. I want you to be comfortable teaching these women. I just know they will be so excited when they have the chance to learn from you; you have so much knowledge." Willa blushed at my words, but she finally looked up at me.

"If this one w-w-w-works, I'll p-p-p-put together something for the next one," Willa said, smiling.

"Since that's settled, let's get started planning." Georgi jumped in, her manner just a bit brusquer and more take charge than I had been.

"I think we should start with a self-defense class. Sparring with my brother Percy taught me a lot, and I can use that knowledge to teach others," I said.

"You know fisticuff fighting and fencing?" Georgi asked.

"Yes, much to my mother's dismay, I took up all things my younger brother was interested in. So I would help him practice boxing and fencing. When his tutor found out, he taught me some moves to help protect myself from anyone bigger and stronger as well. Plus, I have a pretty mean right hook."

"How am I just finding this out? The fencing has been great, but actual hand-to-hand combat could be so useful for all of us," Georgi said.

"I don't talk about it much. My mother was so distraught that I had learned it at all. I decided it was better if no one knew. Every time someone found out, I got in trouble. At least, growing up."

"I will never understand why other women want us to be defenseless," Mads said. "My father taught me some basics, but I've never had the opportunity to really practice, since it was just my sisters and me. He was worried that men would press an advantage because of my darker complexion, assuming I was more forward than a pale Brythionite beauty."

"It saddens me to know that your father was probably correct. My experience with the men here has been horrendous with very few exceptions," Georgi said.

"You're just mad because you have a professor that refuses to acknowledge your genius. A lot of the men here are actually quite forward thinking," I said.

"I will not say you're wrong, but have you met Lord Middleton? He is just awful. It doesn't help that he's handsome. Just adds to his insufferable character," Georgi said.

"Oh, I'll agree that Lord Middleton is quite unpleasant, but that does not make all the men here unpleasant. Just the ones that think like him."

"True, but my exaggerations are more fun. Your friend Colin and of course, Kaiden are probably two of the only exceptions. Okay, enough talk of men. They take up way too much of our daily time, anyway. What if Pippa and Mads teach a beginning self-defense class Sunday? We can have some tea and sandwiches for everyone."

"I could prepare the f-f-f-food," Willa said. "And I would l-l-l-love to be part of the class as well. I think it would be quite useful to have some hand-to-hand c-c-c-combat skills."

"We could also do some modified stick fighting too. I learned early in our lessons that while men had their canes for stick fighting, we could use our parasols with just as much efficacy," I said.

"I love the idea of using the tools that we have at our disposal to help us out. Let's definitely include that," Georgi said.

From there, we dispersed to each go about our day and night, planning for Sunday. Hannah returned and said about ten of her friends could make it to our test salon. It just needed to be held at teatime. Luckily, that was what we had already discussed.

Mads and I sat down together and compared what we knew until we had enough of a lesson plan to get through about an hour of training, which didn't take much since the topic needed physical movement. From there, we retired to our rooms and went to sleep. There was so much to do to prepare, but it felt like we had a lot of it planned for so hopefully it would come together smoothly.

* * *

On Sunday I woke up early, earlier than my body liked to wake up, but there was a lot to get done before the salon. So I stumbled through my morning routine of brushing out my hair and braiding it, brushing my teeth, and getting dressed. I wanted to be comfortable and able to move but still dressed in ladies' fashions so my instructions would make sense.

I settled on my short corset, setting out a spare to show the class this afternoon, a skirt that was shorter than most so my feet could be seen, and my vest-and-blouse top I wore on the first day of class. Well, not the same outfit, since that had burned in the fire, but one that was quite similar and I could move in.

I headed downstairs, and Mads was already in the parlor, moving furniture out of the way. It appeared she had the same idea as me and had found a comfortable but stylish outfit to wear. It even had some flare from her home country, with lovely gold embroidery, and it flowed around her in a way that somehow enhanced her graceful movements. Even though I could see her feet touch the ground, it looked like she floated around the room.

With all the preparations happening, the morning was frantic and passed quite quickly. Willa was to prepare the food and had done a stupendous job. There was an assortment of savory foods, including my favorite, cucumber sandwiches. Then she had somehow thrown together a few sweets, including a lemon tart that looked scrummy.

Georgi and Hannah had worked together to make our dorm look as inviting as possible. A herculean task if there ever was one. I honestly don't know how they did it, but for the first time since we moved in, dull and grey was not the overwhelming feel. They had made the grey sparkle just a bit, probably through some intense cleaning. And had added pops of color here and there with flowers and decorations. Enough that it almost looked cheery. Almost.

Suddenly it was teatime, and women were knocking on our door at an impressive rate. Word must have spread after Hannah did a tally because there were at least twice as many women here than she had said would come. I saw Willa rush off to the kitchen; I assumed to make more food. Georgi took off in the other direction. I swear I heard her muttering, 'more chairs,' but where we would get more, I did not know. That left Mads and me standing in front of about two dozen women. Mads nodded at me, telling me to go on and speak, which, other than teaching the class, had never been my plan. In my mind, Georgi was going to do this part because this was her thing, but she was off playing hostess in a different way. I guess the speaking part was going to fall on me, at least today.

"Welcome ladies," I said, stepping away from the door frame. "Welcome to the first salon of the Women Adventurers' Consortium of Knowledge. All women are welcome here. Our goal is to better ourselves with the exchange of knowledge, whether it be like today when we will learn different skills to protect ourselves, or through discussions of certain philosophical theories, arithmetic, and the knowledge and skills that each of you bring with you everywhere you go."

"Whatdaya mean knowledge and skills that we have?" one of the women asked.

"Well, recently we have been trying to figure out who killed Professor Aneurin, and information that you gave has helped us determine different paths to take. Especially knowing the local gossip about me. The information you have is so valuable, because it is information we would never be privy to. If that is something you are interested and willing to do, I hope you will stay for today and join us in the future. If it's not, I completely understand. While we are not asking you to purposefully spy on your employers, we are asking you to share information you may come across because of your work, due to the fact many employers don't even see you and treat you like you are not there, sometimes speaking about things they would never speak about if they thought someone was listening."

A few women left at that point, but most stayed. I thought it would have been a difficult choice to make, depending on the employer.

"If you are ever not sure about being part of our group, please let us know. We really want everyone to be comfortable. And with that said, let's get started."

I showed the group my modified corset, which greatly interested most of them. I had never really thought how useful it could be to the working class before, but it made so much sense once the women pointed it out. Maybe my stamp on the world would strangely have to do with clothing and not steam engineering. Wouldn't that be ironic?

After showing them the sports corset, Mads and I took turns showing them different moves, starting with the best way to strike. Which Mads showed me last night and involved an open palm and a locked wrist. It was much safer for the wrist than traditional boxing punches. I went through what to do when you were grabbed from behind, which included a headbutt and run, which might not work if the threat was in the household. After every demonstration, we had the women practice with each other.

Our event was loud with laughter and joy. Everyone seemed to have a great time. Which made me smile a proper smile. It felt like the first real, sustained smile since the professor had been killed.

I had just started to teach how to knee someone through all of our petticoats when every single light in the house went off. One woman screamed.

“Try to stay calm and stay where you are,” I yelled over the noise. At once, everyone was quiet, and the shuffling around stopped.

I heard a loud crash above. It sounded like it came from Mads’s room. I hiked up my skirts and ran upstairs into Mads’s room. I don’t really know how I did it in the dark, but I did. The intruder and I made eye contact as I entered the room. The intruder wore a face mask that showed his blue eyes off; unfortunately his eyes were all that I could see. I saw his eyes flick over to where Mads had been keeping the journals. I didn’t know if they were still over there. I lunged for the books. The intruder grabbed onto my skirts, yanking me back. I kicked my leg out as I fell. This movement tripped the intruder but wasn’t enough to do much more, unfortunately. Scrambling to my feet, I lunged and grabbed the intruder by the arm. I swung him around and punched him, cracking him in the jaw. He stumbled but tossed me across the room. I cracked my head on something solid and watched him take the journals as my world faded to black.

Chapter Twenty-Three

"Come on, Pippa, you need to wake up." I heard a male voice say. I recognized that timber. But there was a tremor in his voice I wasn't used to. Was that concern?

I tried to open my eyes. But they really didn't want to open. I licked my lips instead. It seemed like a reasonable thing to do. My throat felt like I had swallowed a cup of sand. Water would be nice if I could open my eyes?

"Pippa, if you can hear me, you have to open your eyes."

Fine, I guess opening my eyes was my only option to be left alone. My eyelids felt heavy and almost glued shut, but I managed to crack one eye open, then the other. Only to find Kaiden mere inches away from my face. His eyes went wide, and he kissed me, if you could call something so brief a kiss. Then he gathered me into his arms, holding me quite tight. It was a nice hug, if somewhat awkward.

"You're awake, thank God. Mads said you took quite the hit to the head trying to be a hero."

"Heroine," I gasped out. "Kaiden, I can't breathe."

"What . . . oh, sorry. But bloody hell Pippa, you had me, I mean us, really worried."

I lightly pushed away as Kaiden's arms loosened. Because

who was I kidding? I would have stayed in his arms all day at the very least if I thought we were all alone. I looked over his shoulder to see Georgi, Mads, and Willa standing there, concern etched on each of their faces. So they saw everything. I could already see the teasing that was in my future.

"Um, what are you doing here? Not that I mind, but you weren't here earlier," I asked.

"I sent one of Hannah's friends to go get him after the attack. With you unconscious, we were struggling to get the lights back on, and this seemed the best option," Georgi explained.

"How long was I unconscious?" I asked.

"Less than a half an hour is my best guess," Mads said. "But we you had us quite worried when you didn't come to right away. Especially seeing you lying on the ground like a rag doll."

"Did he get away with the journals?" I asked.

"Yes, Pippa, he did. But we already have the information out of them, and they weren't all that helpful. You should be more concerned about your health than the journals," Georgi said. She stood back, arms crossed, giving me the look. The look that said, what did you get into this time and I'm not pleased. It reminded me of my mother after a Percy and Pippa escapade.

"They are right, Pippa, now's not the time to worry about lost journals," Kaiden said.

"When is a good time, then? This is something like the sixth attack on this house, and the last two have both led to something from the crime scene being taken. Clearly, we are missing something important. Why are people trying to drive us out? What does it have to do with the Shadowed Sword? And how is it related to the murder of Professor Aneurin?" I tried to stand so I could pace. I was so frustrated. As soon as I made it to my feet, everything started spinning around me and my knees gave out. Kaiden caught me and pushed me back into the bed.

"Pippa, you have to rest, you aren't going to accomplish anything in the state that you are in," Kaiden said.

The death stare I gave him told him exactly what I thought of his restrictions. I had no intention of being waylaid by a slight injury.

"I know you aren't happy about it, but you can't even stand up on your own right now. How do you expect to track down a thief or killer?" Kaiden said.

Was it okay to hate him because he was right? I really didn't feel great, but I hated I couldn't do anything about, well, anything.

"Did the thief take anything other than the journals? The alchemy notes we found, the formula, anything?" I asked. If I had to stay in bed, I could at least try to use logic to figure out as much as possible.

"Nope, just the journals. I can't figure out why they wouldn't have taken more unless it's because you interrupted them. I mean, the notes on alchemy have some really useful theories," Georgi said.

Kaiden gave her a dirty look. I took his hand, because I needed this discussion. He looked down at our hands, and then at me, and sighed. I assume he figured there was no point in trying to stop me. Even if he wanted to.

"So if they took nothing relating to alchemy, either I interrupted the thief, or this isn't related to the alchemy formulas," I said. "And if it's not related to those formulas, then it's probably not Professor Gates that killed the professor."

"Why do you think that, Pippa?" Mads asked.

"When I overheard them arguing, Gates was upset that Aneurin was spending all his time on steam engineering and not alchemy. That Gates needed Aneurin's help, and I was a distraction," I said.

"In addition, Professor Gates was distraught over Aneurin's death. Or so it seemed when we went to talk," Kaiden added.

"I also think that Professor Gates needed Aneurin to finish his work. I got the impression that Gates was at a loss with his research and needed someone else with a different way of thinking to get him to the next steps in his research. Professor Aneurin can't do that now that he's dead. Plus, he said he was home with his sick wife. I wonder if one of Hannah's friends can confirm that?"

"I'll go check with Hannah. If he really was home, then

that really would exclude him as a suspect. With no real motive or opportunity," Georgi said. And then she left the room.

Mads and Willa looked at each other, then looked at me. And both made a beeline out the door, leaving me alone with Kaiden while I lounged in a bed. This did not seem appropriate at all.

"It seems my friends have made themselves quite scarce," I said to Kaiden, trying to decide if it was better to be bold and look at him, or to look at my hands, or really anywhere but at him.

"Indeed, they have, left us alone." He looked at me, raising an eyebrow.

I'd never thought of him as rakishly handsome before, but in that moment he was. Heat rose to my face, my cheeks burned. I was surely turning bright red. In this moment, I wish I could blush gracefully, instead of turning as bright red as my hair.

"Are you all right, Pippa? You are bright red," Kaiden asked, everything about him screaming concern.

"I'm fine. I was just—" My eyes fell to his mouth . . . No, shouldn't look there. "It was, I mean I—" My gaze dropped to his broad shoulders and chest and the arms that had recently been holding me. Nope, nope, nope, not there either. "That is to say, I—" I looked up to his eyes, which I swear were twinkling with laughter, and I stopped.

"You were saying?" he asked, his laughter barely contained. In fact, I swore his shoulders were shaking. He knew exactly all the thoughts that had been running through my head and was laughing at me.

"It's nothing. Kinda like that kiss you gave me." Where did that come from? Seriously, I needed to think before words left my mouth way more often.

"Wait, are you mocking my kiss of relief?" Kaiden asked.

"Is that what you're calling it? I mean, it was over before it started, and while I don't have any personal experience to compare it to, the books I read imply that kissing should be so much more." I might as well continue with the flirtatious teasing. Right?

"No wonder you are disappointed if that was your first kiss.

That won't do at all." Kaiden shifted closer to the top of the bed, the part of the bed where I sat.

"I didn't say any of those things."

"No, but you definitely implied them."

"That was not my intention."

"Oh really, if that wasn't your intention, then what was your intention?"

"I, well, that is . . . Honestly Kaiden, I don't know what my intention was," I admitted. Once again, I didn't know where to look. He was so close and smelled of misty mornings and pine trees. And with all this talk of kissing, I couldn't help but stare at his lips. Which I know he noticed because his lips kept twitching into a smile, as if he knew exactly where my thoughts ran.

"I think I know," he said. Taking my face gently into his two hands, he paused a second as my eyes fluttered shut, and then he gently pressed his lips to mine. I felt one hand curl around to the back of my neck and into my hair as the other dropped to my shoulder and then lower to my waist. The pressure of his lips grew firmer. And then I felt his tongue lick my lower lip as he drew it into his mouth and lightly nibbled on it. I gasped as the sensations ran through my body. Kaiden did not waste my gasp. As my mouth opened, his tongue plundered mine. I hesitantly touched my tongue to his. As I did so, I felt him shudder and pull me close so we touched from chest to waist.

"Ahem . . ."

Kaiden and I broke away from each other, and I looked towards the door. And there was Georgi, standing in the doorway, barely able to contain her mirth.

"Yes, Georgi, do you have something to say?" I asked.

"Hannah is back."

"Well, that didn't take long at all," I muttered.

"The staff at Professor Gates says that Mrs. Gates was home sick, and Professor Gates was there with her the entire night. It appears you are right, Pippa, he couldn't have killed Professor Aneurin."

"Well, then, who did kill the professor?" I asked, frustrated.

Chapter Twenty-Four

I had spent the night tossing and turning, my sleep fitful as I tried to make connections that didn't want to be made. I woke up tired but determined to do more than sit around. It had been too long, and Professor Aneurin's murder should have been solved by now.

Unfortunately, Detective Inspector Radcliffe seemed to have washed his hands of the entire affair. I had come up against one dead end after another. But I had an idea, and since I didn't think anyone was going to like it, I decided to see if I could get my way with some minor manipulation instead of just running off on my own. That, and I didn't trust myself to ride my bike with my head injury. So, I needed another way to get about, especially to get to where I wanted to go.

"Hannah," I called out the door.

"Yes Miss, be there shortly," she responded.

"What are you up to now, Pippa?" I looked back to see Georgi rubbing sleep from her eyes as she tried to sit up in bed.

"Nothing outrageous," I replied.

"Is that so? Nothing outrageous like kissing Kaiden while lounging in bed." She smirked. She wasn't the least bit scandalized by my behavior, just teasing me. I had declared men were too much of a hassle to actually put up with.

"You left me alone with him. All of you left me alone with him. I was bedridden at that specific moment. What choice did I have?"

"I'm sure you had many other choices than passionate kisses."

"But, Georgi, would any of the other choices been as much fun?"

"Haha, Pippa, you are not wrong there. Pretty sure if he was interested in me, I would have kissed him a long time ago."

I threw my pillow at Georgi, blushing. She caught the pillow and fell back into bed with a fit of laughter.

"Oh Pippa, you should not blush in public if you can avoid it. Like many of the things you do, it is not very ladylike."

"Why thank you, it's nice to know you aren't oblivious to the absolutely obvious."

"Miss, what can I do for you?" Hannah asked, interrupting my friendly banter with Georgi.

"I was hoping you could help me pick out something to wear for a long car ride and send someone to see if Kaiden, I mean Lord Fremont, is available today. I think the two of us should go for a drive."

"Of course Miss, I'll send the missive right away and be back to help you dress." Hannah gave a slight curtsy and left the room.

"What is your plan today, Pippa?" Georgi asked.

"I've determined that Edmund's death is somehow related to the professor's, and to solve one, we have to solve both. So, I want to go to where he died and the closest town. It came to me last night that we really don't have that many highwaymen on the roads to and from Grantabridge. To be stopped and killed by one . . . It seems beyond strange and I want to ask some questions."

"Are you sure Kaiden will want to be part of this?" Georgi asked.

"No, but he wants to know who killed his brother, and he doesn't think it was a highwayman. He should go along with my scheme. The real question is, what should I wear so he doesn't feel like he can say no?"

Georgi threw back her covers and leapt out of bed. I knew she would be on board helping me dress for the occasion.

"I know just the thing." She ran to our shared closet. "He liked that minty dotted-Swiss dress you wore, right? The one you went to jail in?"

"Yes, he did. He also likes my leather leggings I wear to ride my bike. So you have a variety of options to choose from."

"What about this one?" Georgi asked.

She had pulled out an aqua wool carriage dress trimmed with copper accents. The neckline was open, but not too low, with long sleeves; the apron and skirt barely had any frills; instead, the fabric elegantly draped because of precise pleats on the side. Then there was a bit of copper trim to tie it all together. It was rather simple, but it had a matching capelet trimmed in a coppery fur, a muff, and a matching hat. It really was the accessories that made this ensemble.

"Miss, Lord Fremont is down in the parlor. I told him you would be down momentarily."

"What did he do, run over here? Hannah, can you do something with my hair so it looks, well, so it doesn't look as wild as its natural state is," I said, trying to manage the buttons on the front of the bodice.

"Of course, Miss, it will only take a moment. Your hair is lovely and so easy to work with."

Within moments, Hannah had my hair in some elaborate braided updo with a few curls framing my face and the hat pinned at a jaunty angle. I really had no idea how she did it. My hair was waist long and wavy; the only thing I was able to do with it was put it into two long braids, and if I was lucky, pin those up out of the way. But it never looked pretty, just practical.

"Thank you, Hannah, you truly are a magician," I said.

"Go Pippa, don't keep that handsome man waiting too long. Although if you do, maybe I would have a chance." Georgi shooed me on my way, all the while laughing at her own joke. At least I hoped it was a joke.

I walked, almost ran, down the stairs. The ache in my head would only let me move so fast before it reminded me I should stay in bed all day, not gadding about. But a headache never stopped me before, and it wasn't going to stop me now. Unless it got worse, but I knew I was going to be in excellent hands.

I walked into the parlor and saw Kaiden try to hide his appreciative glance, but I caught it and thanked Georgi telepathically. Okay, that's probably not a thing, but maybe one day it will be.

"Kaiden, I'm so glad you are here. Did Colin finish your steam carriage? I was thinking we should go for a drive," I said.

"It is done. In fact, I drove it over here, thinking it would be fun to test it out today. I figured the steam carriage would be of interest to you, and you would be upset if I took it out without you."

"You're so right, Kaiden. I would have been upset. Good thing you know me at least that well."

"Why did you ask me over, Pippa?" Kaiden asked. He looked suspicious of my intentions.

"I have an idea." I paused, not really sure if he was going to like it. "We should go to the town outside of where Edmund was killed and see what the locals have to say. I am almost positive that the two deaths are related."

"What I'm hearing is, you want to go on a long steam-carriage ride with me, away from any prying eyes. Are you really just trying to get me alone again?"

"I don't think I would have to scheme much to get you alone again. I mean, you're here alone with me already."

"True. We are alone, aren't we?" he whispered. He then grabbed me by the waist and pulled me close. My arms went around his neck naturally. He bent over and his lips met mine. My mouth opened eagerly under the pressure of his mouth. We kissed until I was out of breath.

"So does that mean you are up for a little day trip?"

"Yes Pippa, let's go investigate together."

I grabbed my handbag and capelet and walked out of the dorm. Kaiden's steam carriage sat on the street, shiny and red. It looked gorgeous. I wanted to drive it so badly. I almost got into the driver's seat but decided against it since it wasn't my vehicle and I was still recovering from a head injury. Kaiden opened the door for me and I climbed into the seat. I settled my skirts so I was comfortable while he walked around the steam carriage to climb into the driver's seat.

"I was prepared with at least three reasons on why you should let me drive today, and I didn't need any of them," Kaiden said.

"As much as I want to drive this beautiful machine, I know with what happened yesterday, today is not the day. But I hope you'll let me drive it in the future."

"How could I say no when you are being so reasonable?" Kaiden leaned over and gave me a kiss on the cheek before dropping the heat stones in and starting the steam carriage.

We puttered down the street as Kaiden familiarized himself with steering. He was also careful to avoid bumps and crevices in the road, as well as pedestrians, but I probably didn't need to include that last bit, as it is quite an obvious thing to need to avoid. Many people stared as we drove by. Some of those stares turned quite hostile when they saw me. I guessed the rumors were still going, and the townspeople were still believing them, which was unfortunate, to say the least.

Once Kaiden had maneuvered his way through town and to the main road between Grantabridge and Shirlock, where Edmund was killed, Kaiden and I put on our goggles. I realized at that moment the face-framing curls Hannah had so carefully placed would not last the drive.

Despite the task at hand, I found the drive quite relaxing. With the wind whipping by, it was too loud to really hold a conversation. But the combination of the wind, the sun, and the company that was fine with the silence, almost lulled me to sleep. It wasn't the freedom of riding my bike, but it was a delightful feeling. I watched as the scenery passed us by. Watching the rolling hills, with stone walls crisscrossing it, relaxed me almost as much as riding my bike. I had never been out this way before, and this was the way to Kaiden's home. The thought entered my head that maybe this would become a common drive for me as well in the future. I pushed it aside. I wasn't sure what was happening between Kaiden and me, but I didn't want to make it out to be something more than it was.

My revelry was abruptly interrupted when I noticed the speed of the carriage. It was going way too fast. I looked over at Kaiden, and I noted the tension in his arms and shoulders, the foot that was pumping the brake pedal with no luck whatsoever. Something was wrong, and if we didn't get out of the carriage, we might not survive a crash. I tugged on Kaiden's arm, trying to get his attention. He eventually looked over at me. I screamed the word jump at him. I grabbed my bag, held my hat, and threw myself out of the carriage, doing whatever I could to avoid the back wheel. I watched from the ground as Kaiden did the same thing. The steam carriage careened down the road, then crashed into a tree, destroying the front suspension.

Sitting on the soft grass, I brushed myself off. I was so very hard on the clothing Georgi bought for me. Not that it was my fault. I glanced up to see Kaiden hovering over me, concern etched on his face.

"Are you okay, Pippa?" Kaiden asked. "How's your head?"

"I think I'm okay," I said, taking the hand he offered and standing. Pausing, I waited for the dizziness to happen, but it didn't.

I walked over to the carriage, noting that in the hectic escape, Kaiden had let the steam escape, avoiding any chance of explosion during or after the crash. I inspected the vehicle the best I could, starting with the brake line. Part of it was frayed, but the other part was sliced clean through.

"Pippa, be careful, I don't want anything else to happen to you."

"Kaiden, the brake line was cut. It appears someone is trying to kill us."

Chapter Twenty-Five

Kaiden and I gathered our things. There was nothing to do for the carriage but leave it there for now. Luckily, the town of Shirlock wasn't too far. It was at least walkable. We did have a slight problem: not having transportation to get us back home tonight. I guessed we would have to figure that out when we made it into town.

"Well, that was quite unfortunate. We will have to find a way to get your carriage back to Colin so he can fix it," I said, walking towards town. I was resolved to accomplish my goal of investigating today, even with this rather inconvenient turn of events.

"Pippa, shouldn't we take a moment to make sure we are okay before heading off?"

"I know you mean to make sure *I'm* okay, which I am. You seem fine, and we can't do anything about almost being murdered until we get to town. So, let's get a move on."

"You know you can be quite headstrong."

"Of course I'm headstrong, what else would you expect?" I asked.

"Maybe just a chance for me to take care of you, just a

little. You are injured, whether or not you like it," Kaiden said.

"You know that's not likely to happen, at least not right now. I mean, really, what do you plan to do, carry me into town? That doesn't seem practical at all, especially since I'm quite capable of walking."

"I know, I know. I'll just have to find another time to be a hero."

"You've already proved yourself to be a hero. You haven't run from me after all the times I've just randomly started crying, and you aren't overly disappointed that I can handle most things on my own." I looked over at him quizzically.

"Of course not, it's actually one of the things I like about you: you are quite capable on your own, and don't need me."

"But I do want you around, which I think is so much better than needing you around," I said with a smile. "Now let's get to town. We are going to need to send a message to Colin to come get the carriage so he can fix it."

"Didn't you suspect him for a brief moment of having murdered the professor? Couldn't he have been the one to cut the brakes?" Kaiden asked.

"I don't think he killed the professor any longer. We had a talk the other day. And while he had the opportunity to cut the brakes, it would be bad for business. I'm sure anyone that came to his shop would have a similar opportunity if they wanted to do something so nefarious."

"Are you sure you didn't just clear him from suspect because you are childhood friends?" Kaiden's questions weren't unreasonable, but they were annoying.

"I'm sure. He really had no reason to kill us, or the professor, or your brother. Plus, who else is going to be able to come out here and get your steam carriage?"

"I have staff, I could send for it."

"Well, aren't you fancy?" I teased. "Do you know how far from town we actually crashed? I know we were close based on the time we had been on the road. But I'm unfamiliar with this area."

"I believe it is just over that hill there," Kaiden said, pointing directly in front of us. "I'm glad we jumped when we did.

I would have hated to injure someone in town."

We walked in silence after that. The Brythionite countryside was just what you would expect, except for the lack of traffic on the road. We didn't pass anyone on our walk. Not a single person on a horse, a wagon, or carriage rode by us. It felt like the entire area was deserted. I would think there would be way more traffic on a road that highwaymen staked out. This one was some pretty slim pickings.

"Have you noticed how no one has come upon us on the road?" I asked.

"It is strange. I was hoping we would be able to ride in the back of a wagon to town, but not a soul has come by."

"Makes me wonder why a highwayman would waylay anyone on this road?"

"It is a strange spot. I really don't think this road is ever busy. Unless my mother hosts an event. We really are quite rustic otherwise."

"Is that Shirlock?" I wanted to hike up my skirts and run. It felt like we had been walking forever. I was quite parched and wanted nothing more than a cold drink and a place to sit. As much as I wanted to, I did not hike up my skirts and run into town. I managed to act with just a bit of decorum. Quite out of character for me, my mother would be so proud.

"It is. Where would you like to stop first?" Kaiden asked.

"Someplace we can sit and get something to drink. I'm parched after our unexpected walk this morning. And then I think our next stop should be to someone who can send a message to my dorm, and to Colin. I'm worried we are going to have to stay the night at this point."

"Should make for an interesting night," Kaiden said. I looked at him, but his face gave nothing away. Although what he said seemed to imply something, I just wasn't sure what. "Let's go to the tavern. I'm sure we can sit and get a cold drink there, and maybe even find someone to deliver our messages."

The town was quite quaint, only taking up a little more than a block. There was an inn, a tavern, plus a few shops for ladies' accouterments, and of course, a general store. I'm sure this town existed because of its location in between larger cities.

We went straight to the Olde King's Head tavern. Kaiden held the door open for me, and I walked inside. It took my eyes a moment to adjust before I could see anything in the dark room. Everything inside was made of dark wood, the bar, the table, the chairs, even the walls. While some light trickled in through some small windows, it wasn't much. I assumed it was to help people forget what time it was so they would stay longer, drink more, and spend more money.

Behind the bar was an old man. He was rotund in a worn waistcoat and white shirt, with his sleeves rolled up and held in place by arm braces. He had hair so dark it looked black and a salt-and-pepper beard. I couldn't decide if he was friendly or foreboding. But he paid little attention to me, focusing instantly on Kaiden.

"How ken I help ye, sir," the man behind the bar said.

"Can I get a lemonade for the lady, and an ale for me. And I was hoping you could point us in the direction of a messenger that can go to Grantabridge today to deliver some messages and wait for a response."

"Yes sir, me boy, Howie, is swift on a horse. He can get your message to Grantabridge today."

"Right, we had a bit of an accident outside of town and walked in. The lady is quite parched. If we can start with the drinks, and the pen and parchment, we can get the message written and on its way directly."

The man brought out the drinks, as well as the pen and parchment. I gulped down the lemonade in a way that was most unladylike, but did it really matter? Kaiden was learning all my foibles, and I didn't really mind if the barkeep found me unladylike. I was thirsty.

I wrote a note to my friends and addressed it to WACK, not knowing who would be home when the messenger got there. I gave enough details to let them know we were fine but needed help to get out of town, if possible. And, if it couldn't be arranged to get here today, to bring with them at least some toiletries so I could freshen up tomorrow before heading back. I then moved on to my note to Colin, letting him know that the brakes had been tampered with and where the carriage was. I included in the missive that we would be in town until we had other transportation back.

I gave the letters to Kaiden, who took them to the barkeep. I saw a younger and somewhat slimmer version of the barkeep come in. He looked quite capable, as long as he didn't dilly dally along the way. I really hoped we could be back to Grantabridge tonight. Although that seemed highly unlikely. Might as well make the best of our stay here, even if it was longer than expected.

It wasn't long before young Howie was on his way. I watched him leave and turned to the barkeep.

"Good sir, I was wondering if you could answer some questions?" I asked, trying to sound as sweet and unimposing as I could.

"Of course, Miss. How ken I help ye?"

"I have some friends that want to come out here and explore, but they heard about the highwayman attack, and some refuse to join because they are afraid. Which is such a pity. I was wondering if you see a lot of crime on the road regularly?"

"Bullocks no, excuse me Miss, the poor man that was killed shouldna had a worry in his head. Other than his death, it's been ages since we have seen crime like that. I dinna know what that highwayman be about. The road is rarely busy. What are your friends planning to do out this way? It's not the most exciting of places."

"Oh, I couldn't tell you. One of them just got it in her head that we needed to come out this way, and the rest of us are always up for exploring, for the most part."

Kaiden settled our tab with the barkeep, and I thanked him for his information as we left. Exiting the tavern was an abrupt reminder that it was still daytime. I could barely keep my eyes open. The sun was so bright. It also caused my head to pound even more. Thankfully, my eyes adjusted, and the pounding subsided to the dull ache I'd felt all day. I looked over at Kaiden; he was watching me.

"Yes?" I asked.

"Where would you like to start? After all, this is your investigation."

I looked at him, trying to judge if he was being kind and letting me lead or if he thought we were wasting our time. I decided to assume the former because it made for a more pleasant day.

"I would think the inn would have the most information if we want to be direct. Or we can just casually go shop by shop and see what they know. I kinda like the latter since we aren't in a hurry at this point. I'm guessing we have at least four hours before we hear back from Howie."

Kaiden nodded, and he offered me his arm. We walked from store to store. Each one we entered, I would make a show of looking for some item or another, depending on the shop. I would direct the conversation to the roads and my friends' fear of highwaymen. And every shop owner said the same thing. There hadn't been a highwayman on this road for decades. They were all shocked and heartbroken over what happened to Edmund Fremont. They hoped my friends and I would come out this way because nothing exciting ever happened. It would be nice to see some young people enjoying themselves. I would thank them, and we would move on to the next shop.

"Kaiden, how far from town was your brother killed? Maybe we should go check that out before it gets dark," I said.

"If I remember correctly, it really wasn't that far, just around that curve in the road I believe."

"Let's go have a look, then. We've exhausted all the shops."

"Let's stop at the tavern first to see if Howie has returned yet, so we can plan on being back at a certain time if necessary."

"Good idea, Kaiden, are you always this intelligent?"

"I try to be, whether I succeed is a completely different story." He shrugged.

Howie had, in fact, just returned from Grantabridge. He handed Kaiden the return missives, who, in turn, handed them to me. I watched Kaiden slip Howie a coin. I read the messages.

Colin could not get a wagon today to carry back the carriage. He could arrange something for tomorrow. He apologized for the delay and wished both Kaiden and me well. Georgi's response was quite similar. She was going to have to rent a horse and carriage and could not make the arrangements today but would be out first thing in the morning. She suggested I use my time alone with Kaiden wisely, which she underlined three times. I rolled my eyes at her not-so-subtle matchmaking scheme.

"Well, Kaiden, it appears we need some rooms for tonight. Our friends cannot make it out until the morning. You would think that there was a shortage of horses in Grantabridge at the moment with their inability to retrieve us today."

"Let's make the best of it, then. Ready to go to the crime scene?"

* * *

Since we were stuck in Shirlock for the evening, Kaiden and I took our time walking to the spot where his brother had been killed. I can't imagine it was easy for him to go there, but he wasn't showing any signs of being bothered by it, at least not yet.

Edmund must have been leaving town when he was accosted. I walked by Kaiden's side, my hand in the crook of his arm, leaning on him more than usual. I wouldn't lie. I was getting tired, my head was hurting, and now that I knew I would spend the night here, I wanted to lie down and have a good nap. After visiting the spot where Edmund had been murdered, of course.

My head continued its light pounding, mimicking the pain in my feet. Then my stomach let me know I was past the point of normal hunger. I had almost asked the barkeep if we could take some sandwiches with us, but picnicking where Kaiden's brother died—well, it seemed gauche.

Kaiden stepped to the side as we cleared the top of the hill and entered a beautiful copse of trees. The sunlight filtered through the leaves, lighting the area with beams of afternoon light. It was absolutely stunning, a place you could bring a blanket and a book and relax for a day.

"This is it; this is where my brother died," Kaiden said.

I mentally slapped myself for my earlier thoughts, but a place this calming shouldn't have bad things happen here. It wasn't right.

"Are you okay?" I asked, trying to see if I could read his mood or not. The answer was apparently not: Kaiden was displaying all the signs of typical Brythionite stiff upper lip. And was rather closed off at the moment. Not that I could blame him. I placed my hand on his shoulder for a moment, trying to give him some sense of comfort. Then I explored.

I knew the sheriff had been over the location after Edmund's death, but I wasn't too impressed with police work after my interactions with Detective Inspector Radcliffe, so I was happy to look for myself even if it was months later.

I started by standing in the middle of the road, where I imagined the carriage would have been stopped. Edmund would have wondered what was happening and, at the very least, looked out to see what was going on.

I looked around and on the side of the road was a fallen tree. I could envision the tree blocking the road and the carriage coming to a stop. Then Edmund asking the coachman what was wrong, learning about the fallen tree, and then getting out of the carriage to help his coachman move it.

"Kaiden, would your brother have helped if a tree was blocking the road?" I asked.

"Of course, he would have only had a coachman with him, and he wouldn't have left the work to just one person."

"Thank you."

I went over to the tree and noted that it appeared to be cut down, at least partially, which made sense with my theory that this was a trap. So now Edmund was out of the carriage and unprotected. The highwayman would appear and order Edmund to do something. I can't believe Edmund would value money or valuables over his life. This implied that Edmund was meant to die from the beginning.

How sad, just a young man trying to get home to his family, cut down in his prime. This really seemed like something out of a gothic novel, if you stopped and thought about it. It made me think the highwayman was not a professional. They had left too much mess behind. The tree itself was still here, with a clear indication that it had been cut down, which was enough to determine this was a trap.

An amateur would have rushed off, maybe left something else behind. I started looking at each tree and bush. The trees had a rough bark that might have grabbed on the clothing of the highwayman. I was methodical in my search, looking for any answers. I felt like I was wasting my time and putting Kaiden through this uncomfortable situation for no apparent reason. That's when I saw the scrap of fabric.

"Kaiden, come here, look at this," I called him over to me.

The fabric had two *S*'s intertwined around a sword embroidered on it. I'd seen that exact pattern before on the journals that Marcus's father had left him. The fabric itself was a faded crimson, and it was stiff and dirty. But it was recognizable. It seemed illogical to think the fabric was here after all these months. But this wasn't a commonly used road, so it was possible.

"That's the Shadowed Sword fabric. The members all have waistcoats made of that fabric, and most of us have a greatcoat lined with it. What is a scrap of it doing out here?"

"I think you know why it's here, even if you don't want to admit it. I'm certain someone at the Shadowed Sword is behind everything that's been happening. All the thefts at my dormitory, the murders, everything."

"I just can't imagine anyone in that group getting their hands dirty, much less killing someone. And why kill my brother? He was such a dedicated member," Kaiden said.

"I honestly don't know. And I don't think there are any more answers to be found here. Let's go to the inn, see if we can get some food and a room. It's been a long day. I mean, someone did try to kill us today—well, at least you—they had no way of knowing I would be in the steam carriage with you."

Kaiden looked at me sharply, raising one eyebrow. "You know, Pippa, you're right. I didn't even think of that."

"Why would anyone want to kill you?" I asked, really just

thinking out loud.

“I do not know, but it is something to think about, isn’t it?”

From there, I walked back to town, Kaiden by my side, in silence. Thinking about why anyone would want Kaiden dead. Especially someone at the Shadowed Sword. It made no sense at all. He had just been trying to figure out what happened to his brother, but not aggressively. And then he had been spending time with me. Part of me thought that would probably put him on someone’s target list more than anything he did on his own.

Chapter Twenty-Six

It didn't take us long to walk back to town and find the inn. Once again, ever the gentleman, Kaiden held the door open for me, then followed me in. He approached a tall, lanky man with silver hair standing behind a small desk.

"Hello, good sir, I was wondering if you had two rooms available for tonight."

"I'm so sorry. We only have one room available right now. Our other room has a leaky roof and we haven't needed to fix it yet," the innkeeper said.

"We will have to make do with one room." Kaiden looked over at me, concerned. I just shrugged my shoulders, dismissing the obvious problem.

"Is there any way we can have some meat and cheeses sent up to the room?" Kaiden asked.

"Of course, I'll see to it right away. Here's the key to your room Mr. . . ."

"Wilson, and this is my wife, Mrs. Wilson." I walked forward as he introduced me but kept my mouth shut.

"Of course, Mr. Wilson, your room will be at the top of the stairs to the right. I hope you find everything to your liking." The innkeeper was too professional to question our story, but I doubted he believed us.

"Thank you, I'm sure that we will," Kaiden said.

Kaiden let me lead the way up the stairs. He unlocked the door, and I walked into a room that had one bed with a clean but worn and faded quilt on it. A small table with two small chairs sat in the corner, and an imposing fireplace took over the small space. There was a small water closet on the wall opposite the fireplace. Thankfully, everything looked quite clean, but there was the issue of only one bed for the night and what we were going to do about it.

"Pippa—" Kaiden was interrupted by a knocking on the door. I answered it. A young maid was there with a giant plate of food.

"Your food, Missus."

"Please put it on the table." I gestured to the small dining area in the room's corner.

"Is there anything else you need?" the young maid said.

"Not at the moment. I will call down if we need anything else." I shut the door behind the young maid, turning back to look at the room and Kaiden. "We should eat. It's been quite a long day, and I don't know about you, but I'm starving." With that, I sat down at the table and prepared myself a plate.

The fare was simple, some ham and cold beef, a hard cheese which was both nutty and salty in flavor, and just a bit of bread. Thankfully, the young maid had also brought up something to drink with our meal. It smelled like a spiced wine of sorts. I would have loved a cup of tea right now, but I didn't really want to call for the maid or anyone else to bring it to me.

Kaiden eventually sat with me at the table and made himself a plate. I could tell he was uncomfortable with our current situation, but really, what was he supposed to do about it? I was about to tell him just that.

"Pippa, I'm sorry, I assumed the inn would have more than one room."

"It's not like the fact we are here is your fault. Did you cut the brakes to your steam carriage so we would have to stay the night? Did you even plan the trip out here at all? I'll hazard a guess and say the answer to both of those questions are no. In fact, I'm the one that convinced you to come out here with me."

"So, what I'm hearing is you planned this all to get me into a compromising position?" Kaiden said, his dimple just peeking out with his slight smile.

"That's not at all what I was implying and you know it." I rolled my eyes at him.

"This definitely could have been an evil plot you planned out last night. Trying to ruin me, I see." He was definitely laughing now.

"I'm sure your reputation can handle it, my lord."

"It probably could, but I'll sleep on the floor tonight. You can have the bed."

"That's nonsense. We can both sleep in the bed without any shenanigans happening. It is plenty big enough. If necessary, you can sleep on top of the covers and I'll sleep underneath," I said. I could not see any reason for one of us to sacrifice the comfort of the bed, even if the bed did look rather lumpy, to sleep on the floor. We were both adults, which I guessed was actually part of the problem.

"I don't know, Pippa, are you sure you can keep your hands to yourself?" His smile implied he didn't want me to keep my hands to myself, and I had to admit, at least to myself, I really didn't want to. But that was a worry for a little later. As for now, I needed to find another way to occupy myself. One that did not involve thinking of undressing in the same room as Kaiden so I could actually sleep.

Drat, that last thought did it. I felt my cheeks heating up, which meant my blush was about the color of my hair.

"Are you overheated, Pippa? I can open a window," Kaiden said.

"Yes please, an open window would be wonderfully refreshing," I said, even though I knew I was not overwarm from the temperature of the room, more like the warmth of my thoughts.

I stood there looking out the window for a moment; I felt

the warmth of Kaiden's body settle behind me. He didn't touch me, but I was pretty sure that I wanted him to. Although even that was outside comfortable thoughts for me, I leaned back anyway until my back came into contact with his muscular chest. Nothing happened for a second, and I almost moved away. Before I did, Kaiden's arms wrapped around my waist, holding me there. It was somehow both scandalous and comforting to stand there like this, and I wanted to see where else this would go if I let it, if it would go any further at all.

I didn't know if I should talk or not, but I really didn't know how to stay silent. "Was it hard to go to the spot where your brother died?" I asked. I felt Kaiden stiffen behind me, and I wanted to kick myself. Why ask such a sad question? Kaiden didn't move away, though, and after a moment, his body relaxed.

"It wasn't pleasant, but it wasn't awful. I think the hardest part was that spot doesn't look sad or scary, or however a spot where someone was murdered is supposed to look. It looked like we could have found fairies peeking around trees, ready to use magic on us. Which is way too whimsical of a spot for my brother to have been murdered."

"I hadn't thought of it that way. I felt bad when I was there, because part of me wished we had a picnic with us. But that felt morbid when I remembered where we were."

"It wasn't morbid. It was a lovely spot that just happened to evoke personal tragedy for me. I doubt I'll want to go there again. Being there did reaffirm my decision to run for president of the Shadowed Sword, though. Edmund would have wanted me to carry on with the changes he was trying to make."

"You're going to run for president? Does Simon know?" I said, tension creeping up my spine.

"I don't think so, at least not yet. I've only mentioned it to a few of Edmund's mates."

"Promise me you'll be careful. I don't want anything to happen to you, especially after today."

"I will. This is something that needs to be done. Seeing where Edmund's life was cut down just confirmed it. It also made me wish my brother was still around. Which that feeling isn't abnormal, but it was stronger today than normal. In some ways, it's hard to remember he is truly gone. In other ways it feels all too real."

"Oh Kaiden, I'm so sorry. I didn't think about any of that when I asked, well, told you to come with me today. I was just hoping for your company, because I rather enjoy it."

I turned in his arms to face him. Then realized that we were now touching down the entire length of the front of our bodies. I tilted my head back to look at him. He really did tower over me. I took a step back, but his arms tightened around me. I bit my lower lip and looked at his full lips.

"Pippa, you can't look at me like that if we are going to make it through the night."

"Look at you like what?"

"Like I'm a dessert you would like to devour."

"Are you a dessert I should devour?" I asked, looking into his heavy-lidded eyes.

Instead of answering me, he let out a low moan. One hand found its way to the back of my head, and I felt his fingers tangle in my hair. The arm around my waist pulled me so close it felt like we were one. And then his mouth caressed mine. I had expected something rougher, but I got soft kisses and light nibbles that left me unsatisfied. I heard a whimper and realized it was me. Rising to my tiptoes, I pressed my mouth to his harder, letting my mouth open so our tongues could tangle with each other as they did before. And I wanted them to again. I felt his hand move from my waist to my derrière, which he grabbed and lifted me up in one fluid motion, and at that point all I felt was hardness pressed against me. His mouth pulled away from mine, and he kissed my neck, licking and nibbling until all I felt was heat. Then he was kissing me again, and I was kissing back, my hands wrapped around his neck, tangling in his hair.

And then he stopped. I stood there, thankful for his support, because I'm pretty sure I would have fallen to the floor if it hadn't been there. My breath was coming hard and fast, as was his.

"Pippa, we have to stop," he said.

I just looked at him, pouting. I'm not sure I wanted anything to stop. Even if that was the smart thing to do. Definitely smarter than anything that was going through my head.

"Okay, we can stop if that's what you want to do," I said. I walked into the middle of the room.

"If that's what I want to do? Good god! I don't want to stop, not even close. But I'm trying to be a gentleman and you are not helping me at all."

"Well, I wouldn't want to take advantage of you, Kaiden. It has been a trying day, after all. Why don't you turn around so I can change into, well, I guess, just undress to my chemise to sleep in. I can't imagine sleeping in all these clothes."

"You can't imagine sleeping in all those clothes? Are you trying to kill me?"

"No, not kill you. I don't think I would like that very much. Now turn around." Watching as he turned around, I laughed to myself. I knew I could test the patience of just about anyone, and it seemed Kaiden was not an exception. I just wasn't sure what sort of trouble I was actually getting myself into. But I was pretty sure I was going to enjoy it.

I undid my bodice, shimmied out of my skirts and petticoats, and removed my sports corset. The boots and stockings came off next until all that I was left wearing was a wrinkled mess of a white chemise that only came down to about midthigh. I had just moved the covers to get under them and let Kaiden know I was decent when I heard the floorboards creak, and he was staring right at me with heat in his eyes.

It took him three steps to get to me, and then we were once again standing so close that if I took in a deep breath, our chests would touch. I stood there staring at him, and he was staring right back at me. I didn't breathe because I was not sure what would happen if I broke the spell. Unbidden, my hands roamed up his chest and grabbed his coat, pulling him down to my mouth. He had other ideas, though. He lifted me up until we were face to face and backed me into the wall, my legs wrapped around his waist, and I felt his hardness press into me and liquid heat pooled there, wanting more.

Our mouths crashed together, a mess of lips and teeth and tongues sparring for control, even though I could acknowledge that I actually had no control. His mouth left mine, and my arms went around his neck and into his hair. He bit my neck. Whether I gasped in pain or pleasure, I wasn't sure, but I wanted more. I felt myself try to rub on his hardness as my heels dug into his firm arse, wanting relief, and my instincts were taking over.

I heard him growl lowly once again, and then the wall was no longer behind me and we were falling right onto the bed. He stood back up, tearing off his coat, waistcoat, and cravat. I pushed myself back to the top of the bed. He pulled his shirt over his head and threw it to the floor. His brown skin glistened, his muscles were more defined than a marble statue, and I wanted to touch. So I did. I reached out and lightly caressed his skin over his stomach. He grabbed my hands and pushed them up around his neck. I pouted slightly but then he was over me, kissing me once again. My mouth, my neck, and he moved lower, holding each one of my breasts in his hands as he worshiped them with his mouth. I felt myself squirm and press myself into whatever part of him was touching me, wanting more contact, more sensations. Because it wasn't enough.

That was, until he went lower still. His mouth was suddenly where I had wanted it most, without even knowing it. My hands didn't know where to go, his hair, his back, the pillows. They settled for grabbing the sheets at my side as he slowly and methodically teased where only I had ever touched in secret. His tongue swirled and licked, he sucked, and then I felt his long finger enter me, all while he continued to lavish attention on that one spot that felt so good. His finger moved in and out in the most magnificent repetitive motion until my toes curled, and I saw stars.

Tingling burst through my entire body in waves that I had no control over; it was delicious, and scandalous, and intense—so much more intense than what I could do on my own. And then the waves receded, and Kaiden was there, smiling at me. I didn't know what to say or do, so I burrowed into his arms.

"That was nice," I said, my voice muffled as I talked into

his chest.

"Nice? That's all it was, just nice? I'll have to try harder next time."

"It was actually exquisite. But isn't there more? I mean, are you okay?"

"I'm fine. While there is more, nothing more needs to happen."

Kaiden lay down next to me, and I settled in next to him, lying on his chest while he was on his back. I had no idea how I was going to get any sleep like this, it was so outside anything I had experienced, but today was full of firsts. His arms wrapped around me, holding me in place.

"So much for not touching," I said and drifted off to sleep.

Chapter Twenty-Seven

I woke up so warm and cozy I didn't want to move. And then everything that had happened the night before came rushing back to me. I felt myself blush, not knowing how I was going to look at Kaiden this morning. Which wasn't a problem right now because his arms were still holding me close. I slowly tried to disengage myself so I could get a drink and maybe use the water closet. Instead, I was pulled closer and flipped onto my back.

"I could get used to waking up like this," Kaiden said, and then he leaned down to kiss me. Honestly, I could get used to it too. I mean, who wouldn't want to be woken up with kisses and cuddles in the morning?

I returned his kisses with fervor, pressing my body into his and wrapping my legs around him. It felt so natural, but I also wondered if I was going about things the right way. Always the academic.

As suddenly as Kaiden was kissing me, he was up and out of bed. He smiled at me and walked right to the water closet. While I appreciated the way the muscles in his back moved as he walked away, I did not appreciate that he had made it there first by distracting me. I got out of bed as well. No use staying if it wasn't the comfy cocoon I woke up to. I poured a glass of water and tried to rinse my mouth as best I could before actually drinking the water; I was thoroughly parched.

It was only when Kaiden came back into the room that I realized I had done nothing to get dressed. I was still in my chemise, which showed more skin than I was used to showing, that's for sure. I would have been embarrassed, but I could see appreciation in his eyes. So instead, I sauntered by him to the water closet. How an inn this small had indoor plumbing, I didn't know, but I was quite thankful for it.

I left the water closet after taking care of my morning needs. Kaiden was lounging on the bed, still shirtless. I was thinking of last night and I felt my face heat up as I stared at his bare skin.

"Are you overheated again, or just thinking naughty thoughts?" Kaiden asked. He sat up, his bare feet resting on the floor. I had never really thought much of feet, but I'm pretty sure there is a wide variety of attractiveness, and his were not unattractive. His bare feet also felt more intimate than if he had shoes on. I have no reason for that feeling, but it was there.

He must have approached me as I was thinking of the fact his feet were bare because the next thing I knew, his fingers were under my chin, tilting it up towards him.

"So Pippa, are you thinking naughty thoughts?" he asked me again. Before I could answer, his lips were on mine. I gasped, and he took advantage of the slight opening of my mouth to plunder it. I matched him with some plundering of my own, throwing my head back, gasping for breath. This just convinced Kaiden other parts of my body need kissing, like my shoulder, my neck, my ear. I felt his hand move lower, touching me there, then parting me, swiping a finger over my sensitive nub, and pressing inside me in one smooth motion. Moaning at the sheer pleasure in that moment, I went to undo his pants, but he moved my hands around his neck. I thought I heard him mutter, "Not yet," but I wasn't sure. His finger, joined by a second, slid into me again. I felt my knees give out at the sensations that ran through my body. I wrapped my legs around him, and his free arm held me tight as I rode his hand to bliss. When it came, I shook from pleasure. I heard Kaiden groan. I wanted to ask if he was okay, but there was no way thoughts could make it from my brain to my lips.

I clung to him, mimicking his kisses, kissing his neck and ear until I fell onto the bed, taking him with me.

"Are you sure?" he asked. All I could do was nod yes.

Kaiden pushed his half-buttoned pants off his hips and kissed me once again. I felt the tension build, then felt something other than his finger press against me, then slowly push inside me. Gasping partially in pain, partially in pleasure, I felt my body adjust to the size of him. I wiggled underneath him as he slid all the way in. He pressed on my hips to stop my wiggle, trying to slow everything down. It might have worked, but I grabbed his head and kissed him, thrusting my tongue into his mouth and tangling with his over and over again. His willpower broke, and he was thrusting inside me hard and fast in a rhythm my body naturally recognized and matched until the sensation that had been building in me burst and Kaiden thrust one more time, muffling his yells of pleasure in my neck. We panted in unison until he rolled over to his side, taking me with him and wrapping his arms around me.

"Well, that was . . ."

"If you say nice, I'm going to think you didn't enjoy yourself, then have to try to prove to you, you did, and I'm just not sure we have time for that."

"I was going to say unexpected. But it was also nice," I said, pushing myself out of the bed. Kaiden growled and tried to drag me back into bed, but I was quicker. I couldn't resist sticking my tongue out, as I felt like I had won this battle.

I grabbed my sports corset and clothes from yesterday and put them on, wishing I had my leather leggings and teal blouse instead of all these layers of skirts. I was putting on the corset when I looked up to see Kaiden watching me; I raised an eyebrow at him.

"You don't wear a full corset?" he asked.

"No, I designed this when I took up fencing with my

brother. Much easier to move in. Since then, I have found it way more practical for day-to-day life. Have I sufficiently scandalized you?"

"No, it's just that you are so tiny, like a wood sprite or water nymph."

"Are you comparing me to fairies, Kaiden?"

"No—yes, I mean . . . You are just so petite and so capable. While one really has nothing to do with the other, most people would probably underestimate you because you appear quite dainty, and almost fragile."

"I hope you know that isn't the case. I don't need you to turn into some overprotective alpha male on me. You know it won't go well."

"Of course not, I watched you jump from a moving vehicle yesterday and come away unscathed. I was just surprised that's all."

"After all you've seen, you're surprised? Not very observant, are you?"

"I was busy observing other things, like the sound you make when I . . ."

Saved by a knock on the door. I answered it before Kaiden could say anything else and make me turn redder than I was afraid I already was. The young maid from last night was there.

"Yes?" I said.

"There are two people downstairs to see you. They said you were expecting them."

"Yes, thank you. Can you tell them we will be down shortly—Actually if you can send the lady in the pair up, that would be quite helpful. I need a little help with my dress."

The maid nodded and headed down the stairs.

"You should head down too, Kaiden. And open the window. It's warm in here and I have a lot of layers to put on."

"It's not that warm, you're probably just overheated from morning exertions," Kaiden said, and then he winked at me as he tightened his cravat and headed out the door.

I took a moment to compose myself and tried to decide if I wanted to put the skirts on myself and then twist them into place when I heard a light tap on the door.

"Pippa, the m-m-m-maid said you needed help," Willa said through the door.

"Yes, Willa, please come in and help me get all these infernal layers on."

Willa opened the door, and she was looking quite delightful in her light lavender gown. Her hair was windswept and her cheeks flushed. It must have been a pleasant drive out.

"Oh Willa, you look lovely this morning. Help me get these skirts on. I'm afraid they are a bit worse for wear, but there's nothing to do about it."

"Actually, Georgi packed a bag for you, said you would be more comfortable in these." Willa handed me a bag. I opened it to find my leather leggings, my teal blouse, and my wide leather belt. I squealed with delight, throwing my arms around Willa.

"This is fantastic. I did not want to put on those soiled clothes. Hopefully, we can squish them into that bag."

I quickly threw on my clothes while Willa, ever the perfectionist, folded each item of my rumpled carriage dress and pushed them into the bag. I braided my hair and in moments, we were heading down the stairs. I almost skipped into the dining room. I was so happy to have not only a change of clothes but ones that were most definitely me. It took but a moment to see Colin and Kaiden sitting together. I hoped Kaiden was over the thought that Colin had cut the brakes. I assumed he was because they appeared to be getting along.

"I see you found a change of clothes, Pippa," Kaiden said.

"Don't be jealous just because my friends know where my clothes live and could pack them."

"You look stunning as always, and quite refreshed," Kaiden said.

"If you think she looks stunning in that, you must be quite besotted," Colin said.

"That I am, Colin, that I am."

* * *

The four of us piled into the carriage; Colin and Willa sat next to each other, going backward. Which was fine by me. I hated traveling backward and avoided it whenever I could. Kaiden sat next to me, filling the space in a way I hadn't noticed before. I felt his leg press against mine, and he didn't make any motion to move away when we touched. Since I was in my leggings, there was no hiding that we were touching. I saw both Willa and Colin note it, not that either of them would say anything.

"A friend of mine is driving your steam carriage back to Grantabridge. We just hooked up some horses to it and told them to get it back to the shop. I should have the brakes fixed in a couple of days if all goes well," Colin said.

"Do you have any idea who could have tampered with it?" I asked.

"I'm sorry to say, but it could have been almost anyone. The last couple of days, almost everyone from the Shadowed Sword has come in to see if I could build them a steam carriage. I even had someone that came in wanting a dirigible," Colin said.

"Oh my, a dirigible! Are you taking them on as a client? Can I help build it? Wait, I need to stay on task. Someone tried to kill us. Figure that out first, then build a dirigible," I said, mostly to myself. "Have you seen Professor Gates at all recently?" I asked, even though I probably could have guessed the answer.

"Professor Gates, no. He isn't interested in steam engineering or that type of scientific progress at all. He's well known around town for his belief that steam power is a passing phase," Colin said.

"I guess that confirms our earlier theory that he didn't kill Professor Aneurin," Kaiden said.

He took my hand and weaved his fingers through mine. I tried to catch his gaze, but he did not look at me. He was either ignoring me on purpose or did not realize what he was doing in front of people.

"I'm sure it's someone at the Shadowed Sword. All the evidence that we had at the dorm that pointed to them was stolen: the poisoned whiskey snifter and the journals. Now, everyone suddenly wants new modern transportation, starting with Lord Middleton. It is highly suspicious. I'm sure it's one of them," I said.

"I just d-d-d-don't understand why any one of them would feel the need to kill somebody," Willa said. "I mean, all the members are wealthy and titled. Don't they have more to lose if they get c-c-c-caught than they have to gain?"

"That's where I'm stuck. Not that you need a motive to kill, but it sure makes more sense if you do. And what good did killing the professor do? Who stood to gain with him gone?"

I watched the scenery pass as I thought about my question. Who benefited from the professor's death? It seemed like no one did. But that couldn't be the case. There had to be something that I was missing, some connection between Edmund and the professor.

"Kaiden, did Edmund and the professor have anything in common?" I asked. At this point, I had accepted that my friends would leave feeling slightly scandalized. Besides, it was nice just to sit and hold hands with someone. It was rather comforting. Of course, that's why I didn't pull my hand away.

It seemed strange, but I was both shaken and kept forgetting that someone had tried to kill us yesterday. In the span of a day, so much had happened, and nothing was resolved. I felt discombobulated and also peaceful. My mental state seemed to war between the two. And the physical contact of holding hands was centering.

"Let's see, they both fought to have women admitted into the University, and were disappointed when they wouldn't let you sit for exams. Then, I think they were both on a committee that was trying to organize lessons for talented commoners. And it seems they both had some connection to the Shadowed Sword. Edmund was a member, as was the professor's father."

"Do you think *both* deaths could have been political in nature? Sounds like both had beliefs that threatened the titled class's superiority."

I almost dismissed the theory before anyone could comment because it seemed so silly. Who would care about social standing enough to kill someone?

"As ridiculous as that sounds, it could be the motive behind everything," Colin said.

I was shocked anyone would agree with me. Such a petty reason to do anything, especially to take two people's lives as if they didn't matter at all.

"That w-w-w-would be so sad. The loss of life over something so unimportant, something that's always fluctuating. What a waste," Willa said.

"I think you summed that up rather nicely, Willa. What an absolute waste," I said.

* * *

It wasn't long before we were back in Grantabridge. The carriage dropped Willa and me off first at our dormitory before taking Colin and Kaiden to their respective homes. Kaiden at least needed a change of clothes after our adventures of the day before, and Colin, well, I'm sure he had actual work to get done.

"Your friend C-C-C-Colin seems quite the gentleman, and h-h-h-he is handsome in an unusual way," Willa said, blushing slightly. I was jealous of how lovely she looked when she blushed. It was a shame I couldn't learn that skill.

"That he is. I've known him since we were children. He's like a brother to me. He's always been very nice. I'm glad he could come help us with the steam carriage. I didn't know how we were going to get it back here."

"It's nice to have friends you can d-d-d-depend on. I've never really had friends I could count on being there for me. It's been so eye opening coming here and meeting you and the others. I've n-n-n-never felt as accepted as I do here."

Without thinking, I pulled Willa into my arms and gave her a big hug.

"Oh my goodness, Willa, you know I absolutely adore you. I mean, who else would give up a morning to save me from myself. Not to mention how intelligent you are, and you're such a gentle soul. I'm pretty sure you're the best out of all of us. I know for a fact you're better than me."

"Oh P-P-P-Pippa, you're going to make me cr-cr-cr-cry, and then I would just be a sappy fool."

"You could never be a fool. And that's why you should sit

down with me and help me plan breaking into the Shadowed Sword. They have to have information there. I'm sure they are part of the murders."

"Why don't you ask K-K-K-Kaiden for help?" Willa asked.

"I'm pretty sure he would say no. And even if he said okay, I don't want him to get in trouble. He is already a member and I wouldn't want him to get in trouble because of me. Which you know is likely. It seems like trouble follows me around, especially lately."

"That is true, I hadn't quite thought of it l-l-l-like that, but it does make sense." Willa nodded in agreement. "But, I think you should let him decide."

"Maybe you're right, Willa. I will think on it," I said. "Here's what I need before I can do this. And some of it I should already know. So, first I need to find the location of the Shadowed Sword. It's one of the only kept secrets about the so-called secret society. Then I need to figure out how to get in. I wish I had lock-picking skills. Then it's just finding the information that I don't even know is there or not, and getting it out without getting caught. No problem, right?" I asked sarcastically.

"We should get Georgi and Mads d-d-d-down here. Maybe one of them has the skills you need to get in. I d-d-d-don't think you should break in at all, but I don't think any of us are good at doing what we should. So I will not be the one that actually stops you. I also think you should contact Kaiden to at least figure out the location."

I knew I should get Kaiden's help, but it seemed so dishonest to get the information and not tell him what I was going to do with it, especially after everything that happened between us recently. I didn't want to cause any sorta rift. But Willa was right. This would go so much smoother with his help.

"You're right, Willa, I'll send a note over to him in a few minutes. Let's get the rest of WACK down here and start planning in earnest."

It took a few minutes to get Georgi and Mads down in the parlor, so I sent Hannah off with a message for Kaiden. Hopefully, he wouldn't be too mad.

"Okay Pippa, what's your plan?" Georgi asked as she breezed into the room.

"It's better to ask, What crazy thing does Pippa want to do now?" Mads asked.

"I think Mads is more accurate at this point. My plan is to break into the Shadowed Sword. I'm sure I'll find more evidence to tie them to these murders, but I need to search it, which means knowing where it is and being able to get in. As much as of a snoop I am, I've limited myself to eavesdropping in the past; actual breaking and entering is not in my skill set," I said.

"Definitely a madcap idea, but I'm not surprised in the least. I can help you with some lock picking," Mads said.

"I don't want anyone else to go with me in case I get caught," I said. "But do you think you can teach me the basics?"

"Of course, but I'll go with you until you are inside. We could keep watch at the very least," Mads said.

"Did you message Kaiden? He should tell you where the Shadowed Sword is," Georgi asked.

"I did, but I'm worried that it will upset him when he realizes what I want the information for. If I tell him, he will try to stop me."

"Of course he's going to try to stop you, or go with you. Which is why you need to tell him we are helping you out, so he has some comfort for your safety. Or you could let him come with us. He would be an incredible asset," Georgi said.

I looked around the room at each one of my friends and realized I really didn't need to do this on my own. Each one of these women knew what was at risk and could decide for themselves if it was worth the risk. I didn't need to decide for them. Just like I didn't need to decide for Kaiden.

"Okay, if we are going to do this, we need a coherent plan. We all need to know the risks, and if it's not worth it, I understand. This is really my mission, and I don't want to drag anyone else down with me," I said.

"Haven't you figured it out yet, Pippa? Your mission is our mission. We are in this together," Mads said.

With that statement, we all got to work on planning, researching, and learning. We knew it would not be easy to get into the Shadowed Sword unnoticed.

Chapter Twenty-Eight

The location of the Shadowed Sword was so obvious once you knew it was there. I walked up to the old brick buildings on the edge of Grantabridge. These were some of the oldest buildings in town. At one point, these buildings were all that existed of the University, which now sprawled throughout the town. But these buildings, with their arched halls, ivy-covered brick walls, and winding staircases, were where it had all started so long ago.

I looked for the arched wooden door that Kaiden had described to me. Finding it, I motioned to my friends it was just up ahead. Mads went ahead since she was still more skilled than I was at picking locks. I intended to practice though; it just seemed like a handy skill to have. And it went hand in hand with my penchant for eavesdropping.

It wasn't long before Mads had the door open. I walked through the hall along with Georgi and Mads. Willa was going to watch the door and signal to us if anyone showed up. I have to say our bird call practice the other day was probably the most humorous of our preparations for today's break-in. I was worried wc wouldn't be able to hear her warning once inside, but better to have someone there than not was the consensus last night.

The three of us made our way through the corridors of the

building, following the directions Kaiden had given us. Those directions led us to a great room. The walls were all stone, as opposed to the brick of the building. In the center of one wall was the society's motto, Seek Knowledge, and taking up the rest of the wall space were different swords, one right on top of another. Some were crossed, indicating that they were a set of dueling swords, like rapiers and foils. The weaponry made it an intimidating room. It wasn't every day you walked into an armory. Really, why did a group seeking knowledge need so many swords? It was a bit of overkill, if you asked me.

The room was large enough to have multiple sections. Closest to the sword wall and motto was an altar, for lack of a better word. Of course, this had me imagining all sorts of gruesome ceremonies. I really hoped my mind was more imaginative than this group of men. Surrounding the altar were wooden benches, with tall torches on either side of each bench. I mean, seriously, who wouldn't picture hooded figures standing around a body, drawing symbols around him, preparing for a sacrifice. Just me? Okay then.

Towards the back of the room there was a row of desks. And behind those was an enormous number of bookshelves filled with books. They were glorious. If it wasn't for my investigation, I probably would have curled up in one of the leather chairs and just started reading, waiting for someone to come bring me back to real life. With all this at your fingertips, how could you not?

"Where do you want to look?" Georgi asked.

"I suggest the offices down the hall," Kaiden said, walking out from behind the corner.

Hearing his masculine baritone, I nearly jumped out of my skin. I wasn't the only one either. Both Georgi and Mads gasped, grabbing each other's hands as Kaiden entered the room.

"Bloody hell, Kaiden! You scared me near to death," I said, swatting at him with annoyance. And deeply relieved it was him, and not another member of the society.

"Did you really think I was going to let you break in here and not help? I thought we understood each other better than that."

Kaiden shook his head, disappointment clearly reflected on his face.

"You're the one that is trying to take over this place, so yes, I thought you would think of that and let us handle it," I sputtered.

"No use arguing. He's here, and will be of tremendous help. Kaiden and Pippa, you go to the right. Georgi and I will go to the left," Mads said, stepping in before things got out of hand.

Kaiden led us to the hall. I went right with Kaiden, Georgi and Mads went left.

"Bird call or scream if anything happens," Mads said.

"Same to you," I responded.

I walked down the hallway, surrounded by more grey stone, Kaiden prowling behind me. When I was done here, the inside of my home would be so brightly colored, not a grey stone would be in sight. Everything around me here just seemed grey. And I loved grey, but it needs some contrast to make things feel alive, and that was just lacking. Because it was lacking, everything felt so melancholy.

Eventually, I came to a room with two doors instead of just one. This seemed like a good place to start. A room that claimed by the size of its entrance that it was important, at least more important than those other rooms. I tried the doors, and they were locked, so I tried my hand at lock picking. It took a few tries, but I was eventually successful. I walked into the room, Kaiden still behind me.

The inside of the room was pleasantly surprising. It was like it had heard my inner monologue. The walls were covered with either bookshelves or a brilliantly green paint. While there was an accent stone wall, it wasn't the only thing around, which made the room seem much more inviting and cozy. It wasn't until I was looking at a pile of papers on the desk that I realized I was in Edmund Fremont's office.

I looked over at Kaiden, unsure what to do. This was his brother's domain here at the Shadowed Sword. Had Kaiden been inside? Did he know the lock I was picking would lead into this room?

"Where should I start?" I asked.

"Edmund always kept what he was currently engaged with on top of his desk. I would start there if I were you," Kaiden said, walking to look out the large window.

"Are you okay?" I asked, concern lacing through my words.

"Just do what you need to do, Pippa. I don't want you caught here." Kaiden's clipped tone told me all that I needed to know.

I sat down in the oversized leather chair behind the desk and just took a moment to see what Edmund would see every time he sat in this seat. In front of the desk were two smaller, but still comfortable, chairs, suggesting this man liked to have company. He wanted them to feel as comfortable as possible. There were two walls of bookshelves, one I had noted as I walked in that was now directly behind me, and one now directly in front of me on either side of the double doors. To my right was a large window with an amazing view of a park and the Granta river. On the wall across from the window was a lovely landscape. None of that super masculine hunting-party paintings, just a lovely country landscape with a river that mimicked his view outside the window. It might have even been a painting of the Granta river. There was a settee under the painting with a side table and a light, which made me think he had spent plenty of time there reading. The room itself gave off the impression of an intelligent and welcoming human.

I stood and looked through the papers on his desk. It felt wrong, invasive. Despite the guilt I was feeling, I continued to snoop. I found a pile of papers towards the back of the desk. Some of it seemed quite innocuous. It looked like Edmund was a treasurer of sorts for the Shadowed Sword. He had numbers on the cost of maintaining the space, food and drinks, custom clothes and journals, along with how much membership dues were and how often they were due. It looked like the Shadowed Sword was hurting a bit for money, which seemed odd for a society of the elite. Typical, though willing to spend their money on frivolous things, but never willing to spend money on what is necessary, like keeping a club running if that was indeed their desire.

The next stack of papers looked way more interesting than something as important as budgeting. This stack was arguments and research on who should be allowed to attend the University. I paged through the papers but soon curled my legs underneath me, making myself comfortable as I read through all of Edmund's notes and theories. He wanted so much more for the University and those of us that had been admitted. Honestly, what he wanted made sense, at least to me. His notes indicated it was his wish that the women admitted be full-fledged students, able to sit for exams, not stopped at studying alone, but actually able to boast a degree from the University.

Edmund had also been pushing to let tradesmen into the University, according to his notes and research. He was especially interested in letting in men that worked in fields that needed more education, so engineering and certain medical sciences greatly interested him. I was both shocked and not at all surprised at how well thought out his arguments were, at least on paper. In his work, I could see so many reasons Kaiden was the way that he was. Edmund's work showed patience, respect for others, and an overwhelming sense of accepting his fellow mankind.

"Your brother was quite the visionary. Have you read through any of this before?" I asked.

"No, I haven't been in this room. I couldn't when I first arrived. After, I just continued to put it off. I knew I would have to face it eventually, but there wasn't any sense of urgency. Of course, he was a visionary. His visions for the future and the power he would have had makes it that much harder for me to take his place."

"You know, I don't think the two of you were all that different. You are all the things your brother was, and you have the benefit of knowing what it's like not to have the power your brother had, which will go into all the decisions you make once you are a duke." I walked over to Kaiden, wrapping my arms around him, holding him for a moment as he continued to work through his loss. I felt his head rest atop mine. Then, as if we both remembered what was at stake, we stepped away from each other. I continued to go through Edmund's papers with Kaiden's help.

It appeared Edmund had hated the compromise that was made when letting women in. He mentioned in his notes that some women attending might have to give up everything, even being disowned by their families, and auditing university with none of the prestige of attending wasn't enough. Reading his words, I didn't know if I had ever felt more seen by someone I had never even met. He was voicing concerns that regularly went through my mind. I had given up so much, and I would not get any sort of acknowledgment of my accomplishment of finishing courses here. None of the women admitted were going to get any recognition. In fact, in the circles we belonged to, our attending university would even be seen as a negative. Just look at what happened with my mother and my sister when I decided to come to Grantabridge.

* * *

I don't know how long I sat there going through Edmund's notes with Kaiden, but it felt way too long. I hadn't heard anything from anyone, no bird calls or screams. The lack of bird calls or screams seemed like a good sign, and we continued to search his office. Glancing up at Kaiden, I shoved his notes into my bag before moving on. Somebody had to take up the position this man had at the University and try to get others to see things the same way he did. Which means I needed to gather more people to support the expansion of the University. A herculean task for a lady that wasn't even wanted here, but why would I let that stop me? Especially if Kaiden was already interested in stepping into the role his brother had left for him.

I found another stack of papers, and while the last one was interesting because it was all about progressive politics in the world we currently lived in, this one was much more close to home—at least Edmund's home, and Lord Middleton's home. It had to do with the internal politics of the Shadowed Sword.

Turned out, I had a decent understanding of the division in the society. There were those that supported the path that Edmund had been pushing them towards. A surprising number were open to admitting other men, especially those that lacked title but had some social standing because of their work in different fields of study.

Edmund had suggested Professor Aneurin for his alchemy and steam engineering, and there was an archaeologist, Braden MacDougal, on his list. I had never heard of MacDougal, but I didn't know much about archeology. Last on the list, and surprising to me, was Colin. I shouldn't be surprised since Edmund had worked with Colin on the steam carriage, but I was. Edmund clearly recognized great minds, which made me feel pretty good that he had recognized my friends for more than just the skirts we wore.

It appeared Edmund was tired of the official stance of the Shadowed Sword: a stagnant belief system he wanted to change. He had spent the time he had here constantly arguing for progress, and it was his belief that if there was a leadership change at the Shadowed Sword, he could argue for the changes he thought were necessary with the backing of the society, instead of fighting against both the society and the school administration. If he had succeeded in his coup, he would just be fighting against the university officials.

It appeared Edmund had it all planned out. He had been campaigning behind closed doors for a while. The members of the society that supported him and what he believed in were firmly on his side.

"Kaiden, you should look at the list of gentlemen Edmund was talking to regarding his grab for power. They would probably support you if you asked," I said.

"Take it, I'll look at it as soon as I know you are safely out of here."

"Edmund hadn't approached many others before his death. Someone must have found out about his plans and took action against him," I said, looking over at Kaiden. "I wonder if Georgi and Mads found anything?"

"Does that mean you're done?" Kaiden asked.

I gave a quick nod. Kaiden grabbed my bag, now full of papers, and my hand.

Kaiden and I left Edmund's office and made our way back to the split in the hallway. I started checking each room, slightly disheartened every time it was empty. Where had Georgi and Mads gone off to? I got to the end of the hallway, and nothing. I hoped they were back in the entry room with all the swords, or back with Willa.

Thankfully, the sword room wasn't all that far away. It was still creepy with the altar circle and all the swords, but interesting if you liked that ready-to-go-to-battle-at-any-moment look. However, it wasn't really for me. Unfortunately, or maybe fortunately, the room was empty. I still hadn't found Georgi and Mads. Kaiden all but dragged me through the sword room and out the door, giving me no time to express my concerns regarding Georgi and Mads.

Once outside, I noticed for the first time that the sun was setting. Kaiden and I had made it out just in time. He had mentioned to me that the society liked to meet at sundown almost every evening. At least, most of its core members liked to gather daily. I looked around for my friends and was so happy to see them sitting on a blanket laid out on the lawn picturesquely. They looked like three ladies out for an afternoon picnic that had just run a little long. It was a relief to see them out, safe, and at least looking like they didn't have a care in the world.

I did my best not to run right over to them. I didn't think it was wise to draw attention to any of us, but I was bursting to tell them my theories. Once at the blanket, I lowered myself to the ground and looked at them, smiling.

"Sorry it took me so long, but I am certain I know who killed Edmund and the professor. And I think I know why," I said.

"I have to go back to our daily meeting. I'll call tomorrow and we can discuss more," Kaiden said.

"I can't wait. See you tomorrow." I almost stretched up on my tiptoes to give him a kiss goodbye. But I remembered where I was before I did.

Kaiden's eyes locked on mine for a moment before he turned and walked back to the secret society.

"Who do you think it is and why?" Georgie said. "I wonder if it matches with our theories. Since we've had forever to sit out here and think about it."

"Well, let me tell you, I found Edmund's office. And he had plans both for the University and the secret society," I said. "Turns out, Edmund wanted the four of us admitted as actual students, meaning we would get to take exams and get a degree upon finishing. But others in the society fought it, as well as others that run the University. He also proposed to let in tradesmen, especially those at the forefront of technology and innovation. Of course, he completely lost the battle and barely won the one that allowed us to attend here. So, here you have a titled man, future duke, throwing everyone for a loop. And he wasn't succeeding how he wanted to."

"Obviously, I would be surprised if he actually succeeded at much of what he wanted. I mean, we have all met Lord Middleton and Lord Bradbury. Those two alone would put a stop to anything that they saw as a threat to their position in society," Georgi said. "And Lord Bradbury's office, it was just paintings of the hunt, including one that showed the actual kill. Seriously, who wants to look at that for any portion of the day?"

"Ugh, he is truly such a fool. I'm glad I don't have more of an acquaintance with him. What I do know of him is enough to keep me away," I said. "Did you two come across anything indicating that Edmund was trying to take control of the Shadowed Sword? Apparently, the society treated the head of the Shadowed Sword kinda like the position of prime minister. That is, the members elected him. And Edmund had started to campaign against Lord Middleton before he was killed. But it was all behind closed doors; he hadn't announced his intentions."

"I saw some notes on this in a few offices. Some in the code we saw in the journals, some just written out," Mads said. "The names of the men that supported him all made sense. I didn't see anything that indicated Lord Bradbury or Lord Middleton showed any support. I don't even know if they knew about it."

"I'm pretty sure they did. At least Lord Middleton—but before I get to that, the other thing that Edmund wanted was new members added to the society. He had suggested the professor, Colin, and some architect, Braden MacDougal, or was he an archaeologist? It doesn't matter." I waved my hand, dismissing Mr.

MacDougal from my mind. "He was pushing the society at every turn. And I bet you can all guess who didn't like it."

"Lord M-M-M-Middleton," Willa said.

"Exactly, it wasn't that long ago Lord Middleton confronted me, saying I was taking up a man's space here at the University. He hated that the four of us were here studying," I said.

"That's the truth. I think we should head back. Let's walk and talk so it doesn't get too dark on our way home. I would hate for something to happen," Mads said. She was always the practical one of the four of us.

"Do you really think Lord Middleton did it? That seems extreme even for him," Georgi asked.

"I do, but my opinion of him is quite low," I said, standing as I spoke. "At the soirée, he left bruises on my arms after I dared to call him out on what he was saying to me. I think he has a streak of viciousness, and probably turns to violence more often than we would think."

All of our things gathered, the four of us began our walk back to the dormitory, passing through town and over my favorite bridge. It seemed strange to notice those things as we discussed murder, but the bridge was my favorite place in the city. It always stood out to me.

"So, Pippa, you really think Simon Middleton is behind all of this? A well-respected duke." I could tell that Georgi was struggling with the idea of someone with so much deciding to murder anyone.

"Actually, I do. I can see him taking stupidly desperate action to stop Edmund from running against him. Whether it was him personally or he hired someone to do the dirty work is still up in the air. And then the fact that Aneurin supported Edmund on university policies and was a suggested new member to the society. His death might have seemed like a super simple solution," I said.

"Taking a life should never seem like a super simple decision, Pippa," Mads said.

"No, it shouldn't, but if you were raised to believe only a

certain portion of society mattered, then the humanity of the rest of society comes into question. If anyone is seen as less than, is their life even worth protecting? I don't agree with it, but I can see an entitled arse absolutely thinking that way. If you think about it, this could even be the answer to the sabotage we have been experiencing."

"Plus the p-p-p-poison, it's the same that the society keeps on hand," Willa said.

"Oh my gosh, Willa, you're right! They have it in the garden outside and they have dried Wolfsbane throughout the building on out-of-reach shelves. Kaiden was telling us about that when your lab was destroyed."

I strode up the steps to our home and held open the door.

"Ladies, I think we are on to something," I said.

Chapter Twenty-Nine

I spent the night going through everything that I had found out yesterday in my head, and I truly didn't think that there was another interpretation of the evidence. I wished I could go to Detective Inspector Radcliffe with my theories, but that man was in the pocket of Lord Middleton. If Radcliffe wasn't in Middleton's pocket, then he wasn't progressive enough to think a woman could have valuable information. At least, not if it was pointing the finger at someone like a duke and not admitting to killing the person themselves.

The sun was just about to peek above the horizon after a night of tossing and turning when I gave up on sleep and decided to see if going for a ride would help clear my head. I threw on my favorite pair of leggings and teal shirt before putting on my large leather belt that cinched in my shirt, and then I threw on my waist pocket before grabbing my leather helmet and goggles and heading out the door.

I was going through my safety check, because really, if you're going to be doing something dangerous, you should be as safe as possible. It was while I was looking at the brakes to make sure they were intact that I heard a noise. I whipped around to see who it was, but there was no one around. I went back to my bike, assuming that I was just on edge, and it was probably a rabbit or squirrel.

Everything looked good, so I put on my helmet and goggles and dropped the heating stones in. It was just moments before there was steam, and I was off. I loved riding through the country towards the ocean. It was always calming and always helped me reset. It also reminded me of home and the shenanigans Percy and I would get into most days.

I stopped near the beach and just sat there, letting the breeze wrap around me and ruffle through my hair after I removed my helmet. Honestly, I didn't really know what to do from here. I wanted to go to the detective inspector with my information, but after our last encounter, it seemed rather pointless. He didn't even pretend to listen to me the last time I was at the station. Even if the police would listen to me, it would be difficult to get anything done. Simon Middleton was a duke, automatically above the law, and that meant justice was not as far-reaching as it should be. The wealthy and titled seemed to always get away with their crimes, even the crimes that were horrendous.

I rode back to Grantabridge, passing by green hills with stone walls and finally a small forest before I was back at the dorm. I parked the bike and released the steam. Taking my helmet off, I attempted to fluff my bangs, but getting rid of the signs of helmet hair was quite difficult. I grabbed my things and walked back to the dorm. The squirrels were at it again; I turned towards the noise and felt like I had walked into a tree branch. I fell to my knees, grabbing my head in pain. Not again. I was really tired of banging my head. As I tried to get up, a sharp pain cracked over my head, and everything went black.

* * *

My head hurt so badly, but I had no clue why. I tried to open my eyes, but a sharp pain shot through my temple. I went to grab my head, but I couldn't move my arms. Struggling, I opened my eyes; I was definitely not where I last remembered. I was surrounded by grey stone and a ton of swords. Somehow, I was back at the Shadowed Sword, and I was tied to the strange altar that was in the center of the room. Definitely not where I thought I would end up this morning when I went for a ride.

I tested the restraints and discovered both my hands and feet were tied to the altar. If I was careful, I could sit up, thankful for all the training WACK and I had been doing on a regular basis. I was tied down with a pretty thick rope. I figured if I was patient, I would be able to get my hands loose. Only because the rope was pretty darn cumbersome in its thickness and I was pretty petite. I thought I would be able, with some time, to slip my wrist through the prickly restraints. I might even be able to slide my feet out of my boots to get them free if it came down to it, but I would rather keep my boots on in case I needed to do more than sneak out of here.

As I lay there, trying to twist my hand out of the bindings, hoping the wetness I felt was sweat and not blood, I wondered how Lord Middleton had figured out I knew he had been committing these crimes. He had to have found out somehow. Unless he just hated me so much, he decided I needed to be taken care of. Which I wouldn't be surprised if that was the case.

I managed to get my right hand free. Then I started untying my left hand. I heard a noise and lay back down and pretended to be unconscious. Whoever had entered didn't approach me, which was strange to me at least. I mean, I would want to see why someone was tied to an altar, but maybe this was a normal thing here. If that was the case, I definitely should be more afraid of the Shadowed Sword than I currently was. I should probably be more afraid, anyway.

I heard the person leave and resumed struggling with the rope. Untying the ropes around my feet was proving to be a bit of a challenge. It was like I was dealing with some crazy sailor knots that tightened every time I pulled on them. I really didn't think Lord Middleton had that type of skill, but one never really knew the skills of another until they shared. I'm sure I surprised people all the time with my knowledge of all things mechanical.

I almost had the last knot untied when I heard someone else come in. Once again I lay there, pretending I was unconscious.

"I don't like this. Why hasn't she woken up yet. Are you sure she's still alive?" said a man I had never heard before.

"Of course I'm sure. It was just a light tap on the head," Lord Middleton said. "I'm sure she would wake up with some persuasion if you are that concerned though."

I knew that egotistical maniac was behind this. It was all I could do to lie there and not move at the sound of his voice. To think he had actually abducted me. What sort of person abducts another person? Not one worth being around, I could tell you that.

Then, out of nowhere, my nose started to tickle. That feeling a person got when their body had decided that they needed to sneeze at the most inconvenient time. It's the worst, in my opinion at least, because the sneeze is there, and I would do anything to hold it in, knowing that I was going to lose the battle. The question was always, When will I lose? I hoped it was after Lord Middleton and his companion left the room. But there was no telling if that was going to happen or not. I felt my entire body tense because the sneeze was coming, and then that feeling dissipated. I relaxed, which in hindsight was a huge mistake.

"ACHOOOO."

Well, bloody hell.

Chapter Thirty

"Did you hear that?" Lord Middleton asked.

"Hear what?" the strange man said.

"I believe our darling Philippa is actually awake. I heard the most unladylike sneeze come from her general direction."

Bullocks, I knew they were going to hear me, and I wasn't quite free yet. I needed to determine how I wanted to play this, and quickly. I had no doubt that Lord Middleton would kill me with very little, if any, guilt if he thought it was necessary. Bloody hell, he probably already thought it was necessary, and he was planning to sacrifice me to the god of young titled arses.

I was definitely going to pretend to be tied here until I could get my feet untied somehow. Or at least get them out of my boots. No shoes would limit me in some ways, but I could make it work. I just needed more time.

"It's no use pretending, Philippa, I know you're awake," Lord Middleton said.

I lay there contemplating how antagonistic I wanted to be because sass was always in order when tied to an altar like a sacrifice to the gods.

"I didn't know we were on a first-name basis, Simon.

That's very, shall we say, modern of you," I said, looking over at him. It wasn't easy lying on the narrow slab, but I could turn my head to see him and saw his sneer before he smoothed over his features.

"I assumed you weren't big on formalities since you seem to push at all of societal norms, attending university, riding a steam cycle, wearing pants." He sniffed in disdain.

"Is that so? Well, I have to say, you have me all wrong. I think certain formalities are quite nice, and then there are those that don't seem all that necessary. But if you feel we are acquainted enough for first names, I really don't mind. It's quite the privilege to call you Simon. That being said, I must ask. What am I doing here, and tied up? That seems quite inappropriate."

"You know why you are tied up, Philippa," Simon said.

"Actually, Simon, I don't know why I'm tied up here or where I am. If I knew, I wouldn't need to ask you. That tends to be how it works. A person asks questions they don't know the answers to. Why ask questions you know the answers to? That's just wasting everyone's time."

I swear I heard him growl in frustration as he turned away from me. As soon as his back was to me, I started working my foot back and forth, trying to loosen the ropes so my feet could slip through. Every now and then I felt the rope give just a little, giving me hope I would be able to untie myself. Throughout all this, I kept my eyes on Simon as he paced and muttered to himself. This man seemed to be losing it. He was not his usual urbane self. Not even close. He stopped murmuring. I stopped moving. He turned back to me.

"Well, that's quite the conundrum. I assumed you had it all figured out. Which meant you were a loose end that had to be tied up, but if you don't know what was going on, you weren't a loose end, just a meddling girl that hadn't gotten far at all. And I didn't need to get you here to finish you. But now that you are here, you are most definitely a loose end that needs to be taken care of," Simon said.

"I swear, Simon, do you even hear yourself? You aren't making any sense at all. Are you feeling okay?" I asked.

"Of course I'm feeling okay. I just figured you knew what I did and, therefore, needed to be silenced. But apparently, you're just a clueless girl. Which, big surprise. I still don't understand why the University let you in. You have no business being here at all."

"Really, Simon, I think you just need to accept that we are here and not going anywhere. Enough people agreed and thought it was a good idea."

"Accept! That I should just accept a change that is completely unnecessary and frivolous. What's next, I should just accept highborn ladies working? Where would we end up? We would be as savage as those over in Eletharis." Simon paced back and forth. I wouldn't be surprised if he foamed at the mouth, he was so enraged.

I knew I had to keep him talking if I was going to get out of this. Especially since no one knew where I was, so no one could come and save me. I could slip one foot out of the ropes, and I was slowly working on the other as Simon paced.

"Since you won't accept, are you planning on getting rid of us? And how are you going to do that?"

"I hoped your run down dormitory and ancient housekeeper would turn you off, but the very clear indication that you weren't wanted did absolutely nothing. It's like you girls forgot your station. None of you even complained." He threw his hands up in frustration.

"Are you telling me you hoped a rundown home would get us to leave here and the opportunity that going to university could provide us? My parents disowned me when I decided to come here. A bit of shabby living wouldn't put me off."

Simon stopped pacing. I stopped trying to get my left foot free of the ropes.

"You mean Edmund was right?"

"What do you mean, Edmund was right?"

"Just before he left on that fateful trip, he said that he wouldn't be surprised if some of the ladies were disowned when they decided to come here. I didn't believe him. The one thing that you have in this life is your status. Why would you risk it to come here? Now you are left with nothing," Simon said.

"Studying what you love is not nothing. Appreciation for your knowledge and skills, rather than a title you have nothing to do with, is not nothing. I think you've always had the wrong reasons for why women want to attend here. You don't understand what it's like for people to treat you with derision because your interests don't align with what they think your interests should be. So, going somewhere and finding others that have that passion in common with you, and then finding someone that respects the way you think and create, was sublime. And then it was ripped away from me."

"And yet you are still here?"

"Where else would I go at this point? I gave up everything to come here, so I will figure out how to stay."

"Why? The only professor in your area of study is dead. Half the town thinks you murdered him. What is left for you here?"

"I'll admit, I've had those thoughts. Especially right after Professor Aneurin's death. It all felt so hopeless and useless. Like what I had been fighting for had been ripped away from me yet again. But I stopped and thought about it. And here I have acceptance, not just acceptance by others, but I've learned to accept others. I've met a group of peers that have the same interest as me. And that interest isn't steam engineering, it's seeking knowledge. And here I've been able to meet so many people that want to do the same thing. Whether it's the three other ladies that were admitted with me, some of your male counterparts, or some of the serving class. It seems like this place creates a desire to learn and know more about the world and each other. So, why are you here?" I said, acknowledging more about myself than I probably ever had in the past.

"That's not what this place is about," Simon sputtered.

"Are you sure?" I asked.

"All of what you said would upset the balance we have in society. And we cannot have that. It would lead to mass chaos. There's a reason things are done the way they are done, or at least have been done. And everyone trying to change that is going to destroy the pillars that this country rests on. It would hand power to those that don't know what to do with power and take it away from those of us that do. The titled class would go down in a flame of meaninglessness if everyone had access. It has to be stopped. And there are those of us that will do what we can to stop it."

"What do you mean?"

"Edmund didn't understand. He would never see reason. He ignored and dismissed what I said constantly. For some reason, he wanted things to change, starting with ladies and commoners attending the university. I don't even know what he was thinking. I managed to limit it with my place in the society, and therefore in the university. But he was going to take that from me. I couldn't let him. The others would never have approved. I had to do what I did to keep my standing here at the university."

"And what exactly did you do?"

"What do you think, Philippa? I shot him. I dressed as a highwayman, stopped his carriage with a fallen log, and removed him from the equation. It was my greatest wish that I hadn't had to take the steps I did. Edmund was a decent bloke, but he didn't see the big picture and was intent on ruining everything," Simon said, like it all made sense and was perfectly justifiable.

"You seriously think taking a life to protect the status quo is fine?" He repulsed me.

"It was necessary. As was the professor."

"Why did you have to murder Professor Aneurin?" I asked.

"That's putting it rather harshly, but true nonetheless." Simon shrugged. "The main reason was he had found out about Edmund's death and my hand in it. He threatened to go to the police with the information he had, and I couldn't let that happen. He was also spending way too much time with you. When I worked with him, it was always Miss Stanhope this, and Miss Stanhope that. I realized nothing that happened at your dormitory would matter as long as you had his support. Then to make matters worse, even after I and some others pressured the university officials to deny your friend Colin a place here, Aneurin still planned on working with him. Where was his sense of decorum and decency? We could not let it stand," Simon said. He responded like it was mostly a matter of practicality and not murdering people.

"So what's next then, Simon? Who else do you plan to murder?" I almost had my foot free, but I could tell I was running out of time.

"Murder is such a harsh word; I prefer, Which problem am I going to take care of next? And if you haven't guessed already, I really am doing the university a favor because you are definitely not as intelligent as they think. It is quite obvious, Philippa, that you are the next problem that I need to take care of." Simon smiled down at me, his blue eyes filled with disdain.

Chapter Thirty-One

I was super grateful my foot came free at that exact moment, and I was no longer bound to the altar, which had become excessively creepy as the time had passed. Especially with Simon telling me he planned to take care of the problem, or, you know, murder me. I just kept imagining some weird ceremony that involved sacrificing me and maybe even drinking my blood. Needless to say, I was thankful to be done with that. Not to mention Simon leering over me like he couldn't wait to snuff out my life. I shivered at the thought.

From my last foray into this chamber, I knew there were swords everywhere, and I thought there was a pair of dueling swords just behind the altar, about ten feet away. I just needed to get off the altar and to the swords in a fluid movement. Well, at least not stumble so much that Simon recaptured me. I was worried that the head injury and being tied to an altar were going to make getting to the sword more difficult than it would normally be.

Simon moved away from me. I didn't wait to see what he was turning to do. Pushing myself up, I swung my legs to the side of the altar that was farthest away from him. I was thrilled that I still had my boots on. Kicking with bare feet really didn't do much good in a fight. As my boots hit the floor, my knees gave out, and I fell. Bloody hell, I knew that was going to happen. I crawled a bit on all fours before trying to push myself to my feet, assuming Simon had heard the thump of my fall.

"Oh, Philippa, I knew you would be a problem since we first met," Simon said.

I didn't say anything, concentrating on just getting to that rapier on the wall. I moved as fast as I could, my head not cooperating one bit. The room seemed to shift on its axis, but I managed to stay on my feet. Holding myself up with one hand on the wall, I reached up with the other and pulled the sword from its sheath on the wall. Unfortunately, Simon did the same thing.

Taking a deep breath, I looked at Simon, holding the sword in front of me. Finally, the world stopped tilting on me and I could let go of the wall.

"It seems you are aware of where to put the pointy end of a sword, Philippa, but do you really know how to fight with one?" Simon said, derision dripping from his voice.

"That's for me to know and you to find out," I said, knowing full well I had trained with the best my father could buy, even if my father didn't know I had been taking lessons with Percy. The fencing instructor was just happy Percy had a sparring partner and didn't have to do it himself.

I slapped Simon's sword away in a flailing move, as if I had no idea what I was doing with the sword. The clang of the weapons echoed through the stone room. It was a well-balanced weapon, on the heavy side due to the ornamentation around the handguard. I was stronger than I looked, though, which gave me another advantage.

I moved away from Simon as he recovered his fighting stance. He came at me and I parried. I stepped past him and pivoted, sweeping my leg out, tripping him. I regained my fighting stance as Simon stumbled a few steps before regaining his balance. Percy's fencing master always insisted that there were rules for competition, and then there was an actual fight. In a real sword fight, you used every advantage.

Simon came at me again, our swords screeching at contact.

I once again ducked and kicked out my leg. I swear I saw steam come out of Simon's ears as he stumbled over my leg. He regained his balance and swung his sword towards my head. I ducked and hit him with a sidekick to the ribs. Advancing after the kick landed, I blocked his sword as he tried to swing it up from the ground, jumping back slightly as he did so. I tried to hit him with the hilt, but he moved out of the way before I made contact.

Facing off, I looked at Simon's face, red with rage. I was at a disadvantage because I didn't want to kill him, and he had no such qualms. Which was quite apparent as he tried to drive his sword through me. I stepped out of the way, raising my sword up, letting his momentum do the damage—in this case, a slight cut to his arm as he stormed past me.

Simon screamed with rage as he regained his control, at least control over his body. His mind might take more than a few seconds to control. He swung low; I jumped over, managing to take a swipe at his other arm in the process. Simon was panting. It appeared he was not used to this type of exertion.

I switched sword hands from right to left as Simon stared at me, panting. I stared at him, waiting for his next move. He came at me; I parried once again, trying to direct his blade off the line. Easier to do than with Percy because Simon's arm was so very straight. How did he even fight like that? Once I had our blades locked, it was time for my right hook. I pulled back and let it fly. I hit him right on the temple as hard as I possibly could. His eyes locked with mine a half second before his sword and body fell to the floor.

* * *

I stood there for a moment, panting, then heard a noise behind me. Now what? Was the cavalry coming for Simon, and I was going to have to fight my way through a bunch of entitled fools?

I moved so I could keep an eye on Simon. I wouldn't want him waking up while I dealt with whoever was coming. It was a shame I didn't have time to restrain him, but such is life. I held my sword up in a fighting stance, ready for whoever was running down that hall.

Instead of entitled fools, it was Kaiden and my dear ladies of WACK. They came to a halt as they burst into the chamber. I watched as each one took in the scene. Me, sword raised, standing over the body of Lord Simon Middleton. Each one's face said something different.

"We are here to rescue you, but it appears you have handled that yourself," Georgi said.

Kaiden had finally picked his jaw off the floor and strode to me, enveloping me in his arms. I heard my sword clatter to the ground as our lips met for one breathtaking kiss.

"Ahem," Georgi cleared her throat, "I think we need to take care of this before you two continue."

I heard Willa giggle and looked up to see Mads rolling her eyes. Georgi was just standing there, looking at me expectantly.

"Get the rope on the altar and tie him up. I would tie him to the altar like I was tied, but why bother dragging him across the floor. Plus, I wouldn't want to wake him up in the process," I said.

Ever-practical Mads brought the rope over, and Mads and Willa worked on restraining Simon. They managed to get him into a chair. Tying his feet to each leg of the chair and strapping his body to the back, they tied his arms behind the back of the chair. Was it comfortable? No, probably not. Did he deserve to be comfortable? Also, no, absolutely not.

"Pippa, it was quite inconsiderate of you to save yourself. How are we supposed to come to your rescue if you are so bloody independent? I'm sure Kaiden is even more disappointed than me at your efficiency," Georgi said, winking.

"If you wanted to rescue me, you should have gotten here sooner. I couldn't just let myself get murdered to allow you to save the day. And I'm sure Kaiden is fine knowing I can handle myself. I told him a while ago I had a mean right hook," I said, smiling at the inane conversation.

"That you did, and I guess the proof is here in front of me, you were not lying. I should probably endeavor not to upset you, if that's how you handle the men who do upset you." Kaiden seemed to realize that all of us needed some levity after the past few weeks and was happy to play along.

“Did anyone think to contact the police before rushing over here?” I asked.

“You mean the worthless Detective Inspector Radcliffe? No, we didn’t, but it appears that he is going to be needed,” Georgi said. “We were much more concerned with finding you. Next time you are kidnapped think of our poor nerves and leave some clues. If Kaiden hadn’t stopped by to see you, I’m not sure we would have figured out you were even missing until later tonight. It was Kaiden that noticed your overturned steamer bike and suggested Simon might bring you here.”

“I’ll try to be more considerate next time.” I sighed and rolled my eyes at Georgi’s nonsense.

“I’ll go get him.” Mads sighed. “If either of you try to get him here, you’re likely to end up arrested. We already know that’s what will happen to Pippa, and I don’t think she needs another night in jail. It just made her more reckless, not less.”

“Are you g-g-g-going to tell us what happened?” Willa asked.

“Well, it’s nothing we didn’t expect after breaking in here yesterday. Simon murdered both Edmund and Professor Aneurin. He felt Edmund was trying to take his place in society, and the professor had found some evidence against him. He called them problems that needed to be taken care of,” I said.

“How d-d-d-did you end up here?”

“Oh, that. Well, I went for a ride this morning over to the ocean. It was supposed to clear my head but didn’t. When I got back, I was attacked and knocked unconscious. I woke up tied to that altar. Which had me picturing all these different evil ways to kill me.”

“So this man that pretended to be my friend attacked you, tied you up, and threatened to kill you, and he killed my brother and the professor. Why? He has everything,” Kaiden asked.

“Fear. Every bit of what we consider progress, he saw as a threat. A threat to his status, control, and lifestyle. He saw society falling apart because of all the changes, so he did what he could to prevent more change. And what he could do was rather extreme.”

"I wish you hadn't knocked him out, so I could," Georgi said.

"You might get your chance, he could wake up." I shrugged like it was the most reasonable thought.

"You'll have to get in line. I have next punch," Kaiden said.

* * *

It wasn't long before Mads was back with Detective Inspector Radcliffe. He walked into the chamber behind her and looked around. He saw Simon tied to the chair, and then me. At least he looked somewhat contrite. Maybe he wasn't worthless after all.

"Who wants to tell me what happened?" Detective Inspector Radcliffe asked.

"I'm probably the best one to explain, at least until Lord Middleton wakes up," I said, taking a deep breath. "This morning I was getting back from a trip on my steamer bike when I was attacked. They brought me here and tied me to that altar over there while I was unconscious. While tied up, Simon—I mean, Lord Middleton—admitted to killing the former Lord Fremont and Professor Aneurin. I was able to get loose and subdue Lord Middleton. Then my friends arrived to help me keep Simon from escaping."

The detective inspector looked at each of us individually. I felt like he was questioning the veracity of what I said. But each of my friends nodded at his unsaid question.

"Somebody wake up Lord Middleton. I need to ask him some questions."

I don't know where Kaiden found a bucket of water or how he came about it so quickly, but I could tell he quite enjoyed dumping it over Simon's head. Simon came to, spluttering as water ran down his face and into his fancy clothes. He immediately tried to stand up and found himself tied to the chair, and tied rather well, if you were to ask Mads and Willa.

"Do you have an explanation for this, Lord Middleton?" the detective inspector asked.

I watched as Simon looked up at the detective inspector. I could see the contempt he had for the man on his face moments before he got control of himself.

“I have been accosted by that girl over there. She challenged me to a duel and then knocked me out, and apparently tied me up,” Simon said.

“Are you admitting to dueling, Lord Middleton?” the detective inspector asked.

“What? Yes, I mean no. I didn’t have a choice.” Simon looked around, his eyes crazy.

“So you’re telling me the redhead who barely comes up to your shoulder not only bested you at sword fighting but knocked you unconscious?” Detective Inspector Radcliffe was incredulous.

“I mean, it’s hard to believe, but why else would I be tied to the chair,” Simon said.

“These individuals, including Lord Fremont, have told me you confessed to killing Edmund Fremont and Professor Aneurin.”

“Why would I ever admit to such a thing?” Simon said.

“Because you didn’t think you would get caught. Miss Stanhope said you were planning on killing her. So I could see you telling her all about it, believing she wouldn’t survive to tell anyone.”

The rest of us just watched as this played out. For me, it was entertaining to see the turn the detective inspector had taken, from literally keeping me in jail overnight because Lord Middleton had told him I was guilty to questioning Lord Middleton about the murders as a suspect. It wasn’t an actual apology, but it was pretty close to one. Probably as close as I would be to getting an apology.

It wasn’t long before Simon broke under the pressure of the questions and admitted it all. Detective Inspector Radcliffe untied him, only to handcuff him and drag him off.

Simon stopped the detective inspector right before they were going to exit the chamber.

“You know this isn’t over. As much as I hate to admit it, I’m just a small part of this. You won’t last here, and things will revert back to the way they should be.” With those parting words, I watched Simon dragged out of the Shadowed Sword, hopefully for forever.

Chapter Thirty-Two

Even with Simon's last threat (or warning, depending on how a person looked at it), I was relieved to get back to normal. As the days passed after his arrest, I realized I didn't actually know what my normal was going to be. Right now, I was admitted and studying at a remarkable university that didn't have a professor versed in what I wanted to study. I had limited funds, so it didn't seem right to stay around if I wasn't going to study anything, but I couldn't go home after everything that had happened here. My mother would not understand what to do with me at this point. While I felt even more secure with who I was, I wasn't even sure I knew what to do with myself.

I sighed, letting Hannah dress me in a lovely bright-blue silk skirt, with a matching blue corseted vest and a white blouse. It surprised me to see the others downstairs already; it wasn't like Mads to be up this early, and Willa was normally already tending her garden.

"Okay Pippa, enough of your moping," Georgi said, hands on her hips, squaring off for an argument.

"I'm not moping." I sighed again, flopping onto the settee and instantly regretting it. "What I am is lost now that we have solved the murder. I put all my effort into finding the professor's murderer and forgot to plan for my life." I had been quite mopey lately, but it wasn't polite to point it out.

"What options do you have? What do you want to do?" Mads asked.

"Well, Colin offered to let me work with him at his shop. I told him I wanted to, but I don't know if he really meant it. I asked him if he had killed the professor. If I were him, I wouldn't want to work with me. What kinda friend am I to even ask those questions? I think I would enjoy working with him the most though," I said. The thought of seeing Colin again set my nerves on edge. I couldn't stop myself from rambling on.

"Colin w-w-w-would love for you to work with him. He d-d-d-doesn't understand why you haven't stopped by since, you know," Willa said.

"Willa, have you been keeping in touch with Mr. Finnigan? How absolutely delightful." Georgi clapped her hands with glee. Turned out, Georgi was quite the matchmaker. Just one of the quirks of our general's character.

Willa blushed prettily. Bloody hell, her skin was perfect. I half expected Willa to deny it, but she said nothing more on the subject. Which had me wondering if Colin had met his match.

"I should go see him then," I said. Was I really going to go talk to Colin? I hadn't actually planned on it.

"You should, and you should decide what you want to study here until they hire a new steam engineering professor. I'm sure it won't take too long," Georgi said.

"You're right. I need to make some decisions. Enough with my aimlessness." With that, I stood, wiping my hands down the front of my skirt. "I'll head to Colin's now."

I grabbed my hat and matching parasol, looking every inch the Brythionite lady my mother had always wanted me to be. I walked towards Colin's mechanic shop in order to take a job, the exact opposite of everything my mother wanted me to be. I half shrugged, dismissing any thoughts of her.

I paused at my favorite bridge and stood a moment taking in Grantabridge in the morning. The mist was still hugging the

Granta river, and in typical Brythion fashion, the sky was still grey from the cloud cover. I wondered in earnest if it was going to rain. I didn't really want to get caught in it if it did. So I hurried the rest of the way to Colin's shop.

As always, Colin was tinkering away in his shop. He looked up as I entered. He smiled when he saw me, and the tension in my body melted away. If he could smile at the sight of me, he really must not be mad at me for asking if he had murdered the professor.

"Hi Colin, I hope you don't mind me stopping by," I said, the apprehension returning as soon as I opened my mouth.

"Of course not. I've been thinking about you since the arrest of Lord Middleton. I hope you are okay after everything."

"Well, yes, I'm fine. Just floundering a bit at the moment. In fact, that's why I came by." I took a deep breath. Everything was fine when we ended things the last time I was here, but I felt so bad for ever questioning Colin. "I was wondering if you still wanted me to work here? I really don't know what to do now that there is no steam engineering professor. But I don't want to leave. That would feel like announcing my failure."

"Bloody hell, Pippa, I thought we went through this. I would love your help here. In fact, you will make me a better engineer because you know more than me, and you think differently than I do. Plus with an extra set of hands building the steam carriages, I could get so much more done."

"I just . . ."

"None of that. I understand why you asked, and I'm not offended. I've moved past it, so should you," Colin said.

"You really are the best, Colin. Thank you." I flung my arms around his neck, giving him a great big hug.

"Ahem . . ." I heard someone clear their throat. Leave it to me to clear my name and get caught immediately in a compromising position. I extricated myself from my exuberant hug and saw Kaiden standing there, looking at the floor rather awkwardly.

"Kaiden, what are you doing her? Is your steam carriage fixed?" I asked.

"I actually came to see you. Madeline told me you would be here. I hope I'm not interrupting anything." Kaiden seemed very stiff and almost awkward.

"Of course not, Colin just asked, or confirmed, that I could work here with him on the actual build of his projects, and I would have a space to work on my personal ideas," I said, excited to share the news.

The stiffness in Kaiden's body left almost as soon as I told him why I was here. I thought I might have just witnessed some jealousy on his part. But I wouldn't tease him about it . . . yet.

"If you can spare a moment, do you have time to go for a walk with me?" Kaiden asked.

"Of course. Why would I not have time? Colin, I'll see you tomorrow, early in the morning."

* * *

The two of us walked side by side through the market and down towards the river. The mist from earlier had cleared, the rain clouds had dissipated, and the sky was a rich, bright blue.

"I'm thrilled to work with Colin. I don't need to stop exploring the subject I love so much. Now I just need to decide what I want to study at the university," I said, bouncing with excitement now that I was planning my future.

"Are you still thinking about alchemy?" Kaiden asked.

"I don't know. It probably makes the most sense at this point. At least I have the professor on board, but part of me wonders if I should continue at all, or try to focus on something else altogether."

"You should continue. If you don't, Simon actually wins, and we can't have that," Kaiden said.

"Of course I have to finish. I can't let that entitled man affect what I do here. I was thinking about looking into studying the luminiferous aether. While it's not steam engineering, it is related in a way. It could help build better dirigibles or create other ways to communicate. I mean, can you imagine if we could send messages through the aether? We could communicate over long distances."

"Is there a professor here that specializes in the subject?"

"I honestly don't know. I had never thought of studying it before. It's just an idea. I'll probably start with alchemy, and see if I need to be learning more."

I looked around, only to find myself standing with Kaiden on my favorite spot in Grantabridge, over the river. The two of us had stopped here naturally, or Kaiden had directed us to this spot. I wasn't quite sure which.

"Pippa, I have a question for you."

"Uh oh, you seem so serious," I teased. Then saw his expression and shut my mouth.

"Pippa, over these last couple of months, I feel that we have gotten to know each other really well. In fact, I would say we've become fond of each other."

"I would concur; I might even say more than a little fond of each other." I smiled.

"I was hoping you would say that, Pippa." Kaiden began patting all the pockets in his blue frock coat, then his waistcoat, and finally found what he was looking for. He pulled out a delicate gold ring with a large red garnet surrounded by diamonds. Without thinking, my hand went up to my mouth. "Since you lectured me on needing better taste in friends, I have been utterly enthralled with you, if you haven't noticed. You're intelligent, inventive, sensitive, strong, extremely independent, and capable. I love that you can take care of yourself, but aren't afraid to lean on your friends, and hopefully me, when things are overwhelming, and you encourage me to lean on you. In short, I love you and want to marry you. Will you spend forever with me?"

I felt the tears in my eyes and the desire to say something sassy well up inside me. But before I blurted out something that wasn't a resounding yes, I said, "Yes, yes of course I'll spend forever with you." And then I added, "And to think my family said it wasn't like I was going to find a duke to marry by going to university, and look at us now."

I threw my arms around his neck and reached up for a kiss, which Kaiden obliged me with. And once again I was risking scandal in this small town, but couldn't have cared less.

Chapter Thirty-Three

To say I was bursting to the brim with news by the time I got back to the dorm would be an absolute understatement. Somehow, I managed to walk back rather sedately with Kaiden by my side. Okay, sedately is a vast exaggeration of my pace. I was practically skipping; I might have thrown in a twirl here and there. Things were just so, well, so superb.

As soon as we were in front of the dorm, I kissed Kaiden again for good measure, and then sent him on his way. He didn't need to see my friends and me in a titter over him proposing.

"My dear ladies of WACK, get your hats and parasols. We are going out for ices to celebrate," I said as soon as I walked through the door.

"What are you going on about now, Pippa?" Mads asked.

"You sent me out to stop wallowing, and I am done with that, so let's go and I will tell you all the news over a delicious ice."

"But . . .," Willa started to say.

"No buts. Georgi, you too. I want all of us together," I said.

After a bit of hustle and bustle, all four of us were on our way to Jarrin's Glace Parlor. We were a rainbow of color walking down the street. I was still in my bright blue silk. Willa was in the most adorable violet confection of frills, much more stylish than she normally wore. Mads was wearing a daring, deep red dress that's top mimicked the lines of a man's suit. And Georgie was looking divine in a buttery yellow dress with just the right amount of ruffled peach lace. Once again, it felt like the town at least accepted us. Shop owners and other perambulators waved as we walked by. My dearest friends tried to get me to talk about my news on our way to Jarrin's, but I would have nothing of it. I was just happy to be out with them and with a brilliant smile on my face.

Once we were at Jarrin's, with its pink-and-cream striped walls, cream iron table and chairs, and chocolate brown accents, we all ordered our favorite flavors. Mine was lemon, Willa enjoyed lavender ice, Georgi insisted on chocolate, and Mads ordered bergamot. All different, just like us.

"Okay, Pippa, spill it. What has got you so bubbly? You're like a champagne bottle ready to burst," Georgi asked.

"Well, first, Colin is happy to have me working with him. He needs the help, and isn't upset with me for accusing him of murder—well, not so much accusing him, as just asking him if he did it," I said slowly, taking off my gloves.

"I t-t-t-told you, Pippa, he wants you at his shop," Willa said.

"That's not enough to have you this effervescent," Mads said, always the practical one.

"Well, Kaiden showed up at the shop and asked to go for a walk. He helped me decide to continue my studies here. Probably in alchemy, but I'm also thinking of doing some research into the aether. I don't know if there is a professor here who studies it. But the implications of what it could do are endless," I said. I might have been waving my hands around a bit more than usual as I talked.

"What's that on your finger?" Georgi asked, grabbing my hand as she spoke.

"What, this?" I pulled my hand away from her and held it up. "Just a token of Kaiden's affection, and a promise to be married and spend our lives together." And like only the best of friends can do, they squealed in happiness for me, oohing and aahing over my new jewelry. After I had all the congratulations I could take, I rather abruptly changed the subject. They should be used to the way my brain worked by now.

"What do you think Simon meant when he said that this wasn't over?" I asked.

"I think he is working with others, not just with men in his secret society. And we might be in for a bit of an adventure staying here," Georgi said. "We need to take precautions to protect each other. If he was willing to murder for this cause, can you imagine what else we are up against?"

"D-D-D-Do you really think there are others? Why w-w-w-would anyone be so opposed to us studying here?" Willa asked.

"I agree with Georgi. There are sure to be others, and I bet who they are would actually surprise us. As to the why, the four of us are a threat to the way things are, and anyone that is satisfied with the world as it is doesn't want us to succeed. Which means we have to, for all the other women that wish they could be where we are."

I looked at the others, and they all nodded in agreement.

* * *

From Jarrin's, the four of us took the circuitous way back to the dorm. With the knowledge and fear that there was someone, or someones, out to destroy our future, we wanted to do whatever we could to make an impact while we were here.

"Ladies, I think we need to continue with the WACK Society. Host different salons and teas. Target both the working class by teaching them the skills that will help them in life, but also do something for society ladies: show them we are not a threat to them, but are like them in a lot of ways. We can have lectures or literature readings or discussions on the uses of different plants," I said.

"Pippa, you beat me to it. I was just about to suggest that we not only continue but expand the salons we talked about. The first one was almost a success. Or would have been if there hadn't been a side of sabotage," Georgi said.

"At least you know what I think," I said. "What about you, Mads? Willa?"

"It may be hard for me to speak in p-p-p-public, but I think they are a good idea. I'm willing to challenge myself."

"I personally cannot wait for another self-defense class. Giving these maids the skills to take control of a small part of their life is so worthwhile," Mads said.

"Think of all the different things we can teach. I mean, my right hook took out the bad guy, as well as my fencing skills," I said, laughing as I watched my friends both roll their eyes and laugh with me.

"Hopefully those skills won't ever be needed, but they are good to have," Mads said.

* * *

Walking and planning what was going to happen in the future distracted me until we were almost in front of the dorm. The acrid smell of smoke hung in the air, which reminded me of coming back here with Kaiden and finding all my things destroyed. The four of us looked at each other. We all smelled smoke. As one, we lifted our skirts and ran the rest of the way to our dorm.

The flames were out, but what was left of the building wasn't much more than a burned-up pile of rubble. Ironically, the pile of rubble had more color to it than the building that once stood there.

It was quite clear at this point Simon Middleton was not the only one trying to get us to leave, and whoever that person was had left the four of us homeless.

Acknowledgements

This book isn't one of those books that's been in my mind for a while, but it is one that stuck with me once I started thinking of it, which was October 2020. I was supposed to be going on a cross-country road trip, starting in California and driving all the way to Maine and then back with my two dogs and my mom. The pandemic limited what was possible, but my mom and I, and my two dogs, still went on a leaf-peeping trip. It just didn't make it all the way cross-country where quarantines and such were still in effect. The thing about driving in the car all day is it gives you a lot of time to think, talk, and think and talk. So, my mom and I started talking about a book she has had in her mind for a long time, she keeps saying 30-plus years, but it's more like 20 plus, on the trip we started plotting it out, talking about character development, family lines, you know all the things. Then she asked me about the book I started in 9th grade, and while I remember a lot of it, what I remember most was my main character was young and whiny. Not something I felt like writing about at all. I had another main character name I had been obsessing over, though. Ever since I had stayed in Colorado with my friend Charlotte and she had rattled off all her sisters' names, and one of them went by Pippa, because no one pronounced Phillipa correctly. The truncated road trip that still involved long stretches of road and an obsession with the name Pippa was how the idea for this book started. So thank you, Mom and Charlotte, little did you know you were creating a monster at the time.

The idea for one book quickly became an idea for four and a prequel as I pulled together women's names that could all have nicknames and created a historical world based on the premise what if everything was powered by steam? Throw in Victorian England values and a university system, allowing a handful of women in for the first time. Would these ladies get along? Would the powers that be challenge the shift in power? How would they do it? Would these ladies have the support of their family or not?

So many questions which, of course, lead to character development and an actual plot. I want to thank my mom, Jacqueline Clemens, for talking all of this through with me in my Jeep.

I didn't actually start working on the book when I got home from our trip. I tried. But I didn't really know where to start. In May, I started with a writing group, the Author's Journey, with the goal of starting a book and have it published in 12 months. A schedule is like gold to me. Once I had it, I had goals I could work with and a cheerleader in my court. I have to thank Joy for cheering me along the entire way.

By September I was sending my manuscript out to people to read, and all the feedback was in valuable. Thank you: Simi, Rachel, Jamie and Christyn for reading my very messy manuscript and giving me the feedback, I needed to make it a more cohesive story.

From that point on, it was editing, and more editing, then maybe even another round of editing. It helped to work with Jamie Dalton, Magnetra's Designs, on my gorgeous cover. Her designs inspired me to keep going. Then, my editor, Sarah Hawkins, with all of her encouraging words and comma placements, really made everything come together so I could actually publish my book. Thank you everyone for all your help! Without you, I would probably still be doing character sheets.

About the Author

Stephanie K. Clemens is known for many things: an author, photographer, dog mom, instagrammer, adventurer, teacher, lawyer, and more. When she's not sitting behind her laptop she can be found on some adventure. Most of the time it's a road trip with her two doggos, but recently it has been in the pages of a book.

You can find her on Instagram and TikTok under the username @bookishstephaniek

Also by Stephanie K. Clemens

The Alex Granger Files - Available on Amazon Vella

Ladies of WACK series

A Study in Steam

A Practicum in Perjury ... *Coming Soon*

www.ingramcontent.com/pod-product-compliance
Lightning Source LLC
Chambersburg PA
CBHW020335310726
48979CB00015B/2384/J

* 9 7 8 1 9 5 7 5 0 8 0 2 3 *